"Jennifer has a bun in her oven,"

Teresa piped up, a gap-toothed smile splitting her eager face, her brown eyes sparkling.

Jennifer's heart stopped and her jaw dropped. Orange juice, halfway down her throat, came back up with a cough and she pressed her napkin to her mouth, her eyes watering.

"*Niña,* we all know Jennifer is not so good in the kitchen," Carmen said, ruffling her daughter's hair.

"No, she is," Teresa insisted. "I think she's taking cooking lessons."

"Teresa, shh!" Jennifer hissed, watching as the rest of the guests began to turn their attention toward her youngest sister.

Ryan handed the little girl a sweet roll, waving it in front of her face. "Have something to eat, Teresa. Aren't you hungry?"

Teresa took the roll. "Jenny and Ryan were in the garden last night and she told him she had a bun in her oven. I was listening from my tree house."

Carmen's eyes were wide. "And what else did Jenny say?"

"She said she's knocked up, too. *And* she's going to have a baby."

"Oh, God," Jennifer

D0958196

Dear Reader,

I've always welcomed the chance to add a little variety into my writing life, so when my editor at Harlequin asked me to contribute a book to the TRUEBLOOD, TEXAS series, I couldn't refuse. In the nearly thirty books I've written for them, I've never set a book in Texas. And the chance to learn more about Mexican-American culture was an added bonus!

A chance inquiry at my local library put me in touch with Cristina Capatillo-Fischer. She graciously agreed to help me "get it right," and we spent many mornings at the library discussing Mexican wedding traditions, *quinceañera* celebrations and dinner menus. It wasn't long before this Wisconsin girl knew the proper time to serve corn tortillas versus flour.

I hope you enjoy the next installment of TRUEBLOOD, TEXAS. The story of Jennifer Rodriguez, Ryan Madison and the baby between them, was so much fun to write. I hope it's as much fun to read! And after you're finished, I'd like to invite you to visit my new Web site at www.katehoffmann.com for information on my upcoming and past releases.

Happy reading,

Kate Hoffmann

TRUEBLOOD, TEXAS

Kate Hoffmann

Daddy Wanted

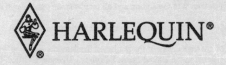

HARLEQUIN®

TORONTO • NEW YORK • LONDON
AMSTERDAM • PARIS • SYDNEY • HAMBURG
STOCKHOLM • ATHENS • TOKYO • MILAN • MADRID
PRAGUE • WARSAW • BUDAPEST • AUCKLAND

Kate Hoffmann is acknowledged
as the author of this work.

For Cristina, with thanks for your friendship
and all those mornings at Mead.

HARLEQUIN BOOKS
225 Duncan Mill Road, Don Mills,
Ontario, Canada M3B 3K9

ISBN 0-373-65081-7

DADDY WANTED

Visit us at www.eHarlequin.com

Printed in U.S.A.

TRUEBLOOD TEXAS

The Cowboy Wants a Baby	Jo Leigh
His Brother's Fiancée	Jasmine Cresswell
A Father's Vow	Tina Leonard
Daddy Wanted	Kate Hoffmann
The Cowboy's Secret Son	Gayle Wilson
The Best Man in Texas	Kelsey Roberts
Hot on His Trail	Karen Hughes
The Sheriff Gets His Lady	Dani Sinclair
Surprise Package	Joanna Wayne
Rodeo Daddy	B.J. Daniels
The Rancher's Bride	Tara Taylor Quinn
Dylan's Destiny	Kimberly Raye
Hero for Hire	Jill Shalvis
Her Protector	Liz Ireland
Lover Under Cover	Charlotte Douglas
A Family at Last	Debbi Rawlins

THE TRUEBLOOD LEGACY

THE YEAR WAS 1918, and the Great War in Europe still raged, but Esau Porter was heading home to Texas.

The young sergeant arrived at his parents' ranch northwest of San Antonio on a Sunday night, only the celebration didn't go off as planned. Most of the townsfolk of Carmelita had come out to welcome Esau home, but when they saw the sorry condition of the boy, they gave their respects quickly and left.

The fever got so bad so fast that Mrs. Porter hardly knew what to do. By Monday night, before the doctor from San Antonio made it into town, Esau was dead.

The Porter family grieved. How could their son have survived the German peril, only to burn up and die in his own bed? It wasn't much of a surprise when Mrs. Porter took to her bed on Wednesday. But it was a hell of a shock when half the residents of Carmelita came down with the horrible illness. House after house was hit by death, and all the townspeople could do was pray for salvation.

None came. By the end of the year, over one hundred souls had perished. The influenza virus took those in the prime of life, leaving behind an unprecedented number of orphans. And the virus knew no boundaries. By the time the threat had passed, more than thirty-seven million people had succumbed worldwide.

But in one house, there was still hope.

Isabella Trueblood had come to Carmelita in the late 1800s with her father, blacksmith Saul Trueblood, and her mother, Teresa Collier Trueblood. The family had traveled from Indiana, leaving their Quaker roots behind.

Young Isabella grew up to be an intelligent woman who had a gift for healing and storytelling. Her dreams centered on the boy next door, Foster Carter, the son of Chester and Grace.

Just before the bad times came in 1918, Foster asked Isabella to be his wife, and the future of the Carter spread was secured. It was a happy union, and the future looked bright for the young couple.

Two years later, not one of their relatives was alive. How the young couple had survived was a miracle. And during the epidemic, Isabella and Foster had taken in more than twenty-two orphaned children from all over the county. They fed them, clothed them, taught them as if they were blood kin.

Then Isabella became pregnant, but there were complications. Love for her handsome son, Josiah, born in 1920, wasn't enough to stop her from growing weaker by the day. Knowing she couldn't leave her husband to tend to all the children if she died, she set out to find families for each one of her orphaned charges.

And so the Trueblood Foundation was born. Named in memory of Isabella's parents, it would become famous all over Texas. Some of the orphaned children went to strangers, but many were reunited with their families. After reading notices in news-papers and church bulletins, aunts, uncles, cousins and grandparents rushed to Carmelita to find the young ones they'd given up for dead.

Toward the end of Isabella's life, she'd brought together more than thirty families, and not just her orphans. Many others, old and young, made their way to her doorstep, and Isabella turned no one away.

At her death, the town's name was changed to Trueblood, in her honor. For years to come, her simple grave was adorned with flowers on the anniversary of her death, grateful tokens of appreciation from the families she had brought together.

Isabella's son, Josiah, grew into a fine rancher and married Rebecca Montgomery in 1938. They had a daughter, Elizabeth Trueblood Carter, in 1940. Elizabeth married her neighbor William Garrett in 1965, and gave birth to twins Lily and Dylan in 1971, and daughter Ashley a few years later. Home was the Double G ranch, about ten miles from Trueblood proper, and the Garrett children grew up listening to stories of their famous great-grandmother, Isabella. Because they were Truebloods, they knew that they, too, had a sacred duty to carry on the tradition passed down to them: finding lost souls and reuniting loved ones.

PROLOGUE

"MR. MADISON? Are you all right?"

Ryan Madison heard her words, even registered the concern in her voice, but the strange buzzing in his head made it impossible to form a reply.

Was he all right? This morning, when he'd walked into the trailer at Number 59, he hadn't really bothered to consider the question. On the whole, his life was going pretty damn well. He was almost twenty-seven years old, considered a decent-looking guy without any major dental problems or personality disorders. He owned a very successful business in Midland, Texas—Madison Drilling and Oil—and made a good living. They'd just opened their fifty-ninth well. And though he wasn't happily married with two point four children and a dog, he came from what he thought was a loving, supportive family—until now.

"I know this must be startling news," she said, her voice lilting slightly with just a hint of a Spanish accent. "And I'm sure it will take some time to sink in."

His attention was fixed on her mouth and he watched her form each word, as if in slow motion. She had a beautiful mouth, a shapely upper lip, like a Cupid's bow, complemented by a soft, full lower lip. She'd introduced herself when she'd walked into the trailer, but suddenly, he couldn't remember her name. Jane? Janice? No, Jennifer. He drew a slow breath and focused his thoughts. That was it. Jennifer Rodriguez.

When his drilling foreman had shown her in, Ryan's

curiosity had been piqued. Beautiful women didn't wander into his trailer every day, or every month for that matter. Beautiful women were in short supply in the oil fields of the Permian Basin. And there was no arguing that Jennifer Rodriguez was beautiful. A breath of fresh air in the hot, dusty oil fields of West Texas.

When she'd introduced herself as a private investigator, he'd nearly laughed out loud. P.I.s were supposed to be balding, middle-aged men with potbellies, cigar-stained teeth and a world-weary attitude. Jennifer Rodriguez wore a pretty flowered dress that skimmed her slender figure. Her long dark hair tumbled in messy waves around her shoulders and her eyes were so brown they were nearly black. Her skin, kissed golden by the sun, looked so soft he was tempted to reach out and touch her face. Without thinking, he raised his hand and—

"Mr. Madison, perhaps it might be best if I leave you to think about everything I said. I'll just wait—"

"No!" Ryan replied. If she left he'd be forced to face a reality he wasn't ready to acknowledge. As long as she was here, he could allow himself the safety of a fantasy or two when doubts overwhelmed his common sense. Reluctantly, he glanced down at the sheet of paper in his hand—a birth certificate. It didn't look anything like the document he had seen when he applied for his first passport. "I don't understand. This isn't me. This baby was stillborn. Why would you think this is me?"

"I'm working for a man named Ben Mulholland," she said. "He was born on October 23, 1974, outside Austin. That's the birth certificate of his twin brother."

"I was born on October 23, 1974 in Austin, at a hospital," Ryan said numbly. "And I'm an only child."

"I'm sure if you look at your birth certificate, you'll see the same doctor's signature, nearly the same time of birth. We think you're Ben Mulholland's twin brother."

Ryan shook his head. "Wait a minute. First, you tell me I'm adopted, that my parents really aren't my parents. And now you tell me I have a twin brother? This doesn't make any sense."

"The doctor who delivered you was a baby broker. When he delivered you to your adoptive parents, he gave them a forged birth certificate. I think if you check closely, you'll see that the doctor couldn't have been in two separate places delivering two different babies."

He raked his fingers through his dusty hair. "I—I don't know— Why do you think—"

Jennifer reached out and placed her fingers on his forearm. "Mr. Madison, I realize this is—"

"Madison?" Ryan asked. He stared down at the spot on his skin where her fingers rested. They were warm and soft, delicately boned and oddly comforting. "You're telling me my name isn't Madison, it's Mulholland." A soft chuckle slipped from Ryan's throat. The sheer absurdity of the situation was more than he could take in. "You're wrong. You're looking for someone else, some other guy born on October 23, 1974. Not me." He pushed the birth certificate back at her. He was the son of Jeffrey and Rhonda Madison.

She held out another item and he noticed it was a photograph of himself—or was it? He snatched it from her fingers and stared at the image, the face so like his, yet just a bit different.

"That's your brother, Ben. Your twin."

"This is not my brother," Ryan insisted. "I don't have a brother." But though he said the words, he wasn't certain they were true. The man in the photo looked remarkably like the man he saw every morning in the mirror as he shaved.

"If that's true, we can clear this up very quickly. I need

you to come to San Antonio with me. There's a doctor there waiting to give you a blood test."

Ryan shook his head. "If you're so sure of your proof, why do I need a blood test?"

"I haven't told you everything," Jennifer said. "There's another reason we need to go to San Antonio."

Ryan raised his eyebrow, then stepped away from her, shoving his hands into the pockets of his faded jeans to keep from touching her. "You mean, there's more?" he asked, a sarcastic edge to his voice. He wandered over to his desk and idly began to flip through a stack of geological surveys. "Let me guess. There's probably a case of amnesia involved. Maybe some family insanity, a few underworld connections. Hell, according to you, my life has suddenly become a cheesy soap opera."

She grabbed his elbow and gently turned him until he faced her. "This isn't some silly television show. This is real life. Ben Mulholland has a five-year-old daughter who has been diagnosed with leukemia. She needs a bone marrow transplant and the doctors haven't been able to find a donor match through the network. Her father can't donate because of a bout with malaria. If worst comes to worst and the right donor can't be found soon, they're hoping you might agree to help."

He stared at her for a long moment, saw the emotion in her eyes, the hopeful expression. He'd always known someday a woman would walk into his life and change him forever. But he'd expected to fall madly in love and get married. He didn't expect her to turn his whole world upside down and make him question who and what he was!

His gaze dropped to her mouth and he fought the temptation to kiss her. It had been so long since he'd kissed a woman, but he hadn't forgotten how easy it was to lose himself in a warm and willing female. All the confusion that muddled his brain would slowly dissolve and he'd be left with only desire and the sweet taste of her mouth.

"She's your *sobrina*," Jennifer said quietly. "Your niece."

"That, Miss Rodriguez," he murmured, letting her name linger on his lips, "is yet to be determined."

"Then come with me," she urged. "If you're sure it's a mistake, we'll prove it and you can get back to your life." She reached into the pocket of her purse and produced a plane ticket. "We've got a flight out of Midland in two hours."

"You were awfully certain I'd agree to come with you."

A tiny smile curved the corners of her mouth, charming, enticing, revealing an impish streak that she'd kept hidden until now. "If you didn't come willingly, I was going to knock you senseless and stuff you in the trunk of my car." She turned and started toward the door of the trailer.

"You must be getting paid very well by Mr. Mulholland," he said.

She turned back, her expression suddenly cool, but her eyes betraying a startling depth of determination. "This isn't about money, Mr. Madison. This is about a little girl's life." With that, she stepped outside into the blazing sun, heat pouring into the air-conditioned trailer like a blast furnace.

Ryan smiled and smoothed his hands over the front of his sweat-stained T-shirt. He was tempted to slam the door behind her and refuse to follow her to San Antonio. But something in the way she looked at him, in the stubborn set of her mouth and trusting look in her eyes, made him want to do as she asked.

"I guess I'm going to San Antonio," he murmured.

And even if he did prove Jennifer Rodriguez wrong,

he'd still manage to come away with something worthwhile. He'd have spent the day with an incredibly intriguing and beautiful private investigator.

CHAPTER ONE

JENNIFER RODRIGUEZ stared up at the office building in downtown Midland. Inside was her salvation, the only person in the world who might be able to help her in this time of crisis. Though she hadn't seen him since that day almost a month ago, she was hoping Ryan Madison remembered his promise to her as she'd left him at the hospital in San Antonio.

If there's ever anything I can do for you, don't hesitate to call.

He'd taken her hand as he thanked her, though she couldn't understand his gratitude. She'd walked into his life, dropped a bombshell of atomic proportions, then walked away. The chaos she'd wreaked on Ryan Madison's life would reverberate for years to come. Jennifer sighed softly. The only satisfaction she'd found in the completed assignment was that she'd tried to help a little girl who wanted nothing more than to grow up strong and healthy. Ryan had been tested but was only a remote match.

But then just days later, a compatible donor had unexpectedly been found, a nearly perfect match for Lucy. Yesterday, Carolyn St. Clair had called from the San Antonio office of Finders Keepers, her voice filled with excitement, to say Lucy was so much better that she would be going home the very next day. She also passed on the good news that she and Ben Mulholland had exchanged wedding

vows in Lucy's hospital room. They'd be a real family
now.

Jennifer thought back to the day she met Ryan, a day
so full of startling revelations. She'd never expected to
become so emotionally entangled in a case, her concern
for both Lucy Mulholland and Ryan Madison weighing
heavily on her mind. In truth, she hadn't had a case of
such magnitude since she'd started working in the tiny
private investigations firm in downtown Odessa. That was
probably because the Mulholland case *had* been her first
real case—sort of.

She'd begun work at Budnicki-Morales Private Investigations a week after she'd graduated from the University
of Texas-El Paso, leaving her family and hometown for an
exciting life of her own in a brand-new city. The two vet-
eran investigators had advertised for a bookkeeper and office manager at the campus job placement center and she'd
found the possibility of working for private investigators
intriguing. And Odessa was just far enough away from El
Paso—282 miles to be exact—that her parents' interference in her life was minimal.

Carmen and Diego had been so proud. She was the first
Rodriguez to graduate college. And with a degree in accounting, she'd always be able to find work, setting a fine
example for her four younger siblings. But from the first
time she'd balanced the books for the two crusty old P.I.s,
she'd known that she wasn't cut out to simply count the
company's pennies. She wanted to be an investigator, just
like Ralph Budnicki and Roy Morales.

She got her first break when Lily and Dylan Garrett
started referring work from Finders Keepers in San Antonio. The workload doubled almost instantly with missing
persons cases for the two licensed P.I.s and Jennifer found
herself doing more and more investigative work. Recently
she'd been promoted to assistant investigator by Ralph and

Roy and had begun taking night classes to get her P.I. license.

She'd worked the Mulholland case from start to finish, and though a licensed investigator should have been the one to approach Ryan Madison, both Ralph and Roy thought Jennifer better suited to handle such a highly charged emotional situation. There was a benefit to being the only woman in the office.

Right now, Jennifer was thankful for the fates that had put her in Ryan Madison's path. She smoothed her palms over the bodice of her cotton dress, ran her fingers through her perpetually windblown hair and started toward the front entrance to the office building. She'd reviewed her strategy over and over again, planning the exact words she would say to him, the perfect way to convince him to go along with her plan.

But there was one part of her plan she still hadn't refined—the exact moment to tell him she was pregnant. Should she just blurt it out at the start or should she chat for a few minutes before carefully steering the conversation in that direction? Should she offer an explanation about the baby's father or would it be better to gloss over that particular lapse in judgment?

At this point Ryan seemed her only hope. The prospect of telling her parents had been hanging over her head like a dark cloud for months, and it was only after she met Ryan Madison that she'd decided on a strategy. He had a good heart. Though he'd wanted to deny all she'd told him about his parentage, in the end, he'd done the right thing. He'd tried to give Lucy Mulholland a chance at life.

She stepped inside the quiet, air-conditioned lobby and headed toward the elevators, plucking at the damp fabric of her dress. For early October, the weather in West Texas had been unbearably hot. Though she wanted to appear fresh and confident for this meeting, she knew she looked damp and wrinkled.

As she rode the elevator to the seventh floor, she tried to slow her pounding heart. Was she really so nervous asking for his help, or was the prospect of seeing Ryan Madison again too much to bear? She couldn't deny she found him attractive. Not just physically, though his broad shoulders, narrow waist and long legs were not lost on her. Nor was his handsome face, the high forehead and sculpted cheekbones, the impossibly straight nose.

On the outside he appeared supremely confident, but she'd seen a side of him that Jennifer suspected he didn't show to the rest of the world. A side he kept hidden behind his striking hazel eyes. There was a vulnerability about him, and a depth of character that wasn't apparent at first glance. He'd probably had his share of women, but she wondered if any of them knew the real Ryan Madison.

Jennifer stepped off the elevator and came face-to-face with a wide glass door. Fine lettering told her she'd found the place—Madison Drilling and Oil. Drawing a deep breath, she stepped inside and crossed the plush reception area to the front desk. "Good afternoon. I'd like to see Ryan Madison."

The receptionist frowned. "Do you have an appointment?"

"No," Jennifer said. "But I called earlier and his secretary told me he'd be in the office after lunch."

"Then you have a delivery for him?" she asked.

"Not exactly. At least not right now. But I do need to talk to him."

"I'm sorry, miss, but I'm afraid he can't see you without an appointment."

"Can you just tell him that Jennifer Rodriguez is here? I'm sure he'll agree to see me."

The receptionist regarded her suspiciously, then nodded

and pushed a button on her phone. "Connie? Would you tell Mr. Madison there's a Jennifer Rodriguez here to see him." She waited, examining her perfectly manicured nails as she did. Jennifer glanced down at hers, nibbled short and unpolished. "What? Well, yes. I'll show her right in."

Jennifer gave her a smug smile before she trailed after her toward Ryan's office. He met them both at the door, a look of astonishment on his face. "Miss Rodriguez. This is a surprise."

"You remember me," she said, gulping down the tremor in her voice.

He took her elbow and showed her into his office. "Of course I remember you. Though that whole day was a blur, I do remember you."

She sat down in a chair and watched as he circled the desk. He wore a tailored suit and silk tie. His tanned skin contrasted sharply with his starched white shirt, and his hair, just a bit too long, brushed the collar of the shirt in boyish waves. The difference between the man she'd met at the drilling site and this man was startling. She'd remembered him as solid, rugged, with a blue-collar attitude about him. But this man was smooth, sophisticated, nothing like the man she'd pictured as she laid out her plan.

Jennifer pushed out of the chair, realizing that she was completely out of her element here. "I—I shouldn't have disturbed you. I know you're probably very busy and—"

"Please," he said, "don't go. I've actually been thinking about you."

She slowly lowered herself back into the chair. "Did you know Lucy is going home from the hospital today?"

"Really?" Ryan asked. "I haven't talked to Ben since that day in San Antonio. I took the blood tests, then came home the next day. Carolyn called me later in the week to tell me they found a match. I'm glad Lucy's doing well."

"Carolyn and Ben got married," she commented.

"They were engaged once, a long time ago, and the case brought them back together." She drew a deep breath. "Kind of like it brought us together."

"Right," he murmured.

A long silence spun out around them as Jennifer scrambled for another topic. "How are things going with your parents? Have they explained everything?"

"They've tried to rationalize their side of the story," Ryan replied, "but I'm not really interested in hearing their excuses. The bottom line is they paid ten thousand dollars for me in a supermarket parking lot. That's all I really need to know."

"They're your parents," she said, distractedly fiddling with the strap of her purse. "They've loved you for twenty-seven years. I think that should count for something."

"Thanks to them, I'll never know my real parents…the Mulhollands. They're both dead." He met her gaze squarely. "Did Rhonda and Jeffrey ask you to come here? Or are you here for Ben and Lucy?"

Jennifer shook her head. "I have a…personal reason for coming." She clasped her hands on her lap and drew a steadying breath. "Remember, at the hospital, you told me that if there was ever anything you could do for me, I should just ask?"

"Don't tell me you've got a client who needs a kidney transplant," he teased.

His smile warmed her blood and made her heart beat a little faster. Asking for a kidney would probably sound less ridiculous than her own request. Was she crazy to think he'd agree? Maybe it was all the hormones racing through her body that had rendered her temporarily insane. With a silent curse, she rose to her feet, ready to make her excuses and leave. But the moment she turned toward the door, a wave of dizziness washed over her.

Jennifer covered her eyes with her hand and reached back for the chair. She hadn't eaten lunch, and with the baby, if she didn't eat something every hour or two, she got light-headed. In a heartbeat, Ryan was out of his chair and around his desk. He grabbed her arm and slowly helped her over to the sofa. "My God, you're as white as a sheet."

"I—I'll be fine," Jennifer murmured. "I just need something to drink. A glass of juice maybe. Or a cookie."

"Lie down," he said, fluffing a pillow behind her. "I'll go get you something."

Jennifer groaned and flopped back on the pillow as he hurried out. "Why not just barf on his shoes?" she muttered. "That would get his attention." She closed her eyes and swallowed back a wave of nausea. For most of the day, she managed to forget the implications of her pregnancy—telling her parents about the baby, preparing for childbirth, raising a child as a single mother. And then the baby would speak to her from the womb, reminding her of how radically her life had changed over the past four months. And how much it would change over the coming months.

"*Ay, chica estúpida,*" she murmured. "You stupid girl. How did you ever get yourself into such a mess?"

"I NEED JUICE," Ryan said, frantically rummaging through the refrigerator in the employee lunch room. "Why don't we have any juice?"

Ryan's secretary stood behind him, anxious to help. "There's cranberry juice in the vending machine," Connie said.

"I don't know if she likes cranberry juice. Most people prefer orange juice. Or a piece of fruit. An apple would be good." Ryan stared at the wide array of drinks they kept to offer to guests during meetings. Designer water, pop, some kind of cold coffee drink. But no juice. "Get me the cranberry juice," he said, gathering up the lunch bags left inside the refrigerator. "And see if we have any cookies. She wants a cookie."

Ryan turned and hurried back to Jennifer, lunch bags clutched in his hands. There had to be something decent to eat in them. By the time he got back to his office, some of the color had returned to her face. He sat down beside her on the edge of the sofa and dropped the bags around his feet. Pressing his palm to her forehead, he scanned her features. "Are you feeling better? You don't feel warm. It could be heat exhaustion. It's been very hot lately."

Jennifer opened her eyes and smiled. "I'll be fine."

He let his palm linger for a long moment, delighting in the silken feel of her skin beneath his fingertips, soft strands of hair brushing the back of his hand.

"I don't have a fever," Jennifer murmured. "I'm pregnant."

Ryan snatched his hand away, startled by her sudden confession. He opened his mouth, then snapped it shut. Had he heard her right? Had she just told him she was pregnant? "You're..."

"Pregnant," she repeated, glancing at his hand, which still hung in mid-air. "I don't have the plague. I'm going to have a baby. And it's not contagious."

He coughed softly to cover his embarrassment. "I—I'm sorry. It's just that...well, you don't look pregnant." In truth, he felt a little guilty for his fantasies, considering her condition. It was like lusting after a nun!

She stared down at her stomach with a morose expression. "I am. Nearly five months." Pushing up on her elbow, she stared at him. "I haven't told many people. It's hard to say the words."

"And—and your husband? How does he feel about this?"

Jennifer giggled. "And here I thought you were so smooth," she teased.

"I've got a pregnant woman swooning in my office," Ryan retorted. "And no juice to be had. Give me a break."

"I don't have a husband." She ran her hand over her stomach, a barely noticeable swell the only evidence of her admission. "I don't even have a boyfriend. The father, he doesn't want anything to do with me or the baby, and I think that's for the best."

Connie appeared at the door with a can of cranberry juice and an orange soda. He pushed to his feet and grabbed the drinks, then returned to Jennifer's side. "Here," he said, offering her the juice. "Try this."

She took a long sip, watching him over the rim of the can. "I'm really sorry," she said, licking her lips. "I shouldn't have come. This is my life, my problem, and I'm going to have to deal with it on my own. I shouldn't have brought you into it."

"You got a little dizzy in my office," Ryan said. "That's all."

"That's not all," she said, a contrite expression suffusing her face. "I came here to ask a favor—a favor I probably have no right to ask."

"Ask," he said. "What do you need? Money? A place to stay? Some things for the baby? Whatever I can do."

"I need a fiancé," she said. "I need you."

This time Ryan was taken completely off guard. His jaw dropped and his eyes went wide. "What?"

"My parents don't know yet," she said, the words tumbling out. "And I think it would be easier for them to accept if they thought I hadn't been completely stupid. I need a fiancé, someone I can take home and introduce as the father of my baby. It won't be a long-term job. After a few months, we'll have a fight and then you'll just disappear from my life. Please don't feel any obligation. Like I said, this is my responsibility and I'm going to—''

"I'll do it," Ryan said softly.

"—have to deal with this sooner or later. It's just that I come from a very strict Catholic family, and when Diego and Carmen find out they'll—"

"I said, I'll do it," Ryan repeated.

The rest of her words froze in her throat and she blinked, as if she weren't certain she'd heard him right. A slow smile curled the corners of her mouth. "You will? You'll pretend to be my fiancé?"

"Yes," he replied.

With a squeal of delight, Jennifer threw her arms around his neck and kissed his cheek. *"¡Gracias! ¡Muchísimas gracias! Le estoy muy agradecida."*

Ryan drew back and looked down into her eyes, which were sparkling with excitement and relief. *"Con mucho gusto,"* he said. "You're welcome." Without thinking, he took her face between his palms and dropped a gentle kiss on her mouth. As soon as their lips met, he realized his mistake. But the urge to kiss her had been too much to deny and he couldn't regret his actions.

Slowly, he pulled back, prepared to see indignation, perhaps even anger in her eyes. But her wide gaze showed only surprise—and a tiny hint of curiosity. Ryan was tempted to kiss her again, to see if she'd respond. After all, they were engaged, weren't they? But his better judgment won out. "I'm sorry," he said. "I didn't mean to—"

"No," Jennifer interrupted, placing a finger on his lips. "It's my fault. My family always tells me I'm too impetuous. I shouldn't have kissed you first. I have to learn to think before I act." Her gaze dropped to her lap. "After all, that's what got me into this trouble in the first place."

"But that's what attracted me to you in the first place," Ryan teased in a feeble attempt to lighten the moment.

"Your passion and fire. The way you jump into a situation without even considering the consequences. I'm usually so careful and conservative. It's our differences that made me fall in love with you."

"In love?"

He grinned and brushed a strand of hair from her eyes. "I'm just practicing. Do I sound convincing?"

"Practicing for what?"

"For when I meet your parents," he said, turning to pick up one of the lunch bags. He plucked out a sandwich bag filled with Oreos and handed her one. "I'm sure they're going to wonder how we met. We should have a story worked out."

Jennifer frowned. "I never thought that far ahead. I guess I didn't expect you to agree to my plan."

"See, you are too impetuous. Now, when is this meeting going to take place?"

"I'm supposed to go home to El Paso on Friday afternoon. This Saturday is my sister's *quinceañera*. Her fifteenth birthday. It's a big deal in our culture, kind of like your sweet sixteen and a debutante ball rolled into one. There's a mass Saturday afternoon and a huge party with dancing and food on Saturday night. All the family will be there, my aunts and uncles and cousins. I figure my parents will be so distracted with the party plans, they won't have time to focus on my news."

"So when do we practice? We should at least get our story straight."

"How about dinner at my house?" Jennifer suggested. "Tomorrow night. I'll make *pozole*. It's my specialty. Actually, it's the only thing I know how to cook. It's kind of like a thick soup made of pork and hominy."

Ryan forced a smile. Hominy? He couldn't say that he'd ever tasted hominy. "Sounds good. I'll be there."

Jennifer swung her legs to the floor and Ryan helped

her to her feet, wrapping her delicate fingers in his hand. "I'll drive you home," he offered.

She tugged her hand from his, then shook her head. "I have my car. I'll be fine. I just needed something in my stomach."

"What about lunch?" Ryan asked. "Why don't you let me buy you lunch?"

"Roy and Ralph need me back at the office. I'm working on a big parental abduction case and I've got a lot of work to do before I leave for the weekend."

Ryan didn't want to let her go and searched for any excuse to get her to stay. But in the end, he accompanied Jennifer to the lobby and watched as she walked out. Then he strolled back to his office, stepped inside and closed the door. A satisfied smile quirked the corners of his mouth.

Once again, Jennifer Rodriguez had barged into his life and turned it upside down. Only this time, he planned to make sure she stayed a little longer.

"*Mamá,* I promise, I'll be there in time for Tía Yolanda's arrival. We're leaving right around lunchtime and we'll be there before dinner Friday night." She reached for the spoon and gave the *pozole* a stir, then bent down and adjusted the heat.

"We?" her mother asked. "Who is this we?"

Jennifer drew a deep breath, all too familiar with her mother's nosy nature. "I'm bringing a friend home."

"Ah, you're bringing that sweet Elena? That girl from your building? I like her. She's a good girl. She listens to her mother."

"No, *Mamá,* not Elena. I'm bringing a…a friend. A friend who's a…boy. A man, actually. A man—I mean, a boyfriend. I'm bringing home my boyfriend, all right?" A long silence echoed over the phone lines between El Paso and Odessa. "*Mamá?*"

"Who is this boy you're bringing? What's his name? Who are his parents?"

"He's not a boy, *Mamá*. He's a man. His name is Ryan. Ryan Madison. He's very nice and very successful. *Papi* will love him."

"Madison?"

"Yes, *Mamá*, Madison. Not Ruiz, not Hernandez, not Castillo. Madison, like the fourth president of our country."

"Does he go to church?"

The doorbell rang and Jennifer glanced down at the dish towel tied around her waist. "*Mamá*, that's him at the door. I'm cooking dinner for us tonight. You can interrogate him on his religious beliefs when we get there."

"Well, I'll tell your *Papi* that he isn't in danger of losing his daughter," Carmen said.

"And why is that?"

"Because once this man tastes your cooking, he won't be back."

"Goodbye, *Mamá*. I'll see you on Friday evening. *We'll* see you." She dropped the phone in the cradle, then hurried over to the table and adjusted the colorful hand-painted Mexican stoneware on the bright tablecloth. She reached for the matches to light the candles, then decided candles might not send the right message.

After all, this agreement they had was strictly between friends. But they really weren't friends yet. Perhaps acquaintances was a better description. But then, they were more than—

The doorbell rang again and Jennifer threw the dish towel onto the kitchen counter next to the stove and hurried to the door. At the last second, she raked her fingers through her hair and smoothed her palms over the skirt of her new dress. Though it wasn't a maternity dress, it did have an empire waist. Her clothes had suddenly stopped

fitting yesterday, as if she'd swallowed a basketball for
breakfast, and she'd been forced to buy something new.
Pasting a smile on her face, she pulled the door open.

Jennifer's breath caught in her throat at the sight of him.
She knew he was handsome—in a suit, in faded jeans, it
didn't really matter. Tonight, he wore immaculately
pressed khakis and a pale-blue cotton polo shirt that set
off his dark tan. His hair was still damp from a shower
and it looked like he'd combed it with his fingers. "Hi,"
she murmured, her knees going soft.

He pulled a bouquet of sunflowers from behind his back
and held them out. "Hello, *mi prometido*. I'm sorry I'm a
little late. I got tied up at the site."

Jennifer laughed and took the flowers from his hand.
"Come in. And it's *promitida*. That's the feminine form
of fiancée. You're my *prometido*."

Ryan shrugged. "My Spanish is pretty lousy, isn't it?
I've been trying to learn. That way, when the guys on the
drilling site are talking about me, I'll know what they're
saying."

"Come. Sit down. Dinner is almost ready."

"How are you feeling?" he asked as he closed the
apartment door behind him.

"Fine," she said, grabbing a vase from an end table
near the window. "No more dizzy spells."

"Did you see your doctor?"

Jennifer shook her head, secretly pleased by his concern.
"No, it's nothing. I just have to be more careful about
how I eat. Now, sit down and I'll get you a drink. Would
you like a beer?"

He nodded, slowly sat down, then frowned. "Do you
smell that?"

"That's my *pozole*," Jennifer said proudly.

Ryan stood and stepped around her. "No, I really think

something is—'' He cursed and hurried over to the
kitchen, where flames rose from the stove.

Jennifer screamed and hurried after him. ''¡Ay, Dios
mío! I'll call the fire department. No, there's a fire extin-
guisher....'' She paused, trying to remember where she'd
put it. ''Throw some water on it!''

Ryan calmly grabbed a stockpot from the rack over the
breakfast bar and dropped it on top of the burning dish
towel. Then he grabbed a saucepan and filled it with water,
holding out his arm to keep her back. ''It'll go out in a
few seconds.''

When he was satisfied that the fire was out, Jennifer
hurried to the stove and pulled the cover off the *pozole*.
But in her haste, she forgot to use a pot holder and the lid
burned her fingers. She cried out and let it clatter to the
floor, where it hit her big toe, which was sticking out of
her sandal. The kitchen filled with the smell of scorched
hominy and burned terry cloth as Jennifer's eyes filled with
tears.

Once again, the baby inside her seemed to hold the con-
trols over her emotions, turning her from a babbling idiot
to a blubbering fool in the blink of an eye. She couldn't
stop the tears from coming even though she wasn't sure
why she was crying. It wasn't the ruined meal or her sting-
ing fingers or even the smoke stain on her kitchen ceiling.
It was...everything.

Jennifer buried her face in her hands and slid down to
sit on the kitchen floor. A few moments later, she felt Ryan
beside her, his fingers stroking her temple. ''It's all right,''
he said. ''The fire's out. No damage done.''

She looked up at him through her tears and a giggle
slipped from her throat. ''I don't care about the fire or the
food. That's the least of my worries. I'm such a mess. I
can't seem to control my emotions. I start crying at the

drop of a hat. My life is in chaos and I'm not sure if I'll ever be able to set it right.''

"I know how you feel," Ryan said, tipping her chin up and capturing her gaze with his.

"Yeah, I guess you do."

He grabbed her hand and gave her fingers a squeeze. "Why don't we sit down on the sofa and relax. I'll call for a pizza and we'll get to work. You can make *pozole* for me again some other night."

He gently helped her to her feet and led her over to the sofa, then returned to the kitchen to order the pizza. Ryan found a beer in the refrigerator and brought her a glass of orange juice. Then he settled on the sofa beside her, his arm draped over the back. "So, where do we start?"

"Well, since I know pretty much everything about you, we should start with me."

"How do you know about me?" he asked after taking a sip of his beer.

"I did a pretty extensive investigation before I came to see you at the drilling site. A bachelor's and master's degree from Texas A and M, dean's list, graduated cum laude, bought your first well with money you made in the stock market, built your business into a multimillion—"

"All right, all right," Ryan said. "Let's start with your family."

"My *papi*, Diego, came from Mexico when he was fifteen. He worked picking vegetables in California until he found a job in a factory. He got his high school diploma going to night classes. He lived the American dream, working his way up, saving his pennies, until he and my mother bought a small electronics factory in El Paso. Now it's huge and he makes components for the auto industry. I think you'll have a lot in common."

"And your mother?"

Jennifer slid down to the end of the couch and stretched

her feet out in front of her, leaning back onto a throw pillow. "*Mamá*. She'll be a little tougher. Her name is Carmen and she's the glue that holds our family together. She's lived in this country nearly all her life and she has very high expectations for her children. We all must go to college, find a good job and marry a nice Catholic."

"Well, that will be a problem then," Ryan said. "I'm not a very good Catholic. I haven't been to church in ages, although I used to be an altar boy. That should count for something shouldn't it?"

"It doesn't make a difference since we really aren't getting married," Jennifer said with a smile.

He slipped her sandals off her feet and tucked her bare toes beneath his thigh. "Brothers and sisters?"

"Four. Joe is nineteen, Maria will be fifteen on Saturday, Linda is ten and Teresa is eight."

"And Jennifer?"

"I'm twenty five," she said. "I went to U of T in El Paso and got a degree in accounting."

"Accounting," he said. "Kind of an odd background for a private investigator, isn't it?"

She sat up. "Now, there's another problem we need to discuss. You see, my parents don't know I'm a P.I. They think I'm an accountant for the office. I don't think they'd approve, they wouldn't find it respectable enough. So if the subject of my career comes up, which I'm sure it will, don't tell them the truth."

"I can vouch that you're a good P.I.," Ryan said. "Look how you tried to help Lucy. You couldn't do something so important as an accountant, could you?"

"I guess not. It's just that I've spent my life trying not to disappoint my parents and yet trying to live my own life. You don't know the pressure of being the oldest child, the perfect little girl. I turned into a rebel at an early age."

"You couldn't have been that bad," Ryan said, "to turn out so well."

Jennifer gave him a grudging smile. "As a child, I was a tomboy. Always with tangled hair and skinned knees. In high school, I wore short skirts and ran with a fast crowd. In college, I partied a little too much. And look at me now. I was supposed to remain a virgin until I got married. Breaking that little rule will become quite obvious in another month."

"What about the baby? How do you plan to tell them about that?" Ryan asked.

Jennifer groaned, then closed her eyes and flopped back on the pillow. "I don't know. I was just going to wing it. Wait for the right moment and then tell them the whole thing all at once. I figured with Maria's *quinceañera* and all the guests, there wouldn't be a chance to interrogate me—or you." She drew a shaky breath. "It's probably going to get a little tense when we tell them about the baby and there will probably be a lot of accusations leveled at you." Jennifer sat up and looked at him. "You can back out if you want. I'll understand."

He idly rubbed her leg, his palm sliding from her ankle along her calf and back again. Delicious sensations skittered over her skin at his touch. Though they barely knew each other, the action seemed perfectly natural. After all, he was her fiancé—at least for the next few months.

Still, it felt good to have a man pay attention to her. She'd been so lonely these past months, dealing with her pregnancy all by herself, wondering if she could handle so many changes on her own, frightened of what the future held. She felt safer when Ryan was near.

For the rest of the evening, they traded details of their lives and made up a few memories of their own—the night they met, their first kiss, the special spot where Ryan asked her to marry him, the first time they heard the baby's heartbeat. And when they'd exhausted every subject and eaten the last piece of pizza, Jennifer walked Ryan to the door.

He bent closer and brushed a kiss on her cheek and then promised to be ready by noon on Friday. After she closed the door behind him, Jennifer reached up and touched her cheek, finding it still warm from the contact. She closed her eyes and sighed. Though it had been a nice kiss, she couldn't help but wish that he'd kissed her like he had the previous day, his lips warm on hers, her face cupped between his palms.

For the first time since she'd thought of this preposterous plan, she actually believed it might work. With Ryan's help, she felt as if she could accomplish anything. And it was clear he was a kind and charming man. How could her parents not fall in love with him? She already—

Jennifer sucked in a sharp breath and pushed the words from her brain. Yes, he was a wonderful man, the sort of man she might imagine spending her life with. But when she'd decided to have this baby, she'd also decided to raise it alone. She had her career and her own life and she'd worked hard at independence. She wasn't about to give that all up now just because some guy had been nice to her.

"This will work," she murmured. "I'll tell my parents, I'll come back to Odessa, we'll break up and I'll never see him again."

But the thought of Ryan Madison disappearing from her life caused a sharp pang of regret. Was she really doing the right thing, using him like this? And would she be able to put him in the past and get on with her life as if she'd never known him?

CHAPTER TWO

"I DON'T KNOW what to say, darling. Do you want me to tell you we regret our actions? How can we? We found you. You became a part of our family."

"You didn't find me, you *bought* me," Ryan said, his voice filled with bitterness. When the doorbell had rung, he'd expected to find Jennifer standing on the other side, ready to leave for El Paso. His heart had quickened as he pulled the door open; he'd been anxious to see her again. Instead, his mother had walked in, determined to straighten out everything that had gone wrong between them.

She was an attractive woman, trim and well-dressed, her ash-blond hair carefully styled into a simple pageboy. When he was growing up, he'd always been so proud of her. Rhonda Madison had been the prettiest mother on the block. Unlike some of the other mothers, her entire life revolved around Ryan—his school activities, sports. Anything that caught his interest caught hers as well. In hindsight, it all became clear. She'd been desperate to become a mother, and when she finally did, Rhonda Madison didn't want to miss a single minute.

"Didn't you ask questions?" Ryan demanded. "Like where I'd come from? What had happened to my parents?"

"He told us your mother was a teenage runaway," Rhonda said. "We'd just turned over our entire life savings to this man. Your father might have been a little suspicious, but he wanted to make me happy and a baby was the only thing that could do that. We aren't bad people, Ryan. And if we'd known you'd been stolen from your mother, we would have—''

"You would have bought me anyway?" Ryan asked. He waited for his mother to deny the accusation, but she didn't.

"Have you talked to your…" The word stuck in her throat as if it pained her to say it. "The woman who gave birth to you?"

"You'll be happy to hear she's dead," Ryan said, wanting to hurt her as much as she'd hurt him. "I'll never know her, or my father. I do have a brother, though. And a niece." Impatient to be done with the conversation, he glanced at his watch. "I have to get ready. I'm going away for the weekend."

"Really?" his mother asked in a forced attempt at interest. "Where are you going?"

"El Paso," he murmured. "I'm going to meet the parents of my fiancée." Why he'd said it, Ryan didn't know, for it was a bald-faced lie. Perhaps he'd meant to shock his mother, to draw her into another argument or maybe to drive home the fact that she wasn't a part of his life anymore.

But she didn't take the bait and the pained expression on her face caused a wave of guilt to rush over him. Sooner or later, he'd have to stop punishing her and accept what she and his father had done. But he wasn't ready. Not yet. The wound was still too raw, and even after it healed a bit, he doubted that he'd ever be able to fully forgive them.

"Maybe, after you get back, you can bring your young lady to the house for dinner," she suggested. "Your birthday is coming up. We could plan a barbecue."

Ryan turned away from her and stuffed another shirt into his overnight bag. "Sure," he muttered. He'd missed twenty-six birthdays with his real family, why not spend another one with the people who had been faking it? Suddenly, birthdays didn't seem so important.

He heard her sigh in defeat and approach him from behind. When she placed her hand on his shoulder, he stiffened. He fought the urge to turn to her and gather her into his arms, to forget everything that had happened in the past month. But nothing could erase the lies they'd told.

In the end, she silently walked out the front door of his condo, leaving him to deal with his demons. Ryan furrowed his fingers through his hair and cursed softly. He'd never been a man to act on his emotions, choosing to think every word, every action out first. But since he'd learned of his true parentage, he couldn't rely on his usual dispassionate nature anymore. Nothing made sense, and until it did, he'd just have to operate on instinct alone.

A soft knock sounded at the door and he spun around, ready to rebuff his mother again. But Jennifer stood in the open doorway, dressed in a pretty peasant blouse and a colorful skirt. She wore a straw hat on her head, her long hair tucked up beneath the crown. Like the sun appearing from behind a dark cloud, she instantly lightened his mood.

"What is it?" she asked, frowning. "You look upset."

"Nothing," Ryan murmured, gathering up his overnight bag and tucking his garment bag under his arm. "I just had a visit from my mother. Needless to say, it didn't go well."

"You shouldn't punish your parents for this," Jennifer said softly. "They didn't know."

"They should have asked," Ryan countered.

"You can't know what's in a mother's heart. Sometimes the need to have a child is so strong it hurts."

Ryan's jaw went tight and he fought the impulse to tell Jennifer to mind her own business. But if there was anyone he could talk to about his personal problems, it was her.

And he didn't want to break the tenuous connection they'd built between them. "I thought I'd drive," Ryan murmured. "We can take my Lexus. I've got a CD changer and—"

"But I have a convertible," she said, accepting the change in subject without further comment. "And it's a beautiful day. Besides, I know a short cut through the desert. I bought some lunch for us and we can stop at Red Bluff Lake on our way there."

Though Ryan would have preferred to determine the route and take his own car, Jennifer seemed so excited about the trip, he decided to throw caution to the wind and go along. After all, this was the new Ryan Madison, operating on instinct and emotion. He grabbed his bags and walked out behind her. Her little convertible was parked at the curb. It had to be at least ten years old and didn't look as though it could make it through town, much less across all of West Texas. "Maybe we should take my car," he said.

"Don't worry," Jennifer chided. "We'll have fun."

As they headed out of town, bypassing the interstate that went from Midland-Odessa to El Paso, Ryan realized why she'd chosen the route. It was obvious Jennifer didn't believe in speed limits. Or stop signs or double yellow lines. She was in all probability the most aggressive driver he'd ever seen short of Al Unser or Richard Petty.

He relaxed a bit when they got out of town and sped toward Kermit. "Maybe we should use this time to brush up," he shouted over the sound of the wind racing around them.

She turned and grinned at him, her eyes hidden beneath the brim of her hat and her dark sunglasses. "All right," she said. "Ask me anything."

He considered his first question carefully. He really wanted to ask her about the baby's father, but Ryan knew he ought to leave that question for another time. "Jennifer. That's an odd name for someone of your background."

She laughed. "That's my father's doing. When he first came to this country, he loved to go to the movies. The only movie he'd ever seen in Mexico was *Duel in the Sun*, with Gregory Peck and Jennifer Jones. He saw it at an old *cine* when he was eight. And then he came to America and the first movie star he saw was Jennifer Jones, walking right down the street in Los Angeles. He took it as a sign from God that he was meant to live in this country. And that's how I got my name."

Ryan laughed. "All right, now it's your turn. Ask me anything."

"You were involved," she said. "Nearly married a woman named Elise. Then you broke it off last year. Why?"

"You are a good investigator." He sat back in his seat and stared out at the long dusty strip of road in front of them. "She was a friend of the family and we'd dated since we were in college. It just seemed as if we were together for all the wrong reasons. There was no..."

"Passion?" Jennifer asked.

Ryan nodded. "Yeah. Passion."

Silence spun between them as the scenery sped by. In truth, he'd seen more passion and excitement in a few hours with Jennifer Rodriguez than he'd seen the entire time he'd been with Elise. With Jennifer, life was a series of surprises. He never knew what to expect or how she'd react. And though he'd always assumed he wanted a woman who was prudent and restrained, when he was with Jennifer, he felt more alive than he'd ever felt in his life.

Perhaps it had been the upheaval, the uncertainty that had changed his perspective. His life had been so orderly, so predictable. He knew who he was and where he was going. But since he'd learned the secrets of his birth, he didn't feel like Ryan Madison anymore.

He glanced over at the beautiful woman sitting beside him, tendrils of hair whipping around her face, her lips curled in an impish smile. She glanced his way, then laughed, pressing her foot to the floor, the car accelerating smartly.

Ryan chuckled and tipped his face up to the intense afternoon sun. For the first time in his life, he felt completely free, unencumbered by expectations—his own and his family's. He was a man with no past and an uncertain future, but the prospect of not knowing what was around the next corner didn't bother him in the least.

Whatever had brought about the change, whether it was Jennifer herself or the news she'd revealed, didn't matter. He was beginning to like the new Ryan Madison.

THEY PULLED INTO El Paso right on schedule. They'd stopped at Red Bluff Lake, and a few other towns along the way. Jennifer was beginning to realize that from now on, the baby would prevent these marathon drives. She had to go to the bathroom at least once every hour and there hadn't always been a bathroom available. Squatting on the edge of the road had been a necessity, lightened only by Ryan's good-natured teasing. She made a note to take the interstate home.

Compared with the flat landscape around Midland-Odessa, El Paso was like an oasis. Set on the Rio Grande and split by the Franklin Mountains, it had first been a huge cattle ranch before the railroads brought people and prosperity. On the other side of the river in Mexico was El Paso's twin city, Ciudad Juárez. She steered the car toward the west side of town, to the lovely neighborhoods built around the Rio Grande Country Club.

The anticipation of seeing her family always brought a

rush of excitement. But it was different this time. For all she knew, this might be her last visit. Once her parents learned of the baby, they might kick her out of the family. She looked over at Ryan. "Are you ready for this?"

He reached across and tangled his fingers in the hair at the nape of her neck. "As ready as I'll ever be. I'll just follow your lead, and if I say anything wrong, just give me a sign."

She turned into a subdivision of spacious homes set on large lots and followed the winding streets. When she finally stopped near a sprawling hacienda-style home with melon-colored stucco and a red-tile roof, she drew a deep breath. The sound of music drifted from the backyard on the still air and cars filled the driveway and the surrounding street. No doubt the celebration had begun. "I'm not sure *I'm* ready for this," she murmured.

Ryan leaned over and forced her gaze to his. "You have to do this, Jen. What are they going to say five months from now when you walk in the front door with a newborn?"

"You're right," she said, warmed by the familiar use of her name. She couldn't recall hearing him say her name before and she liked the sound of it on his lips.

He smiled, then pressed a quick kiss to her cheek. "Here, I have something for you." Ryan reached in his pocket and withdrew a small velvet-covered box, then held it out to Jennifer.

"Ryan, what have you done?" she said, snatching the box from his fingers and flipping it open. Inside, a lovely solitaire diamond sparkled in a simple platinum setting. "Oh, no, what have you done?"

"Don't worry. I had big credit at the jewelry store. After Elise threw her ring back in my face, the store wouldn't give me my money back. So, I guess you could consider it a freebie."

She slipped it on her finger. In another, less pregnant time, it would have fit perfectly. But as she pushed it over her swollen knuckle, she wondered if she'd get it off again. Jennifer stared down at the diamond, twinkling in the light of the late-afternoon sun. "Thank you," she said. Then with a soft laugh, she wrapped her arms around his neck and hugged him hard. "This will be perfect. I'll just wear the ring, and when they notice, we'll tell them."

When she finally drew back, her gaze met his. He stared down into her eyes for a long moment. As if drawn by an invisible force, their lips came together in a kiss so exquisitely soft and perfect that it took Jennifer's breath away. She didn't want it to end, the flood of sensation racing through her body like an addictive drug, calming her nerves yet setting them on edge at the same time.

He furrowed his hands through her hair and molded his mouth to hers, deepening the kiss. Desire warmed her blood and she melted into his arms, wishing that the kiss might go on forever. But a few moments later, he drew back and his gaze skimmed her face.

Her hands clutched at the front of his shirt. "What was that for?" she asked, her voice barely audible, her lips damp from his kiss.

"That was for luck," Ryan said, leaning back into his seat.

"Maybe we should just turn around and drive back to Odessa," she suggested.

Ryan gave her hand a squeeze. "We'll get through this."

With that, Jennifer gathered her resolve and opened her car door. Ryan did the same, then grabbed their bags from the back seat and followed her up to the house. But just as she put her hand on the doorknob, the door swung open in front of her.

Maria screamed and launched herself into Jennifer's

arms. "*Mamá, Papi,* Jenny is here!" She pulled her sister inside and Jennifer was swallowed up by her family's greetings. Her brother, Joe, shouted at her from across the foyer and Teresa wriggled through the oncoming crowd of aunts and uncles and cousins to hug her legs. Linda followed close behind and picked Teresa up so that she could kiss Jennifer on the cheek.

As the crowd moved toward the kitchen, where they were sure to find Carmen and Diego, Jennifer looked over her shoulder and sent Ryan a pleading look. "Wait there," she mouthed.

When she'd finally run the gauntlet of kisses and hugs from all the relatives, she made her way to her parents and hugged them both. Her father was a bear of a man, strong and solid, full of the same passion and spontaneity that Jennifer possessed. Her mother was the opposite, cool and controlled, a patrician woman who held her children to strict standards.

"*Niña,*" her father shouted, gathering her in his arms. "Your mother says you've brought a young man home. Where is he? He wasn't scared off already, was he?"

"He's waiting in the foyer, *Papi,*" she said, ignoring his good-natured teasing.

Her mother drew a dramatic breath and smoothed her silver-gray hair. "Well, Diego, let us go meet the boy." She grabbed her husband's arm and started toward the front of the house, giving Jennifer no choice but to hurry after them. Her parents stopped short when they saw Ryan standing in the spacious foyer, bags surrounding him.

Carmen nodded curtly, her gaze raking Ryan shrewdly. "*Bienvenido.* Welcome to our home."

Jennifer quickly stepped around them and took her place at Ryan's side. "*Mamá, Papi,* I'd like you to meet my...friend, Ryan Madison. Ryan, these are my parents, Carmen and Diego Rodriguez."

As the three of them exchanged pleasantries, Jennifer chided herself inwardly. What a wimp she was! Why not just introduce him as her fiancé and get that out of the way? She'd have been halfway there after barely walking in the door. She twisted the ring around on her finger until the diamond was cradled in her palm.

"Mr. and Mrs. Rodriguez, it's a pleasure to finally meet you," Ryan said, reaching out to shake their hands. "Jennifer has told me so much about you."

"Funny, she hasn't told us a thing about you," Carmen murmured, grudgingly impressed with his easy charm and impeccable manners but still reserving judgment for later.

"Carmen, haven't you forgotten something?" Diego teased.

Jennifer's mother looked over at her husband. "And what is that?"

"You've forgotten to tell Jennifer she hasn't been eating." He turned to Ryan and chuckled. "It's part of their little ritual. Carmen tells Jennifer she's too skinny and Jennifer tells Carmen that she eats plenty. Jennifer tells Carmen to mind her own business and Carmen tells Jennifer to mind her elders."

"Well, I didn't say anything because Jennifer looks fine. In fact, she looks as if she has gained weight." Carmen nodded. "You look healthy, *niña*."

Jennifer sent Ryan a sideways glance and he returned a reassuring smile. "Actually, *Mamá*, I have gained a few pounds." She slipped her hand around Ryan's arm. "And I'm sure you have lots of things prepared to fatten me up even more."

"Come along, then, Ryan," Carmen ordered. "We will introduce you to the family and get you both something to eat."

They followed a few steps behind her parents. "Coward," Ryan whispered.

"Don't rush me," she muttered. "All in good time."

But as they were both drawn in to the whirl of the barbecue, the right time never seemed to appear. Jennifer tried to keep an eye on Ryan as she mingled with the guests. He'd found a friend in her eight-year-old sister, Teresa, who dragged him from spot to spot in the backyard, introducing him to curious relatives and showing off her special hiding places. Like Jennifer as a child, Teresa was a tomboy and preferred to spend her time up trees or crouched behind bushes, knees muddied and hair tangled.

When they finally met up near the edge of the swimming pool, Jennifer felt compelled to apologize. "I know this is a little overwhelming. There have to be at least a hundred people here."

"It's quite a celebration," Ryan said, casually slipping his arm around her waist as he stared out at the boisterous crowd. "Are they all relatives?"

"Relatives and friends. Some are Maria's *padrinos*— her sponsors. They help pay for the *quinceañera* celebration, at least in spirit, since *Papi* won't let them pay for anything big. They contribute little things like the bouquet for the Virgin Mary and the souvenirs for the guests and Maria's crown and ring. They also give her the *capias* and the *capia* doll."

"*Capia?*"

"The *capia* doll is like a keepsake, a doll made up to look just like the *quinceañera* in all her birthday finery. And the *capias* are ribbon favors with Maria's name and the date printed on them. The doll is covered with the ribbons, and after they're all distributed to party guests, the doll is revealed."

"And you went through this when you were fifteen?"

Jennifer smiled and shook her head. "No. I was the family rebel. Of course, I had the mass and I was forced to wear a pretty dress. But I insisted on a small party with just close family. And I made my father give all the money he'd put aside for my *quinceañera* to a homeless shelter. Maria, on the other hand, prefers to follow tradition and spend as much of *Papi*'s money as possible.''

''I didn't expect anything quite so elaborate.''

''If you think this is big, wait until tomorrow. There's the mass and then the party. Tomorrow morning the party planners and caterers and musicians will come and transform the backyard into something resembling a fairyland. Maria will have her court of honor—probably fourteen *damas* and *chambelanes,* plus Teresa for her flower girl and Linda for her princess. After the mass, they'll all walk in with her and *Mamá* and *Papi* and the *padrinos.* That's called *la marcha.* Knowing Maria's flair for the theatric, there will be choreographed dancing. It all leads up to the big moment—the presentation, when *la niña* is transformed into *una señorita.* When she changes from a girl to a young lady.''

''How does that happen?'' Ryan asked.

''She changes her shoes,'' Jennifer said.

''No, really, I want to know.''

''That's how it happens. She'll begin a waltz with *Papi* and then the music will stop and she'll walk to a chair in the middle of the dance floor in flats. Then *Mamá* will change her shoes to heels and she'll finish her waltz with *Papi.* And after that, she'll dance with all her *chambelanes,* the boys on the court. Those are mostly cousins and sons of *Papi* and *Mamá*'s friends. She saves the last dance for her *chambelán de honor,* which will probably be my brother, Joe.''

Ryan released a long breath. ''Wow, it's like a wedding.''

''It's bigger than a wedding,'' Jennifer said.

He turned to her and tugged her closer. ''I'm glad you

asked me to come. Meeting your family gives me a keener insight into you.''

''And what have you figured out?''

''That you're a pretty fascinating woman,'' he said.

She playfully bumped against him. ''You are too charming, Ryan Madison. No wonder my sister Teresa is in love with you.'' Jennifer pointed to a tree at the other end of the pool. ''She's watching us. Why don't you go over and ask her to dance. You'll make her day.''

Jennifer watched as he circled the pool and stood beneath the old cottonwood tree. He held up his arms and Teresa jumped into them. He set her down and she wiped the dirt from her hands on her pretty white dress. Before long, they were dancing the night away on the makeshift dance floor.

Jennifer managed to steal a dance with him, a pretty Julio Iglesias ballad, after Teresa was ordered to bed. They moved around the terrace to the soft sounds of the small mariachi combo and the high, wavering voice of the singer. Jennifer looked over to the house to find her parents watching them both from the terrace. ''Maybe we should tell them now,'' she murmured, resting her cheek against Ryan's chest, exhaustion suddenly overwhelming her.

''Not just yet,'' he said, his breath soft on her temple.

She sighed softly, then drew a deep breath, enjoying the scent of his cologne. ''All right,'' she murmured. ''Not just yet.''

In the end, they danced until the band stopped playing, both of them anxious to avoid the conflict that would surely accompany Jennifer's revelations. As the party guests slowly made their way home, she walked with Ryan to the house, then showed him to one of the three guest rooms that her mother had prepared.

''I guess we'll tell them tomorrow,'' she said, standing outside the door. ''Maybe that's for the best.''

Ryan pulled her into his arms and gave her a hug. "I'll see you in the morning," he said, his fingers skimming her cheek. He wanted to kiss her then, she could see it in his eyes. And she wanted him to capture her mouth and send sweet, stirring sensations racing through her body. But during the party, they'd been playacting, pretending to be a devoted couple for the benefit of her family.

Here in the hall outside his room, it was just the two of them. Two people with nothing more between them than a simple favor. "Yes," she murmured. "I'll see you at breakfast."

He slipped inside his bedroom and closed the door behind him. Jennifer groaned inwardly and leaned back against the wall. Then she glanced down at the diamond she'd kept hidden all night long. She'd never thought much about marriage, never dated a man with whom she'd consider spending her life. But this little game they were playing had given her a taste of what a real relationship might be like.

A soft sigh slipped from her lips and she reached up and rubbed her forehead. It would be so easy to fall for him. But was this really the first stirrings of love she felt? Or was it just desperation? Was she looking for a man to spend her life with or was she simply looking for a father for her baby?

She pushed away from the wall and slowly walked toward her room at the end of the hall. The only thing she knew for sure was that she wouldn't figure it all out in one night.

THE NIGHT WAS perfectly silent, so quiet Ryan could almost hear the stars twinkling in the dark sky. He stretched out on a chaise longue at the far end of the pool and stared down into the illuminated water. The reflection cast wavering shadows all around him, lulling him into a contemplative mood.

His thoughts turned to Jennifer and he glanced out across the wide lawn to the house and tried to imagine her lying in bed, her hair tumbled across her pillow in silken waves, her lips parted slightly as she slept, her body warm and inviting.

As he'd tossed and turned in his own bed, he fought the urge to slip into her room. To wake her and spend just a few more hours in her company, holding her, talking in quiet words. He'd grown to love the sound of her voice, the lilting trace of Mexico that made every sentence like a tiny phrase of music. And her eyes, glittering with mischief or filled with emotion, so dark and deep he could disappear inside them...

Ryan closed his eyes, drawing deeply of the cool air. The sounds of the night surrounded him, and when he opened his eyes again, his gaze came to rest on a vision...a dream that had suddenly become real.

She walked down the steps of the terrace, barefoot, her hair blown by the soft breeze, her nightgown made translucent by the light behind her. He watched her limbs move gracefully beneath the thin fabric as she strolled toward him. When she reached the pool, the light from the water illuminated her face. At that moment in time, Ryan was certain he'd never seen anything or anyone quite as beautiful.

"What are you doing out here?" she asked.

"I couldn't sleep," he said, ignoring the flood of desire that had pooled in the vicinity of his lap. "Strange room, strange bed."

"Strange situation," Jennifer added. "But you did a good job tonight. I think everyone believed we were a couple."

"Good. It wasn't too difficult. You're pretty easy to be nice to."

Jennifer smiled. "Have I told you how much I appreciate what you're doing?"

"Yes," he replied. "Several times."

She crossed her arms beneath her breasts. "It seems like a lot to do. I mean, in comparison with what I did for you. I turned your life upside down and you're trying to help me keep mine upright."

"It's all right."

"No, it's not," Jennifer said. "I feel like I owe you an explanation."

He patted the cushion between his legs. "Sit." Jennifer did as she was told, settling between his legs and leaning back against his chest. He wrapped his arms around her waist and rested his chin on her bare shoulder, the scent of her perfume tickling his nose. God, he loved holding her. Her body seemed to fit perfectly against his. "You don't have to say anything. I don't need explanations."

"But I want to tell you," she said. "I haven't told anyone and maybe it's time I talked about it."

"All right," Ryan said softly.

She paused for a long moment, as if putting all the words in order before she began. "We met at a lunchtime concert at Odessa College right before Memorial Day. Our offices are close by and I picked up lunch and decided to go listen to this bluegrass band. He sat down beside me and we started talking." She paused again. "His name was Jim Kestwick and he was a nice guy, clean cut, well-mannered. It turns out he's an officer in the Navy and he serves on an aircraft carrier. He was visiting his parents on leave. We spent three days together and he was charming and exciting and I thought I knew what I was doing. Then he told me he was engaged to a woman who lived out East. God, what a cliché I am! I thought I was smarter than that.''

"It's not your fault," Ryan said, smoothing her hair with his fingers. "Men can be such jerks."

She glanced over her shoulder, twisting in his embrace until she could look at him. "I've never done anything like that in my life. When I realized I was pregnant, I called him. He came home once more before his ship was deployed again, so I met him and we talked. First, he didn't believe the baby was his. Then he didn't want anything to do with either one of us—me or the baby—and I guess I was glad that he'd made that decision. It made my life simpler."

"So you decided to have the baby alone," he murmured.

"There was no decision to be made. I know I can be a good mother. And though this isn't the traditional route to parenthood, I've never been a very traditional person." She drew a ragged breath than let it out slowly. "It feels good to tell someone. I've been so reluctant to talk about it. I didn't want people to think less of me, although they'd have good reason."

"I don't think less of you," he said.

"Somehow, I knew you wouldn't. That's why I wanted to tell you."

"Now you just have to tell your parents."

Jennifer stiffened slightly as she turned back to stare at the pool. "And how do you think I should do that?" She sat up. "'*Mamá and Papi,* I've got a bun in the oven,'" she said in a firm voice, emphasizing the statement with a sweep of her arms. "'I'm knocked up,'" she said a little louder. "'I'm expecting,'" she said, her voice carrying in the still night air. "'Surprise, surprise, I'm going to have a baby!'"

"Any one of those would probably do the trick," Ryan

said. "And if you shout any louder, you'll wake up the entire household. Now, what am I supposed to say?"

"You don't have to say anything," she said.

"But it takes two to make a baby, Jen. Don't you think they'll want some type of explanation…or apology…or a nice pound of flesh? After all, I'm the one who put the bun in the oven—or at least that's what we want them to believe. Your father doesn't own any guns, does he?"

"You're a man. According to my mother, it's part of your nature to seduce every woman in your path. At least that's what she's been telling me since the moment I started noticing the opposite sex. Too bad I didn't listen. I might not have ended up in this predicament."

"And what happens after we tell them?"

"We'll say we want to wait to get married until after the baby's born. After a couple of months I'll explain that we broke up. Maybe we had an argument about my job. Or how to raise the baby. It doesn't really matter."

"They're not going to like me much," he murmured. "That's too bad, because I kind of like them."

"You do?"

"Yeah. Your family is great. I mean, they're so…real. So big—their laughter, their love. It's different from what I'm used to. My parents always seemed so proper, as if they followed some manual on how to be the perfect parents." He smiled. "When I was a kid, I used to ask my mother and father for a brother. All my friends had siblings and I wanted one of my own. I remember once when I asked my mom got all teary-eyed and ran out of the room. My dad said she had a cold, but I knew she was crying. I guess that wasn't in the manual. After that, I didn't ask anymore."

"Was it hard? Growing up an only child?"

"I didn't know any differently."

She placed her hand on her stomach. "I hope that my baby has brothers and sisters."

"I'm sure someday you'll find someone. Someone who'll be a wonderful father to your baby and give you a huge and happy family."

"Do you think so?"

Ryan nuzzled his face into her hair, so gently she didn't even notice. "You're a beautiful, intriguing woman. A man would be lucky to spend his life with you."

Jennifer sighed softly and leaned back against him. He wrapped his arms more tightly around her, and as they sat staring up into the night sky, the truth of his feelings drew into sharp focus.

Though he wanted to believe that Jennifer's happiness was foremost in his heart, he couldn't ignore his own selfish motives. If Jennifer's baby needed brothers and sisters, he wanted to be the one to provide them. And if Jennifer spent the rest of her life with just one man, then he was going to make sure that man was him.

Now he just had to figure out how to make it all happen.

CHAPTER THREE

"WAKE UP, wake up! Today is my *quinceañera!*"

Jennifer groaned, then grabbed her pillow and pulled it over her head. "Go away," she muttered. "It's too early."

"It's nearly ten," Maria countered. "*Mamá* says to come down. Everyone is here for *almuerzo* and *Mamá* won't let us eat until you come down."

More food, Jennifer mused as she rolled over. This time, a late breakfast.

Maria tugged on the pillow. "Your sweetie is up. He and *Papi* are standing in front of the garage having a very serious talk."

She bolted upright, tossing the pillow aside. How could he already be up? They'd stayed outside talking into the wee hours before dawn. It was only after she'd fallen asleep in Ryan's arms that he'd insisted she go to bed, tucking her in before he disappeared to his own room. "What are they talking about?"

"How should I know?" Maria said, scrambling from the bed. She stood in front of the dresser mirror and piled her shoulder-length hair on top of her head. "How do you think I should wear my hair? *Mamá* told me I have to wear it down, but I think I should wear it up. What do you think?"

"I think I'm way too intelligent to get in the middle of an argument between you and *Mamá,*" Jennifer replied, searching her garment bag for a dress that wasn't too wrinkled.

Maria put on a pretty pout. "But you have a way with *Mamá*. She listens to you."

Jennifer glanced over her shoulder. "What? *Mamá* doesn't listen to me."

"Yes, she does. She thinks you're very independent and very together. She's constantly telling me I should be more like you. That I should take my life more seriously and think about my future."

Stunned by the revelation, Jennifer didn't know what to say. She gnawed on her bottom lip. Her mother had always been so disapproving of her choices—at least on the surface. What would she have to say about the very independent notion of a single mother in the family? Jennifer certainly wasn't setting a good example for her younger sisters on that score.

"I think you should follow your own path," Jennifer said, crossing the room to stand beside Maria at the mirror. "And if you want to wear your hair up, then that's what you should do."

"Yes, I think I will."

Jennifer slipped her arm around Maria's shoulders and smiled. "*Feliz cumpleaños, hermanita.* Happy, happy birthday."

Maria kissed her cheek, then ran out of the room, her mind already on other, more important events of the day. Before the late-afternoon mass, she'd be primped and pampered, her hair coiffed, her nails and toes buffed. For today, Maria was the center of the universe. Jennifer tugged her dress over her head. Was it fair to disrupt the celebration with her own news? She glanced at the engagement ring Ryan had given her. Maybe she could wait until right before they left tomorrow morning. That way if things got too heated they could just drive away.

She washed her face quickly and ran a brush through her hair, dabbed on a bit of lipstick and grabbed her shoes before running downstairs barefoot. Following Maria's direction, she found her father and Ryan standing in front of the garage, deep in conversation. She hurried over. "Good morning!"

Her father grinned and opened his arms. "*¡Buenos días, niña!* Did you sleep well?"

Jennifer smiled at Ryan. "Very well, *Papi.*"

As an afterthought, Ryan brushed a nervous kiss on her cheek. "Morning," he murmured. He reached down and wove his fingers through hers. "Your father and I were just having a nice talk."

"Ryan was telling me all about his business. And I was telling him all about mine. This young man has a very bright future. Fifty-nine oil wells. Don't let him get away, *niña,* or he'll make a fine husband for some other girl."

"I—I won't, *Papi,*" Jennifer said. "Maria says brunch is almost ready. Everyone is gathered on the terrace."

"Well, then we better hurry. Your *mamá* has a strict schedule for today. We wouldn't want to do anything to upset it, now, would we?"

"No, *Papi.*"

Diego set off for the backyard and Jennifer and Ryan followed. "How did you really sleep?" Ryan whispered.

"I didn't," Jennifer replied. "Just a few hours. I couldn't stop thinking about my announcement. I've decided we should at least wait until late tonight, after the party. That way, my parents will be so exhausted, they won't have the energy to argue. What do you think of that plan?"

"Whatever you decide," Ryan said.

"And then I was thinking, we could wait until tomorrow morning, right before church. That way *Mamá* can go to the priest for consolation and I can go to confession. That might make it easier. Or maybe, right before we leave for home. That way, we can make a quick escape."

Ryan drew her to a stop and turned her to face him. "Jen, there's never going to be a good time. You have to tell them this weekend, and if you wait much longer, there won't be any weekend left."

"I—I will. I promise."

"Would you rather I took your father aside and told him first? Maybe he could tell your mother and break it to her gently?"

"You'd do that?" Jennifer asked, her voice filled with relief and gratitude. "That might work. *Papi* already likes you. And he has a way with *Mamá*. Oh, yes, let's do it that way. You can tell him tonight, after the party."

Ryan nodded. "All right. It's a plan. Now, let's go get some breakfast."

When they arrived in the backyard, nearly everyone was seated at the long tables her mother had set up. Only close relatives had been invited to share in the meal—Jennifer's aunts and uncles and cousins, totalling nearly thirty. Once again, her mother had gone overboard with the food. The tables were loaded with tasty dishes—*huevos rancheros, jamón* and *salchichas,* and *pan dulce,* her mother's famous homemade sweet rolls. Baskets of corn *tortillas* were placed in the center of the tables and platters of fresh fruit were passed from guest to guest while her mother poured orange juice and coffee.

Jennifer slid into a spot next to Tía Yolanda, her father's only sister, kissing her cheek as she wished her *buenos días.* Ryan sat beside her, and Teresa, hovering in the background, took the last empty spot beside Ryan. She looked up at him with adoring eyes and Jennifer shot her a scolding look.

When everyone was settled, Diego rose solemnly. "*Familia, amigos.* With this meal, we begin a very special day for my *niña,* Maria. I hope you'll join me in wishing her *feliz quinceañera.*" He held up his glass of orange juice. "May the Lord bless this day and may he bless our girl, Maria."

The rest of the guests held up their glasses and joined in the toast. After a short prayer, the meal began in earnest. Tía Yolanda, known for her great appreciation of food, piled Jennifer's plate high. When the *pan dulce* made its way to their side of the table, she took two sweet rolls for herself and handed one to Jennifer. "Your mama has a way with her oven," she said, laughing boisterously. She turned to look for Carmen. "Carmen! I was just telling Jennifer that you have a way with your oven!"

Carmen smiled and made her way over to Yolanda. "Yolanda, you like my baking?"

"*¡Muy buena! ¡Me gusta!*"

"Jennifer has a bun in her oven," Teresa piped up, a gap-toothed smile splitting her eager face, her brown eyes sparkling.

Jennifer's heart stopped and her jaw dropped. Orange juice, halfway down her throat, came back up with a cough and she pressed her napkin to her mouth, her eyes watering.

"*Niña,* we all know Jennifer is not so good in the kitchen," Carmen said, ruffling Teresa's hair.

"No, she is," Teresa insisted. "I think she's taking cooking lessons."

"Teresa, shh!" Jennifer hissed, watching as the rest of the guests began to turn their attention toward her youngest sister.

Ryan handed the little girl a sweet roll, waving it in front of her face. "Have something to eat, Teresa. Aren't you hungry? If you eat that whole roll, I'll play *fútbol* with you after breakfast."

Teresa took the roll. "Jenny and Ryan were in the garden last night and she told him she had a bun in her oven. I was listening from my tree house."

Carmen's eyes went wide. "And what else did Jenny say?"

"She said she's knocked up, too. *And* she's going to have a baby."

"Oh, God," Jennifer murmured.

"There it is," Ryan said.

"*¡Dios mío!*" Carmen stumbled backward, the pitcher of orange juice slipping from her fingers and shattering at her feet. "Is—is this true, Jennifer? Did Teresa hear right?"

Jennifer looked from her mother to her father, who was slowly rising from his chair, then to all the relatives, who were waiting with undisguised curiosity for her reply. Frantic to repair the damage done by Teresa's announcement, she scrambled for a way to cover. She slowly stood and cleared her throat. "*Mamá, Papi,* I—I have something to tell you both." She pasted a bright smile on her face, but it did little to alter her parents' glowering expressions. Then, she glanced down at Ryan and he rose to stand beside her.

Tears pressed at the corners of her eyes, but she brushed them away. Now was not the time to turn into a blubbering idiot. She glanced down at the ring, twisting the diamond onto the top of her finger. Trembling, she held out her hand. "Ryan and I are engaged," she murmured, emotion clogging her throat. "And—and we're going to have a baby."

The guests fell quiet, everyone except Tía Yolanda, who groaned softly and fanned her face with her napkin. But the silence didn't last long.

A wail burst from Maria. "*Mama,* she's ruined my *quinceañera!*"

The guests' silence dissolved into excited chatter. Linda began to whine that she didn't understand what buns had to do with a baby. Joe sat at the end of the table, chuckling and shaking his head. Diego shoved his chair back and stalked around the table to join Jennifer's mother. "Is this true?" he asked Ryan. "Have you ruined my daughter?"

Ryan drew a deep breath and slipped his arm around Jennifer. "Mr. Rodriguez, I love your daughter. And though we may not have followed the traditional route, we are both devoted to each other and to this child. Now, you can accept that or you can send us both from this house. But this baby is your first grandchild and I would hate to think that you're going to miss out on a single moment of his or her life."

Jennifer stared up at Ryan, caught by the power and candor of his words. She couldn't help but wish they were all true. That he *did* love her and that they *were* devoted to each other, that this wasn't all a big lie. Her gaze jumped to her father, whose expression had softened slightly. Her mother, on the other hand, looked completely aghast, as if she'd just seen Tía Yolanda strip off her clothes and dance naked on the breakfast table.

"Can we discuss this in private?" Jennifer asked.

Carmen shook her head. "Diego, this is Maria's day and I do not want anything to spoil it. We will discuss this later." She sent Jennifer a glare that made daggers look dull. "I will deal with you later." Sucking in a sharp breath, she forced a smile and glanced around the breakfast table. "Well, this is wonderful news, is it not? We have many things to celebrate today, but most important is Maria. Now, we must eat. The food is getting cold. Maria, go get your crown and show Tía Yolanda how pretty it is."

With that pronouncement, the guests understood precisely what Carmen Rodriguez expected of them. Jennifer's news was to be pushed aside for the more important events of the day. It was not to be mentioned until after Maria's *quinceañera.*

Jennifer and Ryan slowly sat back down in their places and smiled wanly as the dishes were passed to them.

"Well," Ryan murmured after the conversation had turned back to Maria. "Though that didn't exactly follow the plan, I think it went well, don't you?"

"Yes," Jennifer replied numbly. "I think it went very well."

"THIS BABY will not be born outside the sanctity of marriage! We will plan a wedding for the beginning of November. Four weeks should give us plenty of time to make all the arrangements, to post the banns, and for you to take your classes with the priest."

The house was silent. The last guest had left a half hour ago, just before midnight. The belle of the ball, Maria, had wearily kissed her parents good-night and wandered up to bed, her pretty white dress wilted and her crown askew. Teresa and Linda had retired before ten, and Joe had gone for a late-night pizza with a few of his cousins, who had served as *chambelanes*.

Jennifer groaned. "*Mamá,* we can't possibly plan a church wedding in four weeks. Ryan and I have decided that we'll wait until the baby is born before we get married. That way it won't be so obvious to all the wedding guests."

"Well, it will not be obvious if we rush the wedding along," Carmen insisted. "If Teresa would not have blurted out your condition for everyone to hear, I never would have suspected. Of course, there will be whispers. *Siete mesino.*"

At Ryan's confused expression, Jennifer leaned closer. "Seven-month baby," she whispered. Considering how her plan was going so far, she wasn't about to inform her mother that it would be more like *cuatro mesino,* an even greater scandal. Jennifer had assumed the notion of a pregnant daughter walking down the aisle of St. Benedict's, dressed in the obligatory gown and veil, was something her mother would never endorse. Though her parents would not consider her a married woman unless she exchanged vows in front of Father Juan, the Rodriguezes' family priest, she'd been certain they'd agree to a ceremony after the baby was born.

But this turn of events threw a serious kink into her strategy. She'd have to announce her engagement *and* "breakup" with Ryan in the course of four weeks. Little more than a week or two if she wanted her parents to recover a small measure of their investment in a hastily planned wedding.

"*Mamá,* we can't pretend that everything is proceeding in the right order. The entire family knows, and if they know, most of El Paso will know by tomorrow evening."

Diego exhaled slowly and sat back in his chair. Everyone looked to him, waiting to hear his first words on the subject. Jennifer was afraid he'd tear into Ryan, blaming him for the mess she was in. She reached over and covered Ryan's hand with hers to show her support.

"Though I am disappointed in your behavior, Jennifer, I am happy to see that you've found yourself a fine man to take care of you. You know I've never liked you living alone in a strange city, and now my fears are calmed. With Ryan to watch over you, you won't be making any more mistakes."

His patronizing *machismo* attitude grated on Jennifer's already frayed nerves. She was perfectly able to take care of herself! She'd made a good life in Odessa, she had a good job and a nice apartment. In just a few months she'd be a full-fledged private investigator. She didn't need a husband to run her life in the same stifling way her parents had for the first twenty-one years of her life!

"We will have a small ceremony with family and

friends,'' Carmen said. "Just a church service, no mass. And we will have the reception right here at the house. I can use many of the same people I used for Maria's *quinceañera,* so it will not be difficult to plan. We will need to find a dress. I think ivory would be an appropriate color.''

"*Mamá,* I'm not getting married in four weeks!"

Diego slapped his hands on the kitchen table, startling everyone with the crack of sound. "This is not your decision to make!'' he said. He slowly turned to Ryan. "What is your opinion on this matter?''

Ryan glanced at Jennifer, then shrugged. "Well, I can understand Jen's point.''

Jennifer nodded in agreement. "See, Ryan doesn't want to get—''

"But I think it would be best if we had the wedding in early November,'' he finished.

At first, she wasn't sure she'd heard him right. Jennifer twisted around in her chair to face him. "What did you say?''

"I agree with your parents. I think the sooner we get married the better. After all, why wait? We're going to get married anyway, why not do it now, so the baby can be born with a name.''

"The baby will have a name. Mine!''

"Jen, please, look at this from your parents' point of view,'' Ryan said. "We don't have to wait.''

"Then it's settled,'' Diego said. "He will be your husband. It is his responsibility to make the final decision.'' He stood, his stern expression softened into a wide grin. Then he pulled Ryan to his feet, opened his arms and grabbed him in a firm embrace. "Welcome to the family, son. You will make a good husband for *mi hija.*''

Jennifer jumped to her feet. "Wait a minute here! What about what *I* want? You can't just plan a wedding without me. If you do, then I'll refuse to show up! You'll have a church full of people and no bride.''

Ryan's hand closed over her elbow, his fingers firm. ''Jen, why don't we let your parents get to bed? We won't be making any more decisions tonight. It's been a long day for all of us and everyone is tired.'' He gently pulled her away from the kitchen table. ''Come on, you need your sleep as well.''

Diego nodded and leaned over to Carmen. ''See how he takes care of her. He will make our daughter a good *esposo*.''

Jennifer shot her father a withering look, then reluctantly followed Ryan to the stairs. But as soon as she was out of earshot of her parents, she yanked her arm from his grasp. ''What do you think you're doing? How could you agree with her? We can't get married in four weeks!''

Ryan glanced over his shoulder, then took her hand and pulled her up the stairs. After he'd closed her bedroom door behind them both, he turned to face her.

''Well?'' she said, her arms crossed beneath her breasts. ''What do you have to say for yourself? What were you thinking?''

He took one long step toward her, wrapped an arm around Jennifer's waist and pulled her body against his. Before she could protest, his mouth came down on hers. Jennifer pressed her palms against his chest, twisting in his arms. But Ryan refused to retreat and instead deepened the kiss, his tongue plundering her mouth.

A tiny moan slipped from her throat, the sound mirroring her surrender. How could she possibly be angry with a man who made her feel this way? His mouth moved over hers, his tongue softly invading, probing, dissolving her anger and transforming it into desire. Her knees wobbled, but she had no fear of falling. He held her tight against him, their hips pressed together. And when the last of her resistance faded, he slowly drew back.

But the instant she looked up and saw the satisfied expression on his face, Jennifer's anger returned. She would not allow him to bully her—even if it was with mind-numbing, toe-curling kisses! She gave him a shove and stepped out of his embrace. "You can't just kiss me and expect me to forgive you! In fact, you can't just kiss me! We're not engaged, we're not even involved, and from now on, there will be no more...kissing!"

"We're supposed to be engaged," he said. "Engaged couples kiss, don't they?"

"There's no one here to see us!" she said. A hysterical edge had crept into her voice and Jennifer paused to shore up her patience. "Why did you agree to the wedding when you knew I didn't want it?"

"Your mother was determined," he said. "Nothing was going to change her mind. I didn't want to continue arguing." He reached out and grabbed for her hand, but she refused to allow him to touch her. "This day has been stressful for both of us. I can handle it, but you have the baby to think of."

"You're the one who's causing all my stress," she accused, wagging her finger at him. "Now I only have four weeks to break up with you. If we'd put off the wedding, if you'd supported me on that, then I'd have had more time to make this plan work."

"I'm sorry," Ryan said.

"Yeah, right. You're sorry. A lot of good that does us now." She stared at him, a slow realization dawning. "Wait a minute. You agreed with them because you wanted them to like you!"

"I agreed with them because—"

"No," Jennifer said. "You were worried they'd think badly of you, so you sided with them instead of with me.

Now, when we break up, it will look like it's all my fault, like I was angry because you took their side about the wedding."

"I did what I thought was best," Ryan said.

"Or maybe it was the whole *machismo* thing. I thought at least you would be immune to the smell of testosterone! The strong, forceful man telling the weak, feebleminded woman what she needs."

Ryan crossed the room to the bed and rummaged through the pile of clothes she'd dumped from her suitcase until he found her nightgown. He snatched it up and tossed it at her. "You're tired," he said, his voice low and even. "We'll talk about this tomorrow. Now, it's time for you to get some sleep."

With that, Ryan walked to the door and yanked it open. He turned back to look at Jennifer. "Everything will be all right, Jen. I promise."

The door closed softly behind him and Jennifer bit back a curse. He was acting just like her father, overbearing and autocratic. Why did he care what her parents thought of him? After she broke up with him, he'd never see them again. But then, Ryan Madison was real straight arrow, a Boy Scout. If she'd learned anything about him over the past few days, she'd learned that he liked to be in control.

"Well, if he thinks he can control me, he's got another guess coming," Jennifer muttered.

She heaved the clothes at the door and pulled the covers down, then angrily tossed her dress on the floor and slipped into her nightgown. When she'd settled herself in bed, she punched the pillow twice for good measure, then closed her eyes. But sleep wouldn't come.

Instead, her mind kept returning to the kiss she'd shared with Ryan, to the sweet sensation of his lips touching hers, to the taste and warmth of his tongue and the strength of his embrace. A shiver skittered up her spine and she pulled the covers up around her neck, wondering why her mother kept the air-conditioning so low.

But it wasn't air-conditioning that was causing her current state of distress. It was Ryan Madison, his penetrating eyes and his firm mouth, his hands that warmed her blood with just a simple touch. His voice, so soothing and persuasive. If she didn't know better, she would almost believe that he really wanted to marry her.

Jennifer buried her face in her pillow. What had ever possessed her to carry out such a ridiculous scheme? In hindsight, telling her parents outright, all alone, would have been so much easier. She sighed softly and raised her fingers to her lips. But then she never would have experienced Ryan's kisses, his tender concern and his teasing humor.

And if there was anything good to take away from this whole experience, it was that.

"I HAVE TO GO and I have to go now!"

Ryan glanced over at Jennifer, slouched down in the passenger seat of her car. They'd driven the nearly three hundred miles from El Paso and the only words she'd bothered to throw in his direction had to do with the state of her bladder and her need for food. Beyond that, she'd refused to speak to him.

"We're only a few miles from Odessa," he said. "Can't you wait?"

"I happen to be pregnant," she said, "and when I have to go, I have to go. Waiting is not an option."

He schooled his temper, knowing that Jennifer was spoiling for a fight. "Maybe you should see a doctor about that. That's not normal, is it?"

"How would you know what's normal? And the doctor says it's only going to get worse. Not that you'll be around to experience it."

They'd left El Paso at dawn, before the rest of Jennifer's siblings had risen and long before they could be corralled into attending mass. Carmen and Diego said goodbye at the front door, Carmen promising to call Jennifer the next day to start plans for the wedding. They'd barely gone a block before Ryan knew it would be a long drive back. Luckily, he'd chosen to take the interstate, a route with a greater concentration of bathrooms than the backwater route they'd taken to get to El Paso.

Ryan stared out at the road ahead, wondering if they'd ever speak to each other again. He hadn't meant to get her all upset. But agreeing to her mother's plans for the wedding seemed like the logical thing to do. After all, what fiancé would refuse the chance to marry the woman he loved sooner rather than later?

But was he only playing the part of her loving fiancé? Or was there something else to it? He couldn't deny that he'd relished the role. In just a few short days, he'd come to enjoy being with her. Hell, he could barely keep his hands off her.

Every time she looked up at him with those sultry dark eyes, he felt compelled to pull her into his arms and kiss her. And when she wasn't in his arms, he was wondering whether she'd eaten anything in the last hour, or whether the heat was too much for her, or whether she'd been on her feet too long. Though she didn't demand his attention, he felt compelled to protect her.

Maybe it was because she didn't look after herself. Her diet was atrocious, made up of whatever junk food was in the general vicinity of her mouth. She stayed up too late and got up too early, she drove too fast, she didn't look both ways when crossing the street, and she smiled at perfect strangers. Hell, most women would consider him a wonderful friend.

But he didn't want to be just her friend. Though he

hadn't really thought about marrying her, he had thought about losing her. Ryan knew once she announced their official "breakup," there'd be no reason for them to see each other. According to her original plan, he'd spend the next few months playing the dutiful fiancé, only to be tossed aside when she worked up the courage to end their "relationship."

At least now, she'd be forced to take action. She might even be forced to tell her parents the truth. And after he was officially dismissed as her "fiancé," maybe they could figure out what was really happening between them—for he had no doubt there was something going on, some connection that sparked every time they were near.

"Here's an exit," she said. "And there's a gas station. Pull over, pull over!"

Ryan took the off-ramp and swung the car into the parking lot of the minimart. Jennifer barely allowed the car to come to a complete stop before she hopped out and hurried inside to the ladies' room. He turned off the ignition and followed her inside. Strolling the aisles, he picked up a bottle of orange juice and a package of cheese and crackers, then paid for them at the checkout.

A few moments later, Jennifer walked out of the ladies' room and headed to the car without saying a word to him as she passed. Cursing softly, Ryan stalked out after her and got in the car. But instead of turning the key in the ignition, he turned to face her. "All right," he said. "I'm sorry I messed up your plan. I'm sorry I took your mother's side about the wedding."

"It was a stupid thing to do," Jennifer said.

"Yes," he said.

"And you had no right to butt into my life like that," she added.

"No right." He paused, sliding his hand along the back

of her seat. He toyed with her hair as she stared stubbornly out the window. "And I'll figure out a way to fix this."

She slowly turned, raising her eyebrow dubiously. "You will?"

"Yes," he said. "I promise everything will be just fine." He handed her the bottle of orange juice. "Drink this."

Jennifer shook her head. "I'm not thirsty."

"I don't care," Ryan insisted. "You haven't had anything to eat or drink for nearly two hours. I don't want you passing out on me. Drink the juice."

"No!" she said. "Stop telling me what to do!"

"Is it so bad that I care about you?" Ryan asked.

"I don't need you to care about me," Jennifer said. "I don't need anyone."

Ryan set the orange juice between the seats along with the cheese and crackers. "It's there if you want it." He started the car and pulled back out onto the interstate. As he drove the last twenty miles to his apartment, the silence still hung heavy between them. Why did she have to be so stubborn?

Watching the skyline of Midland glitter in the noonday sun, Ryan realized that her stubbornness was exactly what he liked about her. She was strong and independent, passionate and sexy, sweet and vulnerable all at the same time. And if he knew her for a hundred years, he'd still never know everything about her.

They passed the first exit for Midland and he knew they'd arrive at his condo before too long. After spending the entire weekend with her, he was loath to watch her drive away. Ryan liked having her near. Without Jennifer, he felt alone in the world. After all, who did he really have? Jeffrey and Rhonda Madison weren't his family. His real mother and father were dead. He barely knew his twin brother and Ben had a family of his own. He had no one now...except Jennifer.

Jennifer needed him and he needed her. He could give her a good life and provide for her baby. She wouldn't need to work anymore. He'd buy them a big house with a yard. And he'd come home every night after work and help her with the baby. And over time, they'd come to love each other. Ryan took a deep breath. This was what he wanted, what he needed.

"How long are you going to be angry with me?" he asked as he turned the car off the interstate and headed for his place.

"I haven't decided yet," Jennifer muttered.

"Can you give me a rough estimate? Or should I just drive around the block until you realize how childish you're being?"

She slouched further down in her seat. "You don't understand," she murmured.

"Then explain it to me."

"All my life, I've lived under their thumb. It's been a daily battle, trying to please them and trying to carve out a life of my own. I was never sure what to be—*Papi*'s sweet little girl, *Mamá*'s prim-and-proper daughter, or the rebel that I wanted to be. When you sided with them, I felt like a child all over again, outnumbered and outgunned."

"I do understand," Ryan said. He pulled her car up to the curb in front of his condo. Then he shoved the gearshift into Park and turned off the ignition. "And I'm sorry. I should have sided with you. Now, either you forgive me, or we'll drive around the block a few more times."

"Apology accepted," she muttered.

They sat in silence for a long time, Ryan unable to walk away while things were still unresolved between them. He drew a deep breath, then turned to face her. "Jen, I think I have the solution to all your problems."

She sent him a sideways glance. "I'm on pins and needles," she said. "Especially since your previous solution—a wedding in four short weeks—has made my life so much easier."

"Marry me," he said.

In a single instant it had all become perfectly clear. They didn't have to pretend anymore. They could marry each other and he'd be there to provide for her, to take care of the baby, to make a life for all three of them. Though they barely knew each other, he knew he didn't want to lose her. Jennifer belonged in his life and the only way to make sure she stayed was to marry her. Sure, it might not work out. But he was willing to take the risk.

"Yeah, my parents will really fall for that. Believe me, my mother and father would want to see a notarized license as proof before they'd even consider us husband and wife. It's hard to forge a document like that."

"I mean it, Jen," he said softly, catching her chin with his finger and forcing her gaze to meet his. "Marry me. For real."

CHAPTER FOUR

"Marry you?" Jennifer's words came out on a gasp and she stared at him incredulously. Then a giggle burst from her throat. "You're crazy. *Loco. Demente.*"

Ryan's smile wavered, then disappeared. "Well, this is every man's dream of the perfect proposal. Ask a beautiful woman to marry you and she questions your sanity."

"*¡Pronto!*" she muttered as she pushed open the car door. "*¡Llame al psiquiatra!* He needs a psychiatrist. The man has lost his mind." Jennifer hopped out, slammed the passenger door behind her, then opened the back door to retrieve his bags. But a few seconds later, Ryan was at her side, snatching his bags from her hands and setting them down on the curb.

She met his gaze, watching his reaction shrewdly. Either the drive back from El Paso in her rattletrap car had seriously affected his brain, or Ryan Madison had a very sick sense of humor. Or maybe this was simply his way of lightening her mood after his blunder of agreeing to a wedding at all. She found nothing but indifference in his expression. "We've been stuck in that car for hours, my back is killing me and I need a nap," Jennifer said. "I'm in no mood for jokes."

An odd expression crossed his face and for a moment, Jennifer thought he might actually be serious. Then he laughed. "You're right. This is no time for jokes. I'm sorry." He glanced down at his bag and gave it a kick, his eyes fixed on the toe of his shoe. "But, you know, people do get married on a whole lot less than we have. We get along pretty well, your parents already like me, we've got the ring. And I make a good living. I could provide you and the baby with anything you need. It's not that bad of an idea, in theory.''

''But it's a terrible idea in reality.''

''It would solve all your problems,'' he said.

''Marrying you would be the beginning of my problems,'' she countered, her arms hitched on her hips. ''I'd be walking down the aisle with a certified lunatic! And that's just the start. There are a million other reasons why I can't marry you.''

''Give me the top three.''

''Because I barely know you,'' she replied, holding up one finger. ''Because you have no idea what you're getting into.'' She drew a deep breath. ''And because in a few months, I'm going to have another man's baby.''

Ryan took her hands in his and gave them a squeeze. ''Jen, that wouldn't make a difference to me…I mean, in theory.''

''It does to me,'' she said softly, feeling the weight of her worries dragging her down. His idea of marriage—in theory—could solve all her immediate problems. But it would create just as many new problems. A loveless marriage, obligation that would soon turn to resentment, a child that would never be his.

She'd always dreamed of marrying a man who couldn't stand the thought of living another day without her. Ryan had asked her out of some misguided sense of chivalry. Or perhaps a need to create an instant family for himself to replace the family he'd lost. Jennifer wasn't naive enough to believe that he truly wanted to marry her for love.

She shook her head. ''We made a plan and we're going to stick to it. In a few weeks, I'll tell my parents we had a fight and we broke up.'' She glanced around, then forced a smile. "I really have to go now.'' With that, Jennifer started around the car. But he refused to let go of her hands, pulling her closer, instead.

Gently, he took her face between his palms and placed a kiss on her forehead. "Call me when you get home, okay?''

The warmth of his lips left a tingle on her skin. She met his gaze and that warmth spread through her body. "Why?''

"Because I want to know you got there safely,'' he murmured, stroking her cheek with his fingers.

Though his touch was stirring and so tempting, Jennifer knew she couldn't allow herself to get used to it. Ryan wasn't part of her future plans, not now or ever. And in a few weeks, he'd be part of her past. "I have to go,'' she repeated.

This time he let her, and she circled the car and got in the driver's side. But before she could turn the ignition, he leaned in the passenger window. "Drive safely,'' he warned. "And fasten your seat belt. And when you get home have something decent to eat. And don't forget to call me.''

Irritated, Jennifer reached down and pushed the button to raise the window. Ryan snatched his fingers out before they were pinched. She buckled her seat belt, but she decided to show him who was boss when she threw the car into gear and slammed her foot down on the accelerator. The tires squealed and the car fishtailed and she caught sight of Ryan's glowering expression in the rearview mirror. As soon as she was out of sight, she slowed the car to below the speed limit and let out a deep sigh.

He was right. She should take more care when she was driving and she should always remember to buckle her seat belt. After all, she was responsible for another life now.

Jennifer reached down and pressed her palm to her tummy. With every day that passed, the baby became more and more real to her—the gentle swell of her belly, the tiny flutters she felt when she lay very still in bed, and the endless hunger pangs.

Up until a few weeks ago, she'd barely known she was pregnant, skipping through the morning sickness with only a few bouts of nausea. And now, she was reminded of the baby every hour of every day. Could she really do this all alone? She'd been so confident that this scheme would work, that she'd be able to get past her parents' initial reaction and make a life for herself and the baby—until Ryan stepped in and messed it all up.

Her jaw tensed and her fingers gripped the steering wheel, white-knuckled. "I'm not going to call him," she muttered to herself. "That's what people who love each other do and I'm not in love with Ryan Madison. I'm not."

But try as she might, her denials weren't entirely convincing. She did have feelings for Ryan, feelings that ran deep. How could she help herself? He was sweet and considerate, protective and understanding. And he'd been the only man to propose to her. Like him, Jennifer had imagined the moment a bit differently—a romantic dinner at a fancy restaurant, champagne, a man on his knees with a diamond ring in his hand. Considering her circumstances, she couldn't expect another man to offer marriage anytime soon, maybe not ever.

She glanced at her left hand, her gaze falling on the ring Ryan had given her. It twinkled in the afternoon sun and she twisted it around on her finger. She really ought to take it off. Wearing it seemed almost hypocritical considering her reaction to his proposal. She tried to pull it off, but her fingers were swollen and the ring refused to budge.

Jennifer cursed softly. Nothing was going as planned. It was all supposed to be so simple and now everything was a colossal mess. Tears of frustration pushed at the corners of her eyes, but she refused to allow them to fall. Why did Ryan Madison have to be so wonderful? Why couldn't he just do his job as her pretend fiancé and then get out of her life?

Memories of their weekend together flooded her mind, the nervous anticipation of introducing him to her parents, the relief when they accepted his presence, and then that awful moment when Teresa made her announcement over breakfast. Jennifer's cheeks warmed, the mortification still fresh.

But there were other memories, too. The warmth of his hand holding hers, the soothing sound of his voice, and the long, lingering kisses they'd shared. And his unwavering support.

As she drove back to her apartment, she let those thoughts drift through her mind. If only she could have met him under different circumstances, before she hopped into bed with a philandering sailor. They would have dated and fallen in love and planned a future together. Then he might have proposed to her for real and she might have accepted. And only after they were married and settled would they have considered a child.

Jennifer sighed. She wondered what Ryan would have done had she accepted his proposal. She really should have called his bluff, or at least made him squirm for a while, payback for siding with her parents. But as she fixed her attention on the road in front of her, her thoughts wound back to the look in his eyes when he'd asked.

Suddenly, doubts assailed her. Could he have been serious? Was that look she'd seen flash across his face a look of disappointment? She shook her head, pushing the notion from her mind. But it kept nagging at her until she was forced to reconsider everything he'd said. Jennifer moaned softly. Had she passed on the only opportunity she might ever have for marriage? There were precious few men willing to take on a single mother and her baby. If Ryan Madison was one of them, then she'd really messed up.

When she turned into the parking lot of her apartment, she'd already decided to call him and apologize for her inconsiderate reaction. But as she retrieved her bags from the back seat and walked to the front door, she wondered whether it might be better just to let it go. Her life was already too complicated.

Jennifer unlocked the door and walked inside the stuffy living room. She flipped on the air conditioner, dropped her bags near the sofa, and walked into the bedroom. Suddenly, exhaustion overwhelmed her. She crawled onto the bed, glancing over at her answering machine. The light blinked and the readout told her she had four messages. No doubt there would be several from her mother and maybe one from work. And perhaps Ryan had called to remind her of one thing or another.

She reached for the phone, needing to hear his voice again, longing for the soothing effect his words had on her and wondering what she might discern from his tone. But the moment after she picked up the phone, she dropped it back into the cradle and pulled her hand away. She'd decided to have this baby on her own and she wasn't about to give in to her fears and insecurities. Ryan was a friend and nothing more.

But as she rolled over and stared up at the ceiling, images of him still drifted through her mind. She closed her eyes and moaned softly, pulling a pillow over her face. Fantasies about a man who was supposed to be just a friend would not make her future any easier. If she was going to put Ryan Madison out of her life in a few short weeks, then she'd better find a way to put him out of her head, as well.

RYAN PULLED the rental car up the gravel driveway and stared out the window at the tidy little farmhouse. The directions he'd been given by a helpful gas station attendant had brought him to a quiet rural area on the outskirts of San Antonio. He glanced at the address again, wanting to be certain he'd found the right place. A little girl's bike, fixed with training wheels, leaned up against the porch, and a doll sat abandoned on the steps, her hair blowing in the hot evening breeze.

He reached to open the car door, then hesitated. What the hell was he doing here? He'd come to San Antonio on business, a quick trip in and out, sign a few leases and that was it. In truth, he'd been grateful for the chance to put some space between him and Midland—and Jennifer Rodriguez.

She'd never called back Sunday afternoon. And though he'd left messages for her on Monday, she hadn't bothered to return his calls then, either. He wasn't sure he'd ever hear from her again, especially after his ridiculous proposal. It had seemed like a good idea at the time, but in hindsight, maybe it was all just an overreaction to everything that had happened to him in the past month.

Without any real family, he felt like a man adrift, clinging to whatever might keep him afloat. And a life with Jennifer and her baby was more to look forward to than a life all alone. His hand clenched the car door handle. Maybe that's why he was here, at Ben's place, looking for answers, for a connection to who he was.

Ben was the only real family he had left, Ben and Lucy, and now Carolyn. And though he'd had no intention of seeing his brother during this trip, a night alone in a hotel room hadn't seemed very appealing. He probably should have called, but chances were, with Lucy just out of the hospital, they'd all be at home. Besides, he and Ben had promised to get together again that day in the hospital when they'd first met.

Ryan stepped out of the car and closed the door behind him, then drew in a deep breath. A brisk wind blew up dust devils on the drive and he squinted as he jogged to the house. He reached for the doorbell and rang it, then waited. For an instant, he regretted coming, wondering what he'd say to virtual strangers. But then the door swung open and he saw a green-eyed beauty standing in front of him. She was dressed in jeans and a T-shirt, her auburn-brown hair pulled back and her face freshly scrubbed.

"Are you Carolyn?" he asked.

Her eyes went wide and a smile broke across her face. "Ryan? Oh, my gosh, what are you doing here?" She wiped her fingers on a dish towel, then held out her hand. "Come in. Please, come in. Ben will be so happy to see you."

Though he'd never actually met Carolyn St. Clair, Ryan knew that she'd been instrumental in reuniting him with his brother. As office manager for Finders Keepers, she'd been the one to enlist Jennifer's help in the search. In fact, if it wasn't for Carolyn and Finders Keepers, Ryan might never have met Jennifer. At first, he wondered how she'd recognized him, then remembered his resemblance to his twin brother—her husband.

Reluctantly, he stepped inside the cool interior. He instantly felt comfortable. The farmhouse was decorated in a primitive, log-cabin style, the rough wood floors covered by brightly colored woven rugs. A worn leather sofa sat in front of a television set, which was tuned to a Disney cartoon. Toys were scattered everywhere and smells of a delicious dinner drifted out of the kitchen.

This was home, he thought to himself. *A family lived here. A happy family.*

"Have you eaten yet?" Carolyn asked. "Oh, never

mind, you'll stay for dinner. I've made a huge pot of spaghetti." She turned and hurried down a hallway. "Ben, Lucy. Come see who's here."

An instant later, a commotion began at the rear of the house and Lucy came racing down the hallway, the stuffed pony he'd given her at the hospital tucked beneath her arm. She smiled up at him, dimples appearing on her angelic face. "Hi," she murmured shyly.

"Lucy, this is your Uncle Ryan," Carolyn explained.

She gave him a penetrating look, then held out the stuffed pony. "Did you give me this?"

Ryan swallowed hard, realizing that he hadn't said a word since he'd walked inside. "Yes, I did. It's—it's good to see you, Lucy."

She hugged the pony to her chest. "I named him Ranger," she said.

He nodded, bent down and patted the pony's head. "That's a good name for a pony."

She hugged the stuffed animal tighter. "I have lots of real dogs and cats and a turtle named Samson, but they're staying with friends for a while since I had chemo. And Daddy said he's going to buy me a real pony for my birthday when I'm six." She held out six fingers. "And then you can come and ride it with me, just like you said on the card that you gave me in the hospital."

"Ryan?"

Ryan looked up and watched Ben stride down the hall. He wore a tool belt slung low on his hips and a pencil was tucked behind his ear. Plaster dust coated his jeans and his faded work shirt. Slowly, Ryan straightened, only to be pulled into a bear hug by his brother. When Ben finally let go, Ryan stepped back and stared dumbly into a face that so closely resembled his own he could be looking into a mirror.

"How are you?" Ben asked. "Come on, sit down." He

drew Ryan into the living room and pointed to the sofa. "Can I get you a beer?"

Ryan nodded, then sat down. Lucy plopped down on the sofa next to him and Carolyn sat next to her. A long silence grew between them and Ryan was relieved when Ben returned with the beer. He took the bottle and nodded his thanks while Ben sat across from him. "So what are you doing in San Antonio?"

Ryan took a long sip of his beer. "Business," he said, licking foam off his upper lip.

Ben nodded and another long silence fell upon them. At least when they'd met in the hospital for the first time, they'd had Lucy to talk about. Now, Ryan wasn't sure what to say.

Carolyn broke the impasse. She forced a smile, then took Lucy's hand. "Come on, sweetie. I could use your help in the kitchen. Daddy and Uncle Ryan want to talk."

Ryan watched them leave. "She looks good," he said. He turned back to Ben. "Is she doing all right?"

"So far, so good. The bone marrow transplant looks like it worked. All her tests have been encouraging." He drew a deep breath. "Hey, I want to thank you for showing up at the hospital. Just knowing you were willing to help made a big difference."

"Everything's good then," Ryan said, staring at his hands. "You're happy, that's good. Jennifer Rodriguez told me you and Carolyn got married. She's the P.I. who found me and brought me to San Antonio."

"I know who Jennifer is," Ben said. "I didn't realize you'd been in touch."

Ryan nodded. "Yeah, we've been in touch." He studied his fingers for a long time, then chuckled softly and shook his head. "I'm really not sure why I'm here."

"You're here to learn more about our parents," Ben

said. "I figured you'd come but I didn't think it would be so soon."

"I—I just felt—hell, I don't know what I felt or what I feel." Ryan raked his hand through his hair. "Last night I proposed to a woman I barely know and today I'm sitting here with a brother I barely know. It's like I'm trying to cobble together a family from strangers and I'm not having much luck."

Ben's eyebrow shot up. "So who's the woman?"

"Jennifer Rodriguez."

The other eyebrow joined the first in an expression of disbelief. "You're going to marry Jennifer Rodriguez?" Ben asked.

Ryan took a long sip of his beer, then sighed. "No. Well, maybe. We're pretending to be engaged, but I'm thinking we should just stop pretending and get married for real." He shook his head. "It's a long and complicated story."

Ben leaned back into the sofa, stretching his arm across the back. "I've got plenty of time," he said with a lazy smile.

Over the next half hour, they talked without stopping. The hesitancy that marked the first minutes of their meeting had disappeared, replaced by a newfound ease. Ryan told Ben everything, about Jennifer's plan to fool her parents, about his growing feelings for her and his spontaneous proposal. For the first time in his life, he got a taste of what having a brother might be like. Ben listened and offered advice without judging. And before Ryan knew it, Carolyn had appeared from the kitchen, informing them that dinner was ready.

Ryan stood up, intending to excuse himself and leave, but Ben insisted that he join them. He followed his brother into the kitchen, where Carolyn had set a festive table. "It's only spaghetti and garlic bread," she said, "but this is our first real family dinner with you. I wanted to make it special." She stepped to Ben's side and he slipped his hand around her waist.

Looking at them standing next to Lucy, Ryan felt an unbidden surge of envy. They'd become the perfect family, close, loving, devoted. They'd weathered terrible troubles and come out of it stronger than ever. Why couldn't the same happen for him and Jennifer? Why couldn't he come to love her baby as much as Carolyn loved Lucy?

"Ryan has some news," Ben said as he sat down.

Carolyn took her place, then picked up the basket of garlic bread to pass. "And what's that?" she asked.

Ryan shook his head. "It's really nothing."

"He's getting married," Ben said. "*Maybe* getting married."

"Maybe?" Carolyn asked.

"She hasn't said yes yet," Ryan explained.

"Jennifer Rodriguez," Ben added.

Carolyn's eyes went wide. "You and Jennifer Rodriguez?" A slow smile curved her lips. "That was pretty quick. You only met what—a month ago? It must have been love at first sight. A wedding for you and Jennifer," she murmured, her voice still tinged with disbelief. "Now, that *is* news."

"Can we come?" asked Lucy. "I love weddings."

Carolyn laughed. "Honey, it's really not polite to invite yourself to—"

"No," Ryan said, reaching over to pass the garlic bread to Lucy. "I want you all to be there, if it happens. In fact, I'll make you a promise, Lucy. If and when I really marry Jennifer, you can be a flower girl in the wedding."

Lucy's pretty face broke into a wide grin. "Can I have a new dress? And new shoes?"

"You can have whatever you want," Ryan said. "My treat."

Lucy could barely contain herself and began to chatter about the kind of dress and shoes she preferred. Ben, Carolyn and Ryan listened to her endless enthusiasm, the mood around the table light and teasing. As Ryan glanced back and forth between the members of his new family, he knew that he'd been right to come. He'd found a place where he belonged, a connection that couldn't be broken.

And someday, maybe he'd have a home just like this with Jennifer.

JENNIFER GLANCED at her watch then picked up her step. She was already fifteen minutes late and her mother was nothing if not punctual. The message Carmen left at the office said Jennifer was expected at the restaurant for lunch at precisely noon, no excuses. In truth, she would have liked a little more warning. She'd spent the last two days immersed in a new missing persons case that Lily Garrett had referred to the agency, and had eaten her lunch at her desk.

After Jennifer's success in locating Ryan Madison, Lily and Dylan were even more eager to use her investigative services. She was already developing a reputation and she wasn't a full-fledged P.I. yet. But this case was a bit more difficult than finding Ryan Madison. Wade Randall didn't want to be found, especially since he'd kidnapped his son from his ex-wife.

She glanced at her watch again, then slowed her pace. It wouldn't do to show up all hot and rumpled, either. After all, her mother and sisters had flown in from El Paso specifically to go over wedding plans. The least she could do was to appear interested. Jennifer knew she was in store for a long and excruciating afternoon, but she had a plan. This afternoon, she'd lay the foundation for the "breakup." She'd casually mention that she and Ryan had had a fight the previous evening and she might even discuss the subject of their argument. It would be the first step in preparing her family for the inevitable.

And it wasn't that far from the truth. She hadn't spoken to Ryan since they'd returned from El Paso. As she'd predicted, he'd called on Sunday afternoon and twice on Monday. But she hadn't returned his calls, determined to put some distance between them. Still, Jennifer hadn't been able to put him out of her mind completely. Again and again, she'd come back to his proposal, trying to figure out his true motives.

When she reached the restaurant, a popular spot in downtown Midland, she drew a deep breath, raked her hands through her tangled hair, and yanked the door open. The cool air hit her flushed face and she mentally prepared herself for the oncoming assault. She'd have to keep her wits about her if this was going to work.

Jennifer stepped up to the maitre d's stand. "I'm here to meet my mother and sisters," she said. "They have a reservation under Rodriguez?"

The maitre d' scanned his book then shook his head. "Are you sure it's under Rodriguez?" He glanced up. "I did show a woman and her three daughters to a table around noon. But their reservation was under Madison."

"Madison?" Jennifer asked.

"Yes," he said. "Let me show you to the table."

She reluctantly followed him into the luxurious dining room, then froze the moment she saw her family gathered at a table near the window. They were all there, her mother, Maria, Linda and Teresa—and Ryan. He looked up from his place and saw her standing in the middle of the room. Excusing himself, he quickly strode over to her. "Jen," he said with a smile. "We were beginning to wonder whether you were going to come at all."

Jennifer pasted a smile on her face. "What are you doing here?'' she asked, her words soft and cool, uttered through clenched teeth.

"I'm treating you and your family to lunch," he said, leaning closer to brush a kiss across her cheek. "Come on, they're watching. Act like you're glad to see me."

He laced his fingers through hers and pulled her along toward the table. Jennifer fought the urge to break free and run. How could he do this to her? She was supposed to lay the foundation for their split today. She couldn't do that with him sitting beside her, smiling and charming her mother and sisters.

Her mother stood as she approached. "Hello, *niña*. You are looking well." She pressed a kiss on Jennifer's cheek before Jennifer sat down beside her.

"This is a surprise," Jennifer said, glancing back and forth between her sisters and her mother.

"For us, too," Carmen said. "When Ryan called and offered to fly us all here, we could not very well refuse such a generous gesture. But he only would do it if it was a surprise for you. Isn't that sweet?"

Jennifer turned to stare at Ryan and he shrugged. "I know how hard it is to plan a wedding long distance," he said. "I thought it might be nice for you to get together and talk."

Her gaze narrowed and Jennifer sent him a few well-aimed daggers as she spread her napkin on her lap. "You planned this whole thing?"

"Linda threw up on the plane," Teresa chirped.

"I did not!" Linda cried.

"Are we going to shop for our dresses today?" Maria asked. "I think they should be black. Then I could wear the dress again for one of the cotillions at the club. I'm not going to wear pastels ever again. Now that I'm fifteen, I'm going to start dressing more mature."

Jennifer dropped her napkin at her place and slid her

chair back. "Will you excuse us for a minute, *Mamá?* I need to speak to Ryan." She got up and headed toward the door. A few seconds later, Ryan joined her in the foyer of the restaurant and she turned on him. "You could have at least told me about your little surprise," she said.

"Then it wouldn't have been much of a surprise, would it?" he replied.

"I was planning to tell my mother that we'd had a big fight. I was going to lay the groundwork."

"Groundwork?"

"For our breakup," she said. Jennifer smoothed her palms over her dress, her mind searching for options. "Maybe this could still work. We could have a fight right here, right now. Then you could storm out and I could go in there and try to explain."

"I'm hungry," Ryan said. "And I just spent nearly seven hundred dollars flying your mother and your sisters here. We're not going to have a fight today. We're going to have a pleasant lunch and discuss the plans for the wedding."

"There isn't going to be a wedding!" Jennifer cried. "And the sooner you get that through your head, the better."

"There could be a wedding," he said, "if you'd accept my proposal."

"Your proposal was a joke," she countered.

"What if it wasn't?" Ryan asked.

Jennifer stared at him for a long moment, her mouth agape. "Are you serious? You want to marry me for real?"

"Maybe," Ryan replied. "We should at least consider it. And until you decide for sure, I think we should play along with this wedding thing. What could it hurt? You should keep your options open."

Jennifer cursed beneath her breath. This was crazy. The

fact that she'd even consider marrying Ryan Madison for real meant that somewhere along the line her pregnancy had sucked every ounce of common sense from her brain. "Marrying you is not an option," she muttered.

"All right," Ryan replied. "Then let's get back in there and lay this groundwork you mentioned. We could have a little tiff right there at the table."

"All right," Jennifer repeated, turning back to the dining room. "Just follow my lead."

She hurried back into the dining room and took her place beside her mother, sending Carmen an apologetic smile. Ryan sat down on Jennifer's left and a few moments later the waiter appeared at their table to take their drink order.

"I think we should celebrate," Ryan said. "We could have champagne, but considering Jen's condition, why don't we have a bottle of sparkling cider. That way Maria, Linda and Teresa can join in the toast."

Jennifer groaned inwardly. He was not going to make this easy. He was already marshalling his support with her siblings. Teresa gazed at him adoringly, Linda accepted his gallant offer of a bread stick, and Maria smiled as the waiter returned and filled her glass with bubbly.

"I must say, *hija,* you are going to marry a very thoughtful man," Carmen said, picking up her wineglass. "All of this just to surprise you."

"Oh, I was surprised." She turned to Ryan. "And when did you plan all this, sweetheart?"

"I called your mother on Tuesday to thank her for the lovely weekend and she told me how difficult it was trying to plan the wedding over the phone, especially when you weren't being very cooperative. I thought it would be better to go over the details in person."

"We have so little time, Jennifer." Carmen opened her purse and withdrew a small notepad. "Now, I have made some lists. Here is the guest list from our side of the family. You and Ryan will have to give me your list before the end of the week. I have already ordered the invitations. They will need to go out next week at the latest."

"Next week?" Jennifer asked. Her time really was running out. If she didn't start her disagreement with Ryan right this second, she'd be too late. She swallowed hard. "Well, I've been trying to discuss the guest list with Ryan, but we can't seem to agree." Jennifer sent him a pointed glare. "He insists on inviting all his business associates. Over two hundred guests! And that's not even counting relatives."

Carmen blinked in surprise. "Two hundred?"

"Actually," Ryan interrupted. "I've changed my mind on that, Jen. I think close friends would be enough. So that reduces my list to under twenty."

Jennifer kicked at him under the table, but when she connected with his shin he simply smiled.

"And he won't pick a best man, either," she accused. "I'm starting to wonder if he's having second thoughts."

Ryan chuckled. "Ben will be my best man. My twin brother, Ben," he explained, turning to Carmen. "And if it's all right, I'd like my niece to be a flower girl. Her name is Lucy."

"Perfect!" Carmen cried. "Maria will be maid of honor and will stand up with your brother, Ben. Linda can be a junior bridesmaid, Joe can usher with one of his cousins, and Teresa and Lucy can be flower girls. Very simple. Now, I spoke with Father Juan and he has contacted the priest at St. Ignatius here in Midland. You may take your classes with him. We will need to start shopping for dresses, *niña*. Since we are going to have to buy off the rack, our choices will be limited. Now, here is the menu for the reception and I have a list of the flowers that we will use and—"

"Ryan doesn't want to take classes with the priest," Jennifer blurted out, desperate for anything to stop her mother's rampant planning. Religion was the perfect opening, considering her mother's strict Catholic views.

Carmen went silent, then turned her gaze to Ryan. "Is this true?"

"And he wants to send our children to public school instead of Catholic school," Jennifer added. "And he doesn't want to ask his parents to pay for the rehearsal dinner and—" Jennifer felt a sharp pain on her shin and she cried out.

"First of all," Ryan began, "I'm looking forward to classes with the priest. And I was educated in the public schools and turned out pretty well, so the education matter will be decided after more thought. As for the rehearsal dinner, I'll pay for that myself."

Carmen glanced back and forth between them, clearly confused. "Is everything all right between you two?"

"No!" Jennifer said at the very same time Ryan said, "Yes!"

"Jen has been under a lot of stress at work," Ryan explained in an even tone, reaching out to pat her hand sympathetically. "And with the baby and the wedding plans on top of that, she gets a little crabby in the afternoons."

"Crabby?" Jennifer cried. This time when she threw her napkin, it nearly hit him in the face. "Darling, may I speak with you in private?"

"Sweetheart, we really shouldn't ignore our guests. And we can discuss this later. Just remember what I told you. We need to keep our options open." He paused. "*All* our options."

"Yeah," Teresa said. "Keep your auctions open."

Linda tugged on her mother's sleeve. "Mama, my tummy feels funny."

"So, what color will the dresses be?" Maria asked. "Because I'm not going to wear pastels. Black is really in style for weddings now."

Carmen sent Maria a withering glare. "You will not be wearing black for Jennifer's wedding."

The rest of their lunch passed without incident. Carmen went over the details for the ceremony and reception, Ryan discussed the finer points, and Jennifer dutifully agreed with everything they planned. Though she'd silently agreed with Ryan to keep her options open, by the end of the afternoon, she felt as if she didn't have any options at all. Her head hurt and she couldn't breathe. And her worries had nearly overwhelmed her.

This entire thing was like a little snowball rolling down a mountainside. At first, it was nothing, but now that it had gathered speed, it was becoming downright dangerous. Jennifer moaned inwardly. If she didn't put a stop to this, it was going to roll right over her and take her tumbling down the mountain in a huge avalanche of anger and recrimination.

CHAPTER FIVE

LILY GARRETT BISHOP checked the address she'd written in her day planner, then glanced up at the simple brick facade of the block-long storefront in downtown Odessa. A door emblazoned with the name of Budnicki-Morales Private Investigations led to a narrow stairway and the second floor. She tucked her dark hair behind her ear and folded her jacket over her arm before she started up the stairs.

When she reached the office door, she smoothed her hand over the front of her sleeveless sheath dress, wondering if she ought to put her jacket back on. Every day, she took a long look at herself in her full-length mirror, assessing the state of her pregnancy and wondering when her condition would become evident to everyone else around her. She and Cole had kept the good news to themselves, with the exception of telling her brother, Dylan, and Cole's grandmother, Eve. But Lily was aching to shout the news from the rooftops.

She wanted to dress in maternity clothes, even though she was barely showing. She wanted to drink milk without worrying about explanations for her choice of beverage and she wanted to coo over little babies without having to walk away silently. She even wanted to read baby books twenty-four hours a day and discuss what she'd learned with every mother she met.

But she and Cole had decided to keep the pregnancy a secret for a while, just until they were certain everything was all right. At first, Lily had agreed, but now she woke up every morning hoping that a nice little basketball-size belly would have grown overnight, giving her an excuse to tell the world. "Be patient," she murmured as she reached the top of the stairs.

She stopped on the landing and slipped back into her jacket, pulling it over her nonexistent tummy. Then she opened the door and stepped inside. The office was long and narrow, a large open area backed by two smaller offices. Rippled glass and aged oak and scarred hardwood floors were reminiscent of all the old private eye movies. A pretty, raven-haired woman sat at the desk nearest the door. She looked up from her work and gave Lily a welcoming smile.

"Good afternoon," she said. "May I help you?"

"Jennifer? Are you Jennifer Rodriguez?"

Jennifer slowly stood, a tiny frown knitting her brow. "Yes."

Lily crossed the office in a few short steps and held out her hand, a smile breaking across her face. "We've talked on the phone so many times, but now we finally meet."

"Lily?" Jennifer asked. "Lily Garrett?"

Lily nodded. "Actually, it's Bishop now."

"That's right," Jennifer cried. "You got married last month. Congratulations!" She pointed to a chair on the opposite side of her desk. "Please, sit down. And tell me what you're doing here. I didn't realize you'd be coming. When you walked in I thought you might be some oil tycoon's wife, wondering if her husband was cheating on her. We get a lot of that."

"I'm in town on a project for the Texas Fund for Children, trying to convince a very old and very wealthy oilman to leave us all his money. So I figured I'd kill two birds with one stone." When they'd both taken their seats, Lily pulled a file folder from her shoulder bag. She handed it to Jennifer. "I thought we should talk about that parental abduction I referred to you. I've got some new information."

"The Randall case?"

Lily nodded.

"Well, I'm sure he's in the Midland area," Jennifer explained. "I learned that he'd been working in the oil fields for Anderson Petroleum but he left that job after he had a fight with the boss. One of the guys at the drilling site said he saw Wade Randall in a bar a week later and Randall mentioned he took another drilling job. He's using his real name, but he's keeping a low profile, no phone, no known address. Some of these guys who do day work in the oil fields get paid under the table so there's no way to trace them. But I'm sure he's still in West Texas. Though I'm not sure he has the boy with him. I've been looking for an old girlfriend or a relative he may have left the child with."

"I've been checking that angle, too," Lily said. "Randall's lived in Florida and Arizona and left a trail of girlfriends behind. But that's not what I came here to discuss." She paused. "Wade Randall has outstanding warrants in both states. Assault and battery in both cases. I think you need to turn this over to Morales or Budnicki. This guy is dangerous, Jennifer. There's no telling what he'll do if he's backed into a corner."

"But this is my case," Jennifer said. "I can do the legwork. And once I have all the information, we can call the police and they'll arrest him on the warrants."

Lily hesitated for a moment, remembering how excited she'd been in the early days of her career with the FBI, how confident she'd been in her abilities as a forensic investigator. But with experience came caution, something that Jennifer obviously hadn't learned yet. "What if he catches wind you're looking for him? What if one of his buddies gets back to him that you've been snooping around? You don't want a confrontation with this guy."

"I'll be careful," Jennifer assured her.

Lily considered Jennifer's plea for a moment, then shook her head. "I still want you to keep me updated. And I want you to discuss this with Ralph and Roy. Those two have a lot more experience with guys like Wade Randall than you do. And if anything looks suspicious, you go to the police right away. They can arrest him on the spot under the outstanding warrants. Agreed?"

Jennifer nodded. "Agreed."

Lily leaned back in her chair and smiled. "Well, now that we've taken care of business, do you have anything to eat around here? Maybe a candy bar or some potato chips? I haven't eaten since I got off the plane, and if I don't have something to eat right now I'm going to get really crabby really fast."

Jennifer hurried over to the tiny refrigerator and pulled out one of her frozen Snickers bars, then brought it back to Lily. "I keep a stash in the office. I get crabby in the afternoon, too, if I—" She stopped short, then looked at Lily. "Are you—?"

"Pregnant?" Lily asked. A tiny smile broke across her lips. It felt good to finally say it out loud to someone other than her husband. "I haven't told a lot of people yet, so I have to swear you to secrecy," she said in a loud whisper. "Just Cole and Dylan, and Cole's grandmother, Eve. But, yes, I am pregnant." She rubbed her hand on her belly. "Almost three months, though you wouldn't know it. I keep waiting to start showing so I can tell everyone the good news, but all my clothes still fit."

Jennifer pointed to her own tummy, then smoothed the fabric of her dress tight over her belly. "Five and a half months," she said with a rueful smile. "And believe me, once you start getting a belly, you'll long for the day when you can button up a pair of jeans.''

"You're pregnant, too?" Lily asked with a gasp. "You're barely showing and you're almost three months ahead of me. Gee, I didn't even realize you were married." She groaned inwardly. If she grew at the rate Jennifer did, it would be Christmas before anyone noticed she was pregnant!

Jennifer swallowed hard, then forced a smile. "I'm not. The father of the baby is…out of the picture. Completely."

Lily felt a blush of embarrassment warm her cheeks. Just because she'd found a perfect life didn't mean everyone else had it so easy. "So you're going to raise the baby alone?" she asked in a sympathetic voice.

Jennifer's shoulders rose and fell in a dejected shrug. "I don't know. I have this other option, an offer, I guess you could call it.''

"Adoption?"

"No, a proposal. For marriage. Actually, you know the guy, at least by name. In fact, you and Dylan and Carolyn St. Clair kind of brought us together. It's Ryan Madison. I helped Carolyn find him a few months ago. He's Ben Mulholland's twin brother."

"Yes, I know the case," said Lily, nodding. "But how did a missing persons case turn into a proposal of marriage?"

"Well, he said if I ever needed a favor, to come to him. So I did, and I asked him to pose as my fiancé until I got my parents to accept the idea of a pregnant daughter. And now he's asked me to marry him for real. I've told him no, but he's pretty persistent." Jennifer sighed. "You're so lucky. You have Cole, you're happily married, you have a future to look forward to with your little baby."

Lily laughed softly. "I'm going to let you in on a little secret. Cole and I didn't exactly start off our relationship in the traditional manner. Finders Keepers brought us together, too. Cole's grandmother, Eve, hired me to find him. When I found him, he mistakenly assumed I was there to apply for the job.''

"The job?"

The memories of that first meeting made Lily smile. But at the time she'd thought Cole was just about the most callous and arrogant man she'd ever met. "He was hiring a wife and a mother for his child. Cole had decided he wanted a child but didn't want to waste any effort on finding and falling in love with a wife. It was all supposed to be a business arrangement. I figured I'd stick around and learn a little more about the man I was investigating. Well, one thing led to another and—'' she held out her left hand, the diamond sparkling in the light ''—we ended up falling in love.''

Jennifer held out her own hand. "Ryan bought it for me as a prop when we told my parents we were engaged. The plan was to break up sometime before the baby was born. The only problem was my mother decided we had to get married right away. Now I've got a wedding date set for the third of November and a fake fiancé who actually wants to go through with the wedding.''

Lily laughed. "Well, you'll have to invite me to the wedding. I can't miss the happy ending on a story like that.''

"If there is a wedding," Jennifer murmured.

"Do you love him?" Lily asked.

"Under any other circumstances, I probably could fall in love with him," Jennifer admitted. "But how can I trust my feelings now? I'd never be sure if I was marrying him because I'm afraid to go through this alone, or because I think we actually have a shot at making a relationship work." She paused. "I was brought up to believe that marriage is sacred, and that once a couple marries, they're bound together for life. Unfortunately, Ryan doesn't share my opinion. He looks at marriage as a legal agreement, an agreement that can be broken as easily as it can be made.''

"Maybe you just need to give it time," Lily advised.

"I don't have much time. My mother and sisters were here for lunch earlier this afternoon, a lunch that should have been the beginning of the end.''

"How's that?''

"I tried to pick a fight with Ryan, but he kept bobbing and weaving. I couldn't connect. I came off looking like a harpy and he came off the patient, understanding, long-suffering future husband.'' Jennifer reached down and patted her stomach. "And I didn't eat a thing.''

Lily glanced at her watch. "My flight doesn't leave for another two hours. Why don't we two pregnant ladies go find a nice ice-cream shop and indulge in something sinful.''

Jennifer laughed, twisting around to grab her purse from the back of her chair and switch on the answering machine. "That sounds like the best idea I've heard all day.''

As they walked to the door, Lily slipped her arm through Jennifer's. "This is going to be wonderful. I can talk about all the baby books I've read and all the things I've learned. Who cares about Finders Keepers?'' she said with a smile. "This afternoon is all about babies.''

RYAN PULLED HIS CAR into a parking space near Jennifer's apartment and flipped off the ignition. Then he grabbed the bags he'd set on the front seat and hopped out of the car. Though he hadn't called ahead of time, he hoped that take-out Chinese and a few other gifts would serve as a peace offering of sorts.

As he walked to the door, he noticed a black pickup truck parked across the street from Jennifer's door. The driver watched his approach, his eyes hidden by the

shadow of a battered straw cowboy hat. He flicked a cigarette butt out the window and Ryan's gaze caught sight
of a tattoo on the stranger's left forearm, what looked like
a spider's web. A few seconds later, the driver pulled away
from the curb and Ryan brushed the man from his mind.

He juggled the packages in his arms then pushed Jennifer's doorbell. When the door swung open, he peered
over the top of one of the bags at her lovely face.

"What are you doing here?" she demanded.

Though it wasn't the greeting Ryan had hoped for, he
considered himself lucky that she'd opened the door at all.
After their disastrous lunch with her mother and sisters
earlier that day, Jennifer had refused to speak to him.
When he'd called later that afternoon, she'd been out of
the office. And when he'd tried her at home, she'd hung
up on him. The flowers he'd sent by way of an apology
had been sent right back with the delivery boy.

There had been only one positive side to her anger—
she hadn't written off his proposal of marriage. Not yet,
at least. "Can I come in?" he asked in a soft voice.

Jennifer nodded, then stepped aside. Ryan hefted the
bags he carried, his gaze fixed on hers. How she managed
to look more beautiful every time he saw her, he wasn't
sure. She was dressed in leggings and an oversize T-shirt,
and her hair tumbled around her face. Though she wore
little makeup, her face looked radiant, her skin like silk
and her mouth irresistibly sweet.

"Did I wake you?" he asked.

She shook her head and brushed her hair out of her eyes.
"I was just resting. I had a busy day at work. Lily Garrett
stopped by and we discussed a case I'm working on for
Finders Keepers."

"Another missing persons case?" Ryan asked.

"A parental abduction," she murmured. "A little boy,

seven years old. His father took him nearly two years ago.''

"I brought dinner,'' he said, holding out one of the bags. "And all sorts of other goodies.''

"Is this a peace offering?'' she asked.

Ryan grinned. "I suppose you could call it that. Although I don't think we've really been at war, have we?''

"What do you call that little battle beneath the table at the restaurant? I'm still wounded.'' She rubbed at her shin and put on a pretty pout.

A sigh slipped from him. "Jen, I just wanted you to consider all your options before you made a final decision. And for that, you need a little more time.'' He moved to the sofa and set the bags down on the coffee table. "Why don't you get us something to drink and we'll have dinner? We can forget this afternoon and talk about this calmly and rationally.'' He picked up the smallest bag. "This needs to go in the freezer.''

She gave him another reluctant nod, then padded into the kitchen in her stocking feet. A few minutes later, she returned with a beer for Ryan and a glass of milk for herself, and a pair of plates. Ryan smiled and noted that she was taking his advice about her diet, forgoing soda pop for a healthier beverage.

"I've brought sweet-and-sour chicken and egg rolls and fried rice. And for dessert, I stopped at Roscoe's and got ice cream.'' He opened the cartons and dumped food on the plates, then handed her a plate and a plastic fork. She picked at the food for a few seconds, then set her fork down. "You're not hungry?''

"Lily and I had banana splits at Roscoe's just a few hours ago.''

Ryan grabbed another of the bags he'd brought. "Then you can save dinner for later. I've got something else for you.'' He rummaged inside the bag. "I went out shopping after lunch and I found some things you might need. You've been so worried about the wedding that you haven't had time to think about the baby. Here's a copy of *Expectant Mother* magazine," he said, flipping through the pages. "There's a very good article in here on prenatal vitamins. Has your doctor prescribed vitamins for you?"

In truth, Ryan had spent most of the afternoon reading through the magazines and books he'd bought. To his surprise, he found the entire pregnancy thing fascinating, from the development of the baby to the supplies needed for its first night at home. But the enormity of it all kind of scared him, especially the pictures of childbirth. And he hoped it might scare Jennifer, too. At least enough to accept his proposal.

He knew he was venturing into shaky territory. After all, he had no right to get involved in Jennifer's life, but he had to believe she'd come to her senses and realize how much she needed him and the security of a marriage. He had to find a way to make her see that the next four months were going to be difficult, especially if she chose to face them alone.

"And here's another article on putting together a layette for the baby," he added.

"Layette?" Jennifer asked, her eyes wide, her expression uneasy.

He nodded. "That's all the little clothes and diapers and things you need to have on hand for when the baby comes home from the hospital. And look at this," Ryan said. *Pregnancy Week by Week.* It's a book that tells you everything that's happening every week. See here? This is what your baby looks like right now." He held out the book and she glanced down at the drawing of a twenty-one-week-old fetus. "That's actual size."

"He—he's so big," she murmured, her eyes going wide, her hand dropping to the swell of her stomach.

"And wait until you see this," Ryan said. He reached in the bag and pulled out a tiny pair of pajamas with little green lambs all over them. "It's called a 'onesie.' It looks so small, but the saleslady assured me that the baby will be this small when it comes out. Can you believe that?" He glanced over the top of the onesie to see an uneasy expression cross Jennifer's face.

"I'm not ready for this," she said, her voice small and shaky. "I—I haven't even thought about a layette. And where am I supposed to buy these onesies and how many will I need?" She took the tiny garment from his hand and turned it around. "How do you even get this on a baby? It doesn't have a zipper." Her eyes glistened with unshed tears and she clutched the onesie. "I should have listened to my mother. She always told me I'd grow up and have a family of my own someday, but I never believed her. She'd give me dolls for my birthday and I'd toss them under my bed. I'm paying for it now."

Once again, her emotions shifted like sunlight and shadows on water, one minute bright and cheery, and the next, morose. Would he ever be able to predict her moods? Ryan hooked a finger under her chin and tipped her gaze up to meet his. He took the wadded onesie from her hands and dropped a kiss on her lips. "Sweetheart, you'll learn. You can read books. And there are classes," he said. "When I first started thinking about it all, it seemed a little overwhelming, but you've got lots of time."

"I—I guess I've just avoided all this," she said, motioning to the books and magazines. "Every time I really thought about it, I'd get nervous. So I just stopping thinking about it. But there's you and—and Lily—"

"Lily?"

"She and Cole are going to have a baby and they've already started planning the nursery," she continued in a tremulous voice. "And they've talked about names and

Cole is so excited. That's the way it's supposed to be. A husband and a wife and *then* the baby.'' She shook her head. "It's a lot harder to face alone.''

"You don't have to, Jen. If you marry me, I'll be there for you. I can help.'' He drew her into his arms and pulled her close. A ragged sigh escaped her lips and she nuzzled her face into the curve of his neck. Gently, he rubbed her back and whispered soothing words. "We can make it work,'' he said.

And deep in his heart, Ryan knew that was true. He just needed time with Jennifer, time to make her see they belonged together. Time for her to see that she needed him.

"How?'' she asked.

For the first time since he'd proposed, he saw a crack in her unbending refusal. "However *you* want it to work. You make up the rules and I'll go along with whatever you want.''

She sniffled, then looked up at him through damp eyes. "Really?''

Ryan nodded. Staring into her gaze, he brushed an errant tear from her cheek with his thumb. "Really.''

She reached up and wiped her nose with her wrist, then gave him a wavering smile. "I—I suppose I could consider it. After talking with Lily, I just got so scared. She has Cole to be there with her, to love her and their baby. And I don't have anyone.'' She drew a shaky breath. "What if I'm no good at this? What if I make a mistake and I don't realize until it's too late?''

"All new mothers worry about these things. They all have insecurities.''

"They do?''

"Mmm-hmm. It's perfectly normal.''

A reluctant smile quirked her lips. "How is it you know all these things?''

"I read it in one of those books. Now, why don't you

have a little more milk and I'll read to you while you eat? And I've got a brochure for childbirth and child care classes. We can sign up right away if you'd like.''

"Childbirth?" she said, swallowing hard.

Ryan chuckled. "You didn't think you'd be able to have a baby without going through labor and delivery, did you?"

"There are drugs," Jennifer countered. "At least I know that much. My doctor assures me that I can have drugs if I want them." Her gaze dropped to her fingers and she stared at them for a long time before she spoke again. "I— I go to my doctor's appointments and take my vitamins, but the baby just didn't seem real—until now. Every day, it's getting closer and closer and I'm getting more and more afraid.''

Ryan reached over to the coffee table and picked up the glass of milk. "Come on. Have something to drink. It will make you feel much better.''

She looked at him with wide brown eyes. "Why do you care so much?''

"I don't know," Ryan said. "I just do. Maybe it's because you look so pathetic when you get all weepy.''

That made her giggle, and she gave him a grateful smile. In truth, he knew exactly why he cared. He was falling in love with Jennifer and nothing he did could stop it. He thought about her all the time and he'd begun to think of her baby as his own. Ryan knew it was probably a direct reaction to his own family situation, and a dangerous reaction at that, but he couldn't deny his feelings.

"I'm not thirsty right now," she said.

"Then maybe we should study these books," Ryan said.

"Can you just hold on to me for a while?" she asked.

Ryan had no intention of refusing such a simple and heartfelt request. He gently pulled her back into his arms. He tucked her head beneath his chin and kissed her fragrant hair. This was the way it was meant to be between them, he mused. No indecision, no indifference. Just long, sweet moments of touching and listening. "You know," he murmured. "A lot of women have gone through this before. Your mom, for instance. She went through it five times, and I'm sure when she was pregnant with you, she had a lot of the same worries. Maybe you could talk to her."

Jennifer pressed her palms against his chest and stared up into his eyes. "She expects me to be perfect," she said. "I'd rather talk to you. You like me just the way I am." She drew a shaky breath. "Why is that?"

He brushed a strand of hair from her cheek and tucked it behind her ear. "Maybe because you're stubborn and opinionated and you never listen to what I tell you. Or maybe it's because you're honest and determined and you try so hard to do the right thing. But it's probably because even with red eyes and a runny nose, you're the most beautiful woman I've ever known."

She hiccuped, then sniffled again. "Really?"

This time he didn't answer. Instead, he leaned forward and kissed her, his mouth lingering on hers. At first, the kiss took her by surprise, but he didn't retreat. He gave her time to get used to the gentle touch of his tongue. Teasing and testing, he molded her lips to his until he felt her surrender, bit by bit.

Would he ever grow tired of this? Kissing Jennifer was a heady experience. The sweet sensation of possessing her mouth was sending his desire into overdrive. He wanted her, but not in just a purely sexual way. With Jennifer, there was so much more to their relationship—an intimacy that went beyond the bedroom.

They could talk to each other. He could protect her and comfort her. She could make him laugh. And it was in those intimacies that his desire for her grew. Now he needed her to want him, to ache for him, to lose herself so thoroughly to passion that he was the only man in the world who could satisfy her. Then it would be perfect. Then and only then would he believe they'd have a future together.

His fingers smoothed over her shoulders and spanned her still-tiny waist. He leaned back into the pillows on the sofa and pulled her along with him, settling her on top of him. Her hair fell down around them like a curtain and he slipped his hands beneath her shirt until he felt warm, silken skin. Slowly, he explored the delicate expanse of her back, rubbing and massaging until she moaned softly.

But then she pushed away from him and his hands slid along her ribs to the soft curves of her breasts. For a long moment, Ryan didn't move, enjoying the feel of her flesh against his thumbs. She blinked, her breath catching in her throat, and he knew she wasn't sure, wasn't ready.

"We shouldn't do this," she murmured, her palms pressed against his chest, her eyes hooded with desire.

Slowly, hesitantly, he drew his hands back to her waist, then tugged her shirt down. "Why not?" he countered.

"I—I have a lot to think about. You've asked me to marry you and I need to give you an answer. And when you kiss me and touch me, I can't think straight."

"Then I must be doing something right," he teased.

She pushed her hair back over her shoulder, then carefully climbed off him. Ryan would have preferred that she stay where she was, at least until the evidence of his passion had subsided. But he swung his legs off the sofa and stood. "Maybe I should go," he suggested.

Hell, that was his only choice. If he stayed in the same room with Jennifer, he'd spend an agonizing evening wanting what he couldn't possibly have. At least, not yet. And the last thing he wanted to do was scare her off. "Why don't you let me know what you decide?" he said.

Jennifer nodded. He leaned over to kiss her, then thought better of it. The kiss he'd given her just moments before had started out innocently and look where it had gotten him. Instead, he grabbed his jacket from the back of the sofa and smiled.

When he reached the safety of his car, Ryan sat for a long moment before turning the ignition. There was only one way to make this marriage work. He'd have to get Jennifer to fall so deeply in love with him that she'd actually want to marry him for real. For Ryan knew, in his heart, he wasn't willing to settle for anything less.

THE GLOW from the television illuminated the living room of Jennifer's apartment. She lay on the sofa, curled up beneath an afghan that her Tía Yolanda had crocheted, halfheartedly absorbed in old episodes of "The Newlywed Game." If the show proved anything, it proved that people just didn't take marriage seriously—not now and not then. These couples were supposed to love each other and yet they barely knew each other!

All of them had done it right, though. They'd met, fallen in love, had a wedding—and then appeared on a game show. If she accepted Ryan's proposal, they'd do it backward. And there'd never be a chance to set it right. They'd have met and gotten married all in a few months' time. And the love part might never come.

But after the day she'd had, Jennifer knew she was ill-prepared to face this pregnancy on her own. Ryan was offering her a way to get through the next months without fear and doubt. He'd already eased her worries by simply holding her and stroking her hair. When he was near, she felt safe.

She sat up and ran her hands through her hair. The remains of her dinner were still spread on the coffee table and the bags Ryan had brought over lay scattered on the floor. She picked up one of them and reached inside. Soft fur touched her hand and she pulled out a stuffed bunny with a pink-checked ribbon around its neck.

Clutching the toy to her chest, she leaned back into the sofa and smoothed her hand over its ears. A marriage between them could be simple or it could be incredibly complicated. If Ryan Madison had feelings for her—romantic feelings—then that could ruin everything. A one-sided relationship would never work. He'd resent her lack of feelings, she'd feel trapped by gratitude and sooner or later they'd end up hating each other.

But if they could keep their relationship strictly platonic, there was a chance they could get through the pregnancy without any hurt feelings. And later, when she and the baby were settled, they could file for divorce. Or they could go on as they had. Or maybe… She pushed the thoughts from her mind. Counting on love to rescue them both would be creating false hope.

"It could work," Jennifer murmured. She scrambled off the sofa and hurried over to the kitchen counter. When she found a pen and a piece of paper, she sat down at the dining table and began to scribble out the conditions for their agreement.

She worked on her plan without stopping, perfecting every rule and regulation, carefully considering the wording and the order. And when she glanced up at the clock, she was surprised to see it was nearly midnight. Jennifer knew she wouldn't be able to sleep until this was all settled. She hurried to the bedroom and changed into a dress, then grabbed her sandals and tugged them on.

As she made the fifteen-minute drive to Ryan's condo, she went over her plan in her head, making sure she'd covered all the possibilities. But one thing she couldn't ignore was the way Ryan made her feel when he kissed her. When she thought about Ryan Madison, she didn't automatically think about friendship. She thought about desire and passion, uncontrolled need and warm, deep kisses—like the kisses they'd shared just hours before.

A shiver skittered over her skin, though the night air was warm and humid. It wouldn't do to keep dwelling on these things. It would only harm their chances for making their "marriage" succeed. Now that the decision had been made, Jennifer felt lighter, as if she could finally stop worrying about her future.

When she reached Ryan's condo, she pulled up into the driveway. But she couldn't bring herself to get out of the car. Was this the right thing to do? Marriage was a serious step, meant for people who truly loved each other. She drew a shaky breath, then opened the car door.

The condo was dark, the only light coming from the doorbell. She pressed the bell once, then three more times before the porch light flipped on and the door swung open. Ryan stood in front of her, dressed only in baggy boxer shorts. His hair was rumpled and his feet bare. He squinted, then opened his eyes wide. "Jen? What's wrong?" He stepped out on the front porch and grabbed her hands. "Are you all right? Is it the baby?"

Suddenly, Jennifer knew she was doing the right thing. For deep in her heart was a tiny corner where her love for Ryan had taken hold. No matter what happened between them, she would always be grateful for the time he spent in her life, even if it was only until the baby was born. And she'd honestly be able to say she loved him, a little bit.

"Yes," she murmured.

"It's the baby?"

"No," she said. "I mean, yes. I will marry you. But I just need to know one thing first."

"Anything," Ryan replied.

She swallowed convulsively. "Do you love me?"

The question caused a brief flicker of emotion in his eyes, and for a moment, Jennifer was certain he was about to say yes. But then he shook his head. "No," he said. "I'm attracted to you but I don't love you."

"All right." She gave a sigh of relief. "Then I think this might have a chance of working. We agree to a platonic relationship."

"And what if feelings change?" Ryan asked.

"They can't. And you can't let them. Neither can I. That's part of the agreement. We get married as planned and we stay married until one of us wants out. Then we get an amicable divorce and we both go on with our lives." She reached in her purse and pulled out her list of conditions. "I have everything written down. We need to go over this so you understand."

"It's past midnight," he said, scratching his bare chest.

Jennifer pushed by him and walked through the front door. "I think the sooner we discuss this, the better. That way we can work out any problem areas. After all, we only have a few weeks until the wedding." She settled herself on the sofa and patted the cushion beside her. "I've worked out twelve conditions, and I think if we just stick to them, there won't be any misunderstandings."

Ryan took a seat beside her and draped his arm across the back of the sofa. "All right. What are they?"

"Well," she said, her gaze drifting down his bare legs. Lord, he had nice legs. And an incredible chest, smooth and muscular. And his shoulders were so broad and— Jennifer cleared her throat. "I think we should jump right to number five. No underwear around the house. We should be fully dressed at all times."

"Even in bed?" he asked.

"Point number two. We'll have separate bedrooms."

Ryan laughed. "If that's point number two, I'm afraid to ask what point number one is."

"No kissing," she said. "And no touching."

"At all?"

"Well, platonic touching is all right, but anything else is against the rules."

Ryan snatched the paper from her fingers and scanned the rest of the rules. "By the look of this list, this would be a marriage in name only. Your conditions strictly prohibit any of the good things that go along with marriage. I could marry one of those blow-up dolls and have more fun."

"That's the point," she said. "This isn't supposed to be fun."

"And why not?" he asked. "Why can't I kiss you when I want to kiss you? And why can't I wrap my arms around you and nibble on your neck when the spirit moves me?"

"Because it would only complicate matters," she explained, trying to keep her mind on the rules and off the notion of a little nibbling. "You might expect something more than I can give you. Or I might need something more than you can offer me. If this is going to work, we have to keep it strictly platonic."

He stared at the list for a long time and Jennifer held her breath. He was going to refuse. The rules were ridiculous and she should never have come to him with such an outlandish plan. Her heart pounded in her chest and she tried to steady her nerves. What would she do if he said no? She'd be forced to cancel the wedding and incur the wrath of her parents. She'd have to face her pregnancy all alone. And after the baby was born, she would have no support, no one to help her get through the sleepless nights.

Jennifer gnawed on her bottom lip, watching him with a shrewd eye. Or—or maybe she could just forget the rules and take a chance on marriage on his terms. There would be kissing and touching and lots of underwear around the

house. And maybe, they'd even share a bed. And—and
who knows what that might lead to?

"Can I have some time to think about this?" Ryan
asked.

She sucked in a sharp breath. "Then you'd consider it?"

He shrugged. "Maybe."

Jennifer jumped to her feet. It would probably be best
to leave him to his deliberations. If she stayed, she might
be tempted to convince him of the merits of her plan. Or
he might try to convince her of the benefits of tearing it
up. "Then I'll go. You can let me know."

Ryan stood and grabbed her hand. "You're not going
anywhere," he said.

"I—I'm not?"

"No," he insisted. "I don't want you driving back so
late and all alone. You'll stay here tonight."

"But I—"

He placed his finger over her lips to quiet any further
protest. "This is not up for negotiation. You can sleep in
my bed and I'll sleep on the sofa."

Jennifer nodded. "All right. It will be good practice."

Ryan took her hand and led her through the living room.
As she stepped into his bedroom, she moaned inwardly,
her gaze falling on the wide, comfortable bed. Though she
was determined to stick to her plan, she couldn't help but
wonder what would happen if she threw him down on the
bed and seduced him. Would everything change with just
one night together? Or would she be even more committed
to her plan? She drew a shaky breath, then pasted a smile
on her face. Unfortunately, if she let him walk out of the
bedroom, she'd never know the answer to her questions.

CHAPTER SIX

THE FIRST RAYS of dawn were filtering through the bedroom curtains when Ryan opened his eyes. He leaned over and grabbed the alarm clock beside his bed, squinting to see the numbers in the early-morning light. Jennifer lay curled up beside him, her face nestled in the curve of his shoulder, her leg thrown across his hips. He wasn't sure how they'd ended up tangled in each other's arms and sleeping in the same bed.

He'd simply showed her into his bedroom and they'd begun discussing her twelve-point plan for marriage again, reviewing each point in more detail. Sometime during the discussion, she'd flopped down on the bed, and soon after, he'd sat down beside her. Neither one of them noticed that they'd broken rule number two—the separate bed rule.

He nuzzled his face into her hair and pressed a gentle kiss on her forehead, breaking rule number one. A smile curved the corners of his mouth as he thought about all her goofy rules. Some of them were completely convoluted, like the prohibition on arguments regarding family, finances and the baby. Why she didn't just ban arguments altogether, he wasn't sure. Maybe she wanted to leave open the possibility that they could fight over his leaving the toilet seat up or throwing his dirty socks underneath the sofa.

The agreement was tucked under her pillow and he carefully removed it so he wouldn't wake her. Though he hadn't signed it yet, Ryan would be willing to sign over his soul to the devil just to marry Jennifer Rodriguez. He'd lied to her the night before when she'd asked if he loved her. He'd loved her for quite a while now. All he needed was the time to convince her that she loved him. He figured he had three weeks until the wedding, and during that time he had every intention of testing the limits of her rules.

And if he couldn't convince her to love him before they were married, he'd have all the time in the world after the ceremony. Ryan glanced at the clock again. For now, he had another fifteen minutes before he had to slip out of bed and get to the drilling site. Though he'd love to spend the day with his fiancé, he knew as soon as she woke up, she'd have something to say about the sleeping arrangements. So he'd simply slip out of bed before she awoke and avoid the mandatory punishment per rule number twelve.

Ryan closed his eyes, then opened them again when Jennifer shifted in his arms. He watched her for a long moment, taking in her peaceful and perfect features. His gaze dropped lower, to her belly, the fabric of her dress stretched tight over her abdomen. With a tentative hand, he reached out and placed his palm on the soft swell below her waist.

"Who are you in there?" he murmured. "Will you have beautiful brown eyes like your mother? Or will you look like—" Ryan stopped, the words catching in his throat. It was so easy to forget about the baby's real father. He thought of the baby as Jennifer's now, and someday his. "I don't care who you look like," he continued. "I'll still fall in love with you the very first time I see you. Just like I did with your mom."

At that instant, he felt a movement beneath his palm, a subtle, almost imperceptible undulation of Jennifer's belly. Ryan froze, not sure what had happened. But then the baby moved again and he slowly smiled. "Let me revise that last part," he murmured. "I think I'll love you starting right now."

He brought his gaze back up to Jennifer's face, then leaned forward and pressed a gentle kiss on her lips. He knew it was against the rules, but he didn't care. The rules were made to be broken, wherever and whenever he felt the need. What he didn't expect was to be caught so soon. Jennifer slowly opened her eyes and stared up at him.

Ryan didn't speak, afraid that if he hadn't fully awakened her, his words might do just that. Instead, he bent close and kissed her again. Her lips parted slightly and she sighed, then returned his kiss. Warmth washed over his body and Ryan's hands moved to her hips, pulling her against him until she stretched along the length of his body.

No matter how many times he kissed her, in the past, in the future, Ryan knew he'd never get enough. Her taste was like a drug to him, addicting, creating a hunger that refused to be sated. What was it that made him want her so? From the moment she'd walked into his trailer at the drilling site that day, he'd felt the connection, like an electrical current that popped and crackled between them, a magnetism that couldn't be ignored.

And when she'd come back to him again, he realized that he'd been given a second chance, a chance to see her as something more than just a passing attraction. She'd drawn him into her life and he hadn't resisted. No, he'd never be able to resist her, no matter how many walls she attempted to build between them or how many rules she tried to enforce.

Ryan took her face in his hands as his mouth moved against hers. The kiss had gone from a gentle exploration to a frantic search for more—more heat, more sensation, more intimacy. He murmured her name, his words soft against her lips. But her only reply was the quickening of her breath.

Her body pressed closer, and suddenly, the clothes they'd worn to bed seemed to stand between them. Ryan wanted to touch her, smooth his hands over naked skin. He slipped his fingers beneath the bodice of her dress and cupped her breast in his hand, the warm flesh molding perfectly to his palm. His thumb brushed the nub of her nipple, teasing it to a peak. A tiny moan slipped from her throat and she arched toward him.

For a moment, he thought she really wanted him, really needed him—that she was awake and aware of everything that was happening between them. But though she may have felt every sensation, they were both caught in a fantasy world—until his alarm went off.

The sound cut through the silent room. Jennifer jerked, startled, then stared at him for a long moment, as if she were trying to figure out exactly where she was. Realization cleared her sleepy gaze and she sucked in a sharp breath. "I—I have to go," she murmured, scrambling out of his arms and nearly tumbling from the bed. The loose skirt of her dress was still caught beneath him. She tugged on it and he rolled onto his side, releasing her to nearly fall backward onto the floor.

"Jen, I'm sorry. I just—I couldn't—" He drew a deep breath. "I couldn't help myself."

"Well, you're going to have to start," she muttered, smoothing her dress. "We have an agreement. It doesn't say much for your honor if you break the agreement right from the start."

"I haven't signed it yet," he said.

She glanced around the bed, then saw the paper on the other side of Ryan. Crawling over him, she snatched up her list of rules and waved it in front of his nose. "Sign it now," she said.

"No," he replied. "I want to take a while and think about it."

"Are you backing out?" she asked, shifting uneasily from foot to foot.

Ryan shook his head. "I just want to think about it."

"Well," she snapped, "don't take too long. I might change my mind." With that, she grabbed her shoes from the floor and hurried out of the bedroom.

When he heard the front door slam, Ryan sank back into the pillows and threw his arm over his eyes. If she really expected him to live by her damn rules, she was seriously deluded. There was no way he could be around her every morning and every night and not want to kiss her and hold her. And leaving her to sleep alone would be impossible. Hell, he'd spend every night lying awake and wondering what it would feel like to hold her in his arms again, to run his hands over her naked body, to make her moan the way she had earlier. And after a few nights of that, he'd be too sleep deprived to function.

There was only one thing to do, Ryan mused. He'd have to do some serious renegotiating. And now that she had a good taste of what she'd be missing, perhaps she'd be willing to listen to his ideas about what life would be like between Ryan Madison and his new wife.

CLOUDS OF DUST bloomed behind Jennifer's car as she sped down the access road to the latest drilling site of Madison Drilling and Oil. All morning she'd tried to concentrate on work, running down leads in the Randall case, answering the phones and balancing the books, but again and again, her mind returned to what had happened in Ryan's bed. Or what had almost happened.

This was exactly like him! He'd developed an annoying habit of ignoring her wishes—with her parents and the wedding plans, with her list of rules, even with the way she ate. If this was a taste of what marriage to Ryan Madison would be like, she wasn't sure she wanted anything to do with him.

It wasn't that she didn't appreciate his concern, but there was a point when concern turned to control. She'd worked hard to make a life—an independent life—for herself. And when she kissed Ryan Madison, all that flew right out the window. His lips, his touch, just staring into his eyes had the effect of making her mind turn to mush.

Well, it was time she took a little control. She turned her car into a wide circle, then skidded to a stop in front of the trailer. Workmen had gathered in the parking area to eat their lunches. They sat on the tailgates of their pickups, listening to a radio blaring out a country-and-western tune. When she opened her door, all eating stopped and every eye turned toward her. The last time she'd been at the site, the men had been out in the oil field, but now they watched her as she slowly started toward Ryan's office.

A wolf whistle split the air, then a chorus of laughter. The door to the trailer swung open and Ryan stepped out, dressed in a chambray workshirt and a pair of faded jeans. Like everything else at the site, his boots were coated with dust. His attention was fixed on some kind of map and he didn't see her standing at the bottom of the metal steps.

"Hey, boss," one of the workers called. "You got yourself a visitor."

"And a pretty little filly, too," another man shouted.

"I guess the benefits are better for management than us grunts, right, boss?"

Ryan looked up and blinked in surprise when his gaze came to rest on Jennifer. "Hey," he said, shoving the map into the arms of the man who had followed him out the door. "What are you doing here?"

"We need to talk," she replied.

He reached out and took her hand, then led her up the steps and through the open door of the trailer. The inside was cool and dim and Jennifer was automatically drawn back to that day, when she'd first set eyes on Ryan Madison. All she'd been interested in was completing the job she'd been assigned, bringing Ryan to his long-lost brother and his brother's dying child. In the end, someone else had been a match for Lucy, and Ryan's marrow wasn't needed. She'd often wondered what his life might have been like had she never stepped inside the trailer. Or what turns *her* life might have taken had she been facing her pregnancy alone.

Would she still be hiding the baby from her parents and her bosses? Or would she have worked up the courage to tell them? Jennifer rubbed her arms, the goose bumps more a result of her thoughts that the cold breeze blasting from the air conditioner. No good would come from wondering what-if? Her life was what it was, right here and now.

She wandered over to his desk, then noticed a framed picture of Ryan and a woman. Hesitantly, she reached for it, a flare of jealousy surging up inside her. Why would he still keep a photo of Elise on his desk? But as she studied the photo, she saw that it wasn't his ex-fiancée sitting and smiling next to Ryan. She held up the pretty silver frame. "Where did you get this?"

He crossed the trailer and stared down at the photo. "Your mother took that picture of us at Maria's party. She thought I might like to have a copy. She gave it to me when we had lunch, before you arrived."

"This is exactly what I'm talking about," Jennifer said, slamming the frame back down on the desk.

Ryan scowled. "Talking about? Jen, we weren't talking about anything."

"Well, it's what I came here to talk about."

He rubbed the back of his neck and sighed dramatically. "Are you still angry that I kissed you this morning?"

"I'm angry about a lot of things," she said, his impatient tone piquing her even more. "I'm beginning to I feel like an outsider in my own life. All the decisions about my future are being made by you and my mother. And I'm sick to death of it!"

"Jen, calm down," he whispered. "It's not good for you to get upset. And the baby can hear the shouting."

"What are you talking about?"

He reached out and patted her tummy. "I was reading in a book last night that said the baby can hear sounds outside the womb after week fifteen."

Jennifer pressed the heels of her hands to her temples. "Have you completely lost your mind? Why are you reading books about my pregnancy?"

"Because I want to be prepared," Ryan said, as if it were the most logical reason in the world.

"This is just another example," Jennifer said, wagging her finger at him. "Another way of exerting your control."

He scoffed. "I don't try to control you."

"Oh, no? Well then, why is it the very first time I try to express my opinion on how we should proceed, you decide that you've got to revise my rules?"

"Because your rules are stupid."

"But they're *my* rules," she said, jabbing her finger at her chest. "They're what *I* want. And you should respect that. After all, this is my life you're intruding into."

Ryan opened his mouth, then snapped it shut. Jennifer saw hurt in his eyes and she instantly regretted saying what she had. She cursed inwardly. Lately, her emotions had swung from one extreme to another. If she wasn't crying on his shoulder, she was shouting at him. Jennifer drew a long, calming breath.

"You think I'm intruding in your life?" he asked.

She shook her head. "That's not what I meant. I just feel that I'm not in control anymore. You don't allow me to make any decisions that affect the two of us. You make them all for me."

"All right," Ryan said. "What decision would you like to make?"

"I don't have one ready," she replied.

"Well, then the next decision we make will be made by you." He took her hand and pulled her toward a chair beside his desk. "Now, sit down and let me get you some lunch. I'd be willing to bet you didn't eat anything before driving out here."

Jennifer shook her head, then grudgingly took the offered seat. She brushed her hair back from her eyes and watched as Ryan pulled deli containers out of a small refrigerator. He grabbed two cans of pop, then set everything in front of her. "So, did you come out here just to yell at me or did you have another reason for this visit?" he asked as he pulled the tops off the containers.

Jennifer grabbed the potato salad and jabbed at it with a plastic fork. In truth, she was famished. Part of her bad mood could probably be written off as hunger. "My mother left a message at the office early this morning. She's got a problem with the guest list you gave her for the wedding."

"What kind of problem?" Ryan asked.

"She wants to know why your parents aren't on the list."

A long silence descended over the trailer as Jennifer waited for Ryan's reply. "My parents are dead," he finally said with an indifferent shrug.

Jennifer slowly set her fork down, then dropped the container of potato salad on the desk. She knew this would cause another argument, but it was one she couldn't let pass. Especially since she felt responsible for the rift between Ryan and his parents. "Jeffrey and Rhonda Madison are not dead. And since they aren't, they should be invited to the wedding."

"Absolutely not," Ryan replied, his voice cold. "I don't want them there."

"What you want doesn't make a difference," she said.

"It doesn't?"

"Nope. This is my decision. I get to choose this time, remember?"

Ryan cursed softly. "Can't you decide next time? Can't we just skip over this one for now? I'll give you two decisions if you give up this one."

"I want your parents at the wedding. If they aren't there, then there won't be a wedding."

His brow rose and he set his jaw. "Are you giving me an ultimatum?"

Jennifer smiled, then reached out and patted his hand. The physical contact had the desired effect. His expression softened as he took her fingers in his. "I'm giving you a choice," she said.

"I haven't agreed to your plan yet. And if I do, might I point out rule number six? All family obligations to be negotiated. And rule number eleven—no arguments about money, family, the wedding or the baby. And there are reasons I don't want my parents—I mean, Rhonda and Jeffrey Madison—at the wedding."

"And I don't care about your reasons. They raised you. They made you the man you are today, and they deserve the courtesy of an invitation. And if you can't give them that, then you're not the kind of man I want to marry."

"Maybe I'm not," he muttered, as if the admission pained him to say out loud. "Maybe it's time I cashed in my chips and got out of the game, before I lose it all."

She stared into his eyes, confused by his comments. Did he really mean to back out now? After all this, was he going to let a little disagreement about the wedding guest list change his mind? "I—I should go. I said what I wanted to say." She stood and grabbed her purse. "If you want to back out, I'll understand."

"I don't want to back out," he said in a weary tone. He reached out to take her hand, but she pulled away, unwilling to allow his touch to sway her. If she was going to keep control of her life, she'd have to put her foot down and resist his charms. She reached into her purse, pulled out the crumpled list of rules and tossed it on the desk.

"If you don't agree by tomorrow morning, I'm going to call my parents and tell them the truth."

"We'll talk more about this tonight," Ryan said.

Jennifer shook her head. "I'm working tonight. I've got a stakeout."

"A stakeout? Where?" Ryan asked. "How long will you be gone? Who are you staking out?"

She ignored his questions. He'd already barged into her personal life. There was no way she'd let him control her professional life, as well. "I won't be home until late. I'll talk to you tomorrow morning."

"Jen, I—"

"The choice is yours," she said as she walked to the door. She stepped out into the blazing sun. The men watched as she hurried to the car. She started it and roared back out along the gravel road. When she was out of sight of the trailer, Jennifer pulled over and threw the car into Park.

She sat for a long time staring out the window at the featureless landscape. Then a slow smile lifted the corners of her lips. She'd done it. She'd shown Ryan Madison that she could wear the pants in the family with just as much style and determination as he could. And she didn't intend to take this pair off anytime soon.

JENNIFER SLOUCHED down in the driver's seat of her car and stared out the window at the front door of the tavern. Located in a seedy section of Odessa, the bar was surrounded by run-down commercial buildings. But this was the place and she was determined to sit outside until she caught sight of Wade Randall.

He'd been seen three times at the Lucky Eight Tap, according to a friendly bartender, all on Friday nights between nine and midnight. She glanced at her watch. It was already ten past midnight, but she'd give him another half hour before she threw in the towel and headed for home.

Like the Mulholland case, she'd taken the Randall case to heart. The story was a sad one, a seven-year-old boy kidnapped by his noncustodial parent, a mother left to wonder whether her son was happy and healthy, and a father who had lived on the edge of the law his entire life. Randall had worked the offshore platforms in Louisiana where his ex-wife and son had lived. After the kidnapping, a private detective from New Orleans had tracked Randall all over the southern U.S. until he disappeared into Texas's vast oil business. That's where Finders Keepers had stepped in.

She watched another group of men exit the bar, sinking down in her seat even further. A grainy DMV picture of Randall hung from her dashboard, fixed there by a piece of tape. He looked dangerous, a fact confirmed by Lily. And though Jennifer knew she ought to be careful on this case, she hadn't bothered to tell Ralph or Roy that Randall had a criminal record, only that she was headed out on a stakeout at the Lucky Eight.

The door to the bar swung open again and a single figure emerged. He fit the profile, the right height, the right build. Jennifer fumbled for her binoculars, then peered out the window, focusing on the guy's left forearm as he passed beneath a feeble street lamp. "There it is," she said, tossing the binoculars back on the seat and reaching for the ignition. "A big black spiderweb tattoo." Now all she needed was a license plate, a make on the car and an address. If she tailed him home, she'd have enough to turn over to the police.

A sharp knock sounded on the passenger window of Jennifer's car and she jumped and let out a tiny scream. Pressing her palm to her pounding heart, she glanced over to find Ryan staring at her through the glass.

"Open up," he said. "We need to talk."

Frantically, she looked back at Randall, following his path down the sidewalk to a black pickup. "Go away!" she cried. "I'm working."

"Jennifer, let me in."

The pickup's lights flipped on and the truck started to disappear down the street. She turned the ignition, but her car wouldn't start. A curse slipped from her lips when she realized that she'd left the radio on for the past three hours. The battery must be dead. She scrambled out of the car with her binoculars and stared down the street. She managed to catch the first three numbers of his license plate. Murmuring them over and over, she grabbed a pad of paper from the dash and wrote them down, along with a description of the truck. Once that was done, she turned on Ryan.

"What the hell are you doing here?"

"What the hell are *you* doing here?"

"I'm on a stakeout and you almost blew my cover. How did you find me?"

Ryan shrugged. "I called the agency this afternoon and Roy told me where you'd be. And lucky he did! You don't belong in this part of town, Jennifer. Not alone, at midnight, with a car that doesn't start. What would you have done if I hadn't come along?"

"Oh, I don't know. Maybe I would have hitched a

ride,'' she replied, sarcasm dripping from her voice. "Or I could have gone into the Lucky Eight and asked one of the boys for a lift home.''

Ryan circled her car and grabbed her hand. "Come on, we're getting out of here. We'll come back and get your car tomorrow morning—if it's still here.''

"I have a cell phone. I'll call the auto club.''

"All right," Ryan said, yanking her door open. "I'll wait with you.''

"You don't have to do that.''

"But I want to," he said, helping her back in the car. "Besides, it will give us a chance to talk about your list of rules.''

He closed her door, then jogged around the front of her car and hopped in the passenger side. When he'd settled himself, he turned to her. "Well, aren't you going to call the auto club?''

Jennifer shifted nervously. "Well, I would. But I really don't have a cell phone.''

"No cell phone? You came out here without a cell phone?''

Jennifer covered her ears with her hands. "Don't yell at me! And don't tell me what I'm supposed to do. We already had this discussion earlier today. I'm tired of you trying to run my life!''

Ryan crossed his arms over his chest. "All right. I'm not going to say anything. Since you want to run your own life without my interference, then you'll just have to figure a way out of this.'' He reached in his jacket pocket and withdrew her list. "Until then, we might as well spend our time negotiating. Let's begin with my parents. I've decided that you can invite them to the wedding.''

A satisfied grin quirked her lips. "All right. Good. That's a start.''

"And now you have to compromise on something.''

She looked at him suspiciously. "What do you want?"

"Rule number one. No kissing or touching. I'd like to amend that to no kissing. It will be very hard to stop from touching you. We can't possibly pretend to be engaged or married without touching each other."

"All right, no *romantic* touching."

"Compromise," he reminded her. "No kissing, end of rule one. Unless of course you'd be willing to add a thirteenth rule. No stakeouts until after the baby is born."

Jennifer shook her head. "Stakeouts are part of my job!"

"I'm sure Ralph and Roy would be glad to take over for the next four months."

"No," she said. "Stakeouts are nonnegotiable."

"All right, the no touching rule is out, and if you have to do a stakeout, you take me along with you. And we take my car."

"Why your car?"

"Because I have a killer sound system and your car smells like old burritos."

Jennifer couldn't help but giggle. He was right. Her car did smell like old burritos, probably because of the pile of burrito wrappers she'd collected on the floor of the back seat, remnants of fast-food lunches. "All right. Agreed."

He reached in his pocket and withdrew a pen, then made the alterations on her list. "Now, about the full dress around the house, rule number five. There are times when I want to walk around without a shirt, or maybe watch a ballgame in just my boxers. I suggest we change that to nothing less than what might be covered by conservative beachwear."

"I can live with that," she said. "As long as you don't consider a Speedo conservative." She could more than live with that. If there was going to be no kissing, at least she'd get to watch him walk around the house in his boxers every now and then.

He made the changes, then leaned forward, placed the paper on the dashboard and scribbled his signature on the bottom. "There," he murmured, holding the paper out to her. "I guess it's official."

"We're getting married," Jennifer said as she took the paper. She stared at him for a long moment, unable to believe that they were really going to do it.

His gaze dropped to her mouth and lingered there for a long time. "I suppose we could kiss to seal the deal," he murmured.

"Rule number one," she reminded him. "No kissing." But she wanted to kiss him then. In truth, she wanted to throw herself into his arms and lose herself in the taste of him. She wanted to shiver when he grazed her bottom lip with his teeth or when their tongues touched for the first time. And she wanted the kiss to lead to more.

He leaned closer, his mouth so near that she felt the warmth of his breath on her lips. "And we wouldn't want to break the agreement," he murmured. He moved to her cheek, his lips so close that he might as well have been kissing her. "Although, the agreement isn't absolutely final until you sign." She felt his breath on her ear.

This was crazy! He might as well be kissing her. The desire that raged inside her was even more intense than when he *did* kiss her. If this was what she had to look forward to, she'd never survive. Jennifer grabbed the pen from his hand and scribbled her own name on the bottom. But when she shoved the paper at him, he didn't pull away. Instead, she felt his fingers skim along the curve of her neck and brush her hair out of the way. And then, he nuzzled the skin below her ear, with his nose, not his lips.

Jennifer groaned. "This is not following the spirit of the agreement."

"Who the hell cares about the spirit of the agreement?" he said with a low chuckle. "I'm following a literal interpretation."

He drew back, his mouth just millimeters from hers. A tiny sigh slipped from her lips as her gaze darted between teasing hazel eyes and a mouth that could send all common sense from her head. He was waiting for her to make the first move, to lean into him ever so slightly until their lips met.

A war raged inside her brain, her determination at battle with her sensuality. She'd never considered herself a carnal person, but here she was, willing to give up all she'd worked for just for a few moments of the pure, unadulterated pleasure his lips gave her.

She closed her eyes and tipped her face up, waiting, knowing that he wouldn't be able to resist. But he didn't kiss her. She opened her eyes and found him staring at her, a smile quirking his lips.

"You didn't want me to kiss you, did you?" he asked.

Jennifer gasped, embarrassment warming her cheeks so furiously that she was sure he could see her beet-red face. "N-no. Of course not. That would be against the rules."

"Good," he said. "Because I really want to follow the rules. In fact, maybe I'd better go wait in my car to make sure you're not tempted to break them. I'll call the auto club from my car phone. And after they start your car, I'll follow you, just to make sure you get home all right." He chuckled softly, then opened the door and stepped out.

Jennifer waited until he was inside his own car before she screamed in frustration. She kicked her feet and banged her fists on the steering wheel. She cursed a blue streak, first in Spanish and then in English. And when her anger had faded a bit, she leaned back in her car seat and pressed her hand to her chest.

Beneath her fingers, her heart hammered a rapid rhythm.

What had happened to her single-minded quest for control? She'd made up her rules and he'd signed them, but nothing had changed. All Ryan had to do was come close and she suddenly lost every ounce of her resolve.

Even now, a full minute after he'd left her alone, desire still raged inside her. She grabbed the list of rules where it lay on the dashboard, tempted to tear the paper up and forget it even existed. If this was Ryan's idea of no kissing, then she was in big trouble. Especially if he had the same liberal interpretation of the other eleven rules.

CHAPTER SEVEN

RYAN STOOD OUTSIDE the elementary school and watched as the front doors flew open and children ran out. A line of buses waited at the curb, ready to drive the many miles of road between the ranches outside San Antonio. Though chaos seemed to reign, it took only ten minutes to get every child into the buses and on their way. Only teachers were left standing on the sidewalks, various degrees of exhaustion evident in their postures and expressions.

Ben stood near the front entrance of the school, chatting with another teacher. Ryan walked across the drive slowly. He'd stopped by the house before driving out to the school, only to find that Ben had returned to work that week. Unlike his last trip to San Antonio, this time he'd come with a purpose, a purpose that he wanted to discuss with Ben.

He stepped up next to Ben and gave him a slap on the shoulder. "Hey, brother."

Ben turned, then a grin broke across his tanned face. "Hey, Ryan. What are you doing here?"

"I stopped by the house and Carolyn said you'd gone back to work." He drew a deep breath. "Lucy looks good. She was outside riding her bike." The unease that had plagued the first moments of their last meeting had abated some. Ryan wondered if they'd ever get to a point where they could instantly feel comfortable in each other's presence, like real brothers.

Ben nodded. "Doesn't she? The past few days she's just perked up. She seems to be getting her old energy back.

She's also running Carolyn ragged. She should be able to go back to school soon, and then Carolyn can return to work full-time." He paused. "So…"

"So…" Ryan repeated.

"So what brings you to San Antonio? Two visits a week apart. Must be important business."

"Actually, it's not business at all. It's personal. Can I take you out for a beer? After getting a look at all those screaming kids, you could probably use one."

Ryan's joke seemed to break the ice and Ben chuckled. "I could use a beer. Why don't we head over to Boots? It's a Western bar near where Carolyn works. They've got all kinds of beer and great burgers if you're hungry."

"We can take my car," Ryan suggested. "I'll drop you back here on my way to the airport."

"All right," Ben replied with a nod. "Let me run inside and get my things and I'll meet you back out here."

Ryan jogged back to the car, then pulled it around in front of the school just as Ben was coming out. He leaned over and unlocked the door, then waited for his brother to slide inside. When he'd buckled his seat belt, Ryan pulled away from the curb. As he drove out of the school parking lot, he tried once again to put his thoughts in order, as he'd been doing for the entire flight to San Antonio. Back home, the notion of discussing his concerns with Ben had seemed a logical choice, but now that he was here, struggling to make even the most banal conversation, he wondered whether he should have kept his doubts to himself.

"Do you want to tell me why you're here?" Ben asked. "Do you have more questions about our parents?"

Ryan shook his head. "This is something else." His hands clutched the steering wheel. "I wanted to ask you about Carolyn and Lucy."

"They're doing great," Ben said.

"I know. But this is something different. I—I— This is kind of hard to ask."

"We're brothers," Ben assured him. "You shouldn't be afraid to ask me anything."

"I wanted to know if the fact that Lucy isn't Carolyn's daughter ever causes...problems in your relationship. Because it looks like Jennifer and I are really going to get married, but the fact that I'm not her baby's biological father seems to be standing between us. She thinks it makes a difference to me. But the baby is her baby. And I'm in love with her. So it only reasons that I'm in love with her baby, too."

"The father of her baby isn't around?"

"Nah. And I don't think he'll ever be," Ryan said. "Hell, I hope he never comes back into Jen's life."

"Well, then your situation is a little different. Marissa is around, and even though Carolyn and I are married, she's still a factor in Lucy's life."

"Jen is so damned intent on maintaining her independence. She's made this list of rules we have to follow if she's going to agree to a wedding. And one of them is that I have no input into the baby's life. I'm not sure I can agree to that. I mean, how can you keep yourself from loving a child who is part of your life?"

"I think Carolyn fell in love with Lucy the minute they met. Lucy brought us closer."

"That's what this baby has done for Jen and me."

Ben sighed. "I didn't think I'd ever want to get married again. I was ready to raise Lucy alone. And then she got sick and Carolyn came back into my life and it seemed like the most natural thing in the world to make us all a family."

"That's what I want with Jennifer and the baby," Ryan said. Now, if only there was a way to make it happen, a surefire plan to put Jennifer and the baby in his life permanently.

"Just give it time," Ben advised. "She's pregnant. She's probably scared and unsure of what the future holds. And she's in no position to make life decisions right now. In a few months, her life is going to be turned upside down all over again. And if you're there, at her side, you can be the one to help her put it straight. Like Carolyn did for me. That's a powerful thing, something I'll never forget."

"I'm willing to wait as long as it takes," Ryan said. "Sooner or later, Jennifer will realize how much she needs me and, maybe, how much she loves me." Ryan reached over and patted Ben's shoulder. "Thanks for the advice, brother. I appreciate your honesty."

"That's it?" Ben said. He laughed. "Hell, this big brother stuff isn't so tough. I'm pretty good at giving advice."

Ryan returned the smile. "Hey, I thought I was the big brother."

Ben sent him a sideways glance, one that was laced with regret. "I guess we'll never really know. All I'm sure of is that you were the quiet one. That's why they took you."

The revelation hit Ryan like a slap to the face. Was that it? Was that all that had stood between him and having a life with his real family—the fact that he hadn't cried? It took him a long time to digest that little nugget of news. Ben stared at him from the other side of the car. They didn't need to talk. They both shared the same pain, the same frustration.

"There is something else," Ryan ventured, anxious to change the direction of his thoughts. "Another reason why I came to San Antonio. A favor I'd like to ask."

"I owe you a lot more than one favor," Ben said. "Especially after what you did for Lucy. Name it."

"I thought maybe you could introduce me to someone

at Finders Keepers. I want to find the father of Jen's baby and make sure he doesn't come back.''

"You should talk to Carolyn," Ben suggested. "Hell, she and Jennifer found you. She could probably track the guy down in a matter of days."

Ryan shook his head. "I don't want Carolyn to know about this. She and Jennifer have become friends. This needs to be between us."

"Then we're going to the right place," Ben said, pointing to a spot down the road. "Boots is where Dylan Garrett hangs out, and if anyone can help you, Dylan can."

"And he'll be discreet?"

"I can guarantee it."

Ryan turned off the highway into the parking lot of Boots. The bar was built in a converted barn, and as they stepped through the door into the dim interior, Ryan noticed the straw on the floor. The decor focused on ranch and horse themes, and though it was only four in the afternoon, the place was already busy with the happy hour crowd.

"How do you know Garrett will be here?" he asked.

Ben glanced around. "I don't. If he isn't, we'll drive over to the Double G. Finders Keepers has their offices out there. It's still a little early. Let's have a beer first."

They crossed the room to the long antique bar, then pushed aside a pair of stools. A country-and-western ballad blared from a nearby jukebox, adding to the noise, and Ben had to shout to order a couple of beers. When the bartender slid the mugs across the scarred surface of the bar, Ben grabbed his, leaned back against the rail and took a long sip. Ryan did the same, surveying the patrons of the bar with an unknowing eye.

"Bingo," Ben murmured.

"What?"

"Over there," he said, indicating a table in a dim corner. "The guy in the black Stetson reading the newspaper. That's Garrett."

"So what am I supposed to do?" Ryan asked, straightening and taking another sip of his beer. "Should I just go over and introduce myself? He doesn't look like he wants to be disturbed."

Ben shrugged. "This is business. Come on, I'll introduce you."

Ryan followed Ben to the table, still reluctant to disturb Garrett. But from all he knew about private investigators, doing business in a bar wasn't that unusual.

"Hey, Dylan. How's it going?"

Dylan Garrett looked up from his newspaper, a distant expression on his face. For a moment, Ryan wondered whether the guy even recognized Ben. Then his gaze focused and he smiled. "Hey, Ben. How're you doin'? How's Lucy?"

"Good," Ben replied. "Lucy's doing great. Carolyn should be back in the office full-time before too long."

"We miss her," Dylan said. "Things don't run as smoothly without her there from nine to five."

"Dylan, this is my brother, Ryan Madison."

Dylan stood, took off his hat, and held out his hand to Ryan. "Yeah, right. Ryan. I saw the file on your case. Quite a story. It's good to meet you."

"Ryan needs your help," Ben explained. "He's got a missing person he wants found."

Dylan tossed his hat on the table, then pointed to the chair across from his. "Have a seat. And tell me what you know."

"I'll wait at the bar," Ben murmured, clapping Ryan on the back.

Ryan took a chair, then set his beer down in front of him. "No, I want you to stay." Ben obliged and sat down beside Ryan. "I need you to find a guy," Ryan began.

"His name is James Kestwick. All I really know is that his parents live in Odessa, he's an officer in the Navy, he serves on an aircraft carrier. And he likes bluegrass music. And he's engaged to some woman out East."

"There are only so many aircraft carriers," Dylan said. "And I can't imagine there'd be that many James Kestwicks. Why do you want to find this guy?"

"He's the father of my fiancée's baby," Ryan explained. "And I need to talk to him before the wedding."

"Ryan's fiancée is Jennifer Rodriguez," Ben added.

Dylan's eyebrow rose as he recognized the name immediately. "Shouldn't she be the one asking for my help?"

"She doesn't know that I want him found," Ryan explained. "She wants him out of her life and so do I. I just need to be sure he's going to stay out."

"When's the wedding?"

Ryan gave Dylan an apologetic look. "Two and a half weeks. Can you do it? I'll pay whatever it costs."

"I can try," Dylan said.

And with those words, Ryan held out his hand and Dylan shook it. He knew without a doubt that Dylan Garrett was a man he could trust—to get the job done and to be discreet while doing it.

WHEN THEY'D CONCLUDED their business, Ryan Madison wandered back to the bar with his brother, leaving Dylan to his own thoughts. Dylan glanced down at the front page of the newspaper he'd laid on the table, then tore off the corner that contained his notes for Madison's search. He shook his head. Maybe a new case was just what he needed—anything to get his mind off Julie.

He had every confidence he could track down the guy Madison was looking for, the father of Jennifer Rodriguez's baby. Hell, he'd never lacked confidence. So why couldn't he solve the one mystery that plagued his thoughts day and night? Why couldn't he find Julie?

He still couldn't believe she was dead and refused to acknowledge that he might be searching for a body and not the woman he secretly loved, the wife of his best friend. It had been nearly a year since the car-jacking and he still didn't have much more to go on than the evidence the police had gathered from her car—a few bloodstains—and the accounts of a short list of witnesses. With carjacking determined as the suspected cause of her disappearance, Dylan knew all too well the odds that she'd be found alive after such a long time.

Even so, he refused to believe she was dead. He'd known Julie since college, and though she'd married their friend Sebastian Cooper, Dylan had never been able to completely put aside his feelings for her. And now, he felt himself grieving as deeply as Sebastian was. Frustrated with the stalled case, Sebastian had hired Finders Keepers to look for Julie. At the time, Dylan had assured him that he'd do everything in his power to locate her—but in four months, he'd come to realize he was powerless.

With a sigh, Dylan opened his newspaper and squinted to read it in the low light of the bar. He'd made a habit of scanning the personal ads every day, looking through all the major Texas papers, either at the bar, which had a nice collection of newspapers, or at the library. At first, he'd done it because the personals offered a wealth of potential cases among the missing persons ads. But now he did it for a completely different reason.

He'd found the first verse in September, in the *San Antonio Express-News,* among the pleas for car accident witnesses and notices of unknown heirs and runaway tenants. He'd brushed it off as a coincidence, but then, a week later, another verse of Dylan Thomas poetry appeared. By the time he saw the third, Dylan realized just what he was reading.

His skin had prickled along the back of his neck and he had felt his heart stop for an instant. He had wanted to believe the ads were a clue, a plea for help or at least an assurance that Julie was still alive. So he'd gone back and collected them all, then read them over and over again, trying to make sense of the quotations or reason out a pattern to their selection. He'd even gone to the newspaper, but all they could tell him was that the ads were placed by mail and paid for in cash. There was no way to trace the person who had placed them.

Since then, he'd carried the clippings in his file on Julie, taking them out every day to reread them. "'Do not go gentle into that good night,'" he murmured as his gaze skimmed the column for today. "Come on, Julie. If it's really you, give me another clue."

His eyes stopped, as if drawn to a particular spot amid all the other ads. Dylan's breath stalled in his chest as he read the words, so familiar, almost haunting. "Though they go mad they shall be sane, though they sink through the sea they shall rise again; Though lovers be lost love shall not." He reached out and touched the words with his fingers. "God, Julie, it is you."

Dylan flipped back to the beginning of the classifieds and found the phone number, then fumbled in his jacket pocket for his cell phone. He punched in the number, then waited. "I'd like to place an ad in the personal classified column." He gave the operator his credit card number, then carefully repeated the next line of the verse. "'And death shall have no dominion.' Then, on the next line, put 'DG is waiting.'"

He listened as the operator read the ad back, then confirmed that he wanted it placed in the classifieds for an entire week. When he hung up, Dylan let out a long breath, his heart suddenly lighter. This was it—his first real break in the case. He had no doubt in his mind now that the ads had been placed by Julie. She knew he read the personals, and what better way to catch his attention than with a verse from his namesake and their favorite poet?

He turned back to the paper and tore the ad out, but his attention was drawn away by the entrance of a loud-mouthed patron. Dylan glanced up, only to see Sebastian Cooper stroll in and take a spot near the end of the bar. From his lazy stagger, Dylan could tell his friend had already had a few too many beers. His normally impeccable grooming was forgotten, his suit disheveled and his jet-black hair unkempt. Dylan couldn't blame him. His wife had disappeared without a trace and he didn't know if she was dead or alive. Living with all those questions about Julie had to be much harder than anything Dylan was experiencing.

Perhaps he should show Sebastian the poetry, explain his suspicions that the ads were placed by Julie. At least Sebastian might have hope. But telling him might also raise his hopes, only to have them dashed later. Dylan glanced back down at the newspaper. Besides, if the ads were from Julie, they were directed at him and not Sebastian, for Sebastian had never been a fan of poetry. But that didn't make sense. Why would Julie try to reach him and not her husband?

His gaze returned to Sebastian and he studied him for a long moment. The owner and chief bartender of the bar, a rangy old cowboy named Boots, sauntered up to take Sebastian's order. But one good look was enough for the bartender to realize that Dylan's friend didn't need anything more to drink. Unfortunately, Sebastian didn't agree. When the shouting started, Dylan gathered up his notes, tucked the file beneath his arm, and hurried over to the bar.

"Cooper! Hey, buddy!" he called.

Sebastian turned, his angry expression changing the moment he recognized Dylan. "Garrett! Sit down and let's have a beer. Boots, a beer for my best buddy."

Dylan shook his head at the bartender. "Actually, I was just heading out to get something to eat. I'm in the mood for a steak. Why don't you come with me? I could use the company and you could use dinner."

Sebastian glanced around. "Sure," he muttered. "This place is a drag. Can't even get a drink."

Boots sent Dylan a silent "thank you" as Dylan helped his friend toward the front door. When they got to the parking lot, he steered Sebastian to his own truck. "Why don't you ride with me? I'll drop you back here after we eat."

Sebastian didn't protest and Dylan congratulated himself on keeping a drunk off the road. He slammed the door behind Sebastian, then circled the pickup and jumped in.

"You're a good friend," Sebastian said, his attention fixed somewhere outside the passenger window. "It's good to know who your real friends are."

With that, he leaned back in the seat and closed his eyes. Dylan wasn't sure whether Sebastian had passed out or whether he was just asleep. But the silence gave him time to study his friend as he drove toward Sebastian's house.

There was no reason to be suspicious of Sebastian, but there were two things that had bothered Dylan from the start. Two interviews he came back to again and again. First, the testimony of Hector Gonzalez, the security guard at Sebastian's downtown San Antonio office. The guard had noted that Julie went up to Sebastian's office the afternoon of January 5, just hours before she'd disappeared. An hour later, she'd left in a hurry, not even taking time to say goodbye to Gonzalez, as she usually did.

Sebastian claimed he hadn't seen Julie that afternoon.

But if she was in Sebastian's office for an hour, and Sebastian had been in all afternoon, how could they have missed each other? And why would Julie have left without speaking to her husband?

The second interview was with Dr. Joann Klein, an OB-GYN who had come forward to add another piece to the puzzle of Julie's disappearance. She'd revealed that she'd seen Julie that day as well, just a few hours before Gonzalez had. Though she'd maintained doctor-patient privilege in her police interview, she had told Sebastian later that Julie's pregnancy test had come back positive and Julie had learned the results the day she'd disappeared. Dylan knew how much Julie wanted a baby and that she and Sebastian had been trying for months.

Dylan had to assume that her visit to the office was to tell Sebastian the good news. That made the fact that she hadn't spoken to her husband even more confusing. Dylan sighed then rubbed his forehead. Or had she seen Sebastian and had Sebastian lied to the police? And if he had, was he involved with Julie's disappearance?

Dylan cursed softly. Maybe he should be suspicious. Maybe that was why he couldn't figure this case out, because his friendship with Sebastian was clouding his objectivity. His investigative instincts had been finely honed as an undercover detective in Dallas, and Trust No One had been his motto. Trusting Sebastian Cooper might have been a mistake.

Though he wanted to believe Sebastian, another doubt kept creeping back into his mind. A few months ago, he'd attended a charity ball held by the Texas Fund for Children. Sebastian had been there and Dylan could have sworn he'd seen him deep in conversation with Luke Silva, a reputed mobster. At first, Dylan had brushed it off as a trick of the eye. But now, he had to wonder if Sebastian had some underworld connection that he'd been hiding.

"Hey, where are we?"

Dylan glanced over at Sebastian just as they were turning into the driveway of Cooper's home. He pulled the truck to a stop, then hopped out and circled around the passenger side. "Come on, buddy," he said, helping Sebastian out of the truck.

"I thought we were going to get something to eat," Sebastian said dazedly.

"I figured we could find something at your place," Dylan replied.

Sebastian grinned, then nodded. "I've got some twenty-year-old Scotch inside. We can throw a few steaks on the barbecue and have us a party."

He stumbled toward the house, a modern stone-and-stucco home located in a quiet neighborhood on the outskirts of San Antonio. From the outside, the house didn't hint at the wealth and power of its owner. But once Dylan passed through the front door, that changed in very subtle ways. From the expensive appliances in the kitchen to the high-end entertainment center in the family room, Sebastian preferred to have not just the best, but the very best.

Dylan glanced over at his friend. Sebastian stood in the middle of the large family room and slowly turned in a circle. When he faced Dylan again, tears swam in his eyes. He lowered himself to the sofa. "She's gone," he muttered. "I still come home every evening expecting her to be here." He covered his eyes with his hands. "She took everything with her and now I might as well be dead."

Guilt washed over Dylan. His first thought was to chide himself for his suspicions about Sebastian. Any man agonized by such deep grief couldn't have anything to do with the disappearance of his wife. Dylan glanced around the room. Hell, every reminder of Julie had been removed—every photo and memento, all the special little touches she'd added to the house. He wondered if her clothes and other personal items had been packed away, too.

As he watched Sebastian give himself over to emotion, Dylan felt his own control waver. This had been Julie's home, and though there were no outward traces of her in sight, he could still feel her presence, could almost smell the scent of her perfume.

Dylan swallowed back the lump in his throat and forced a smile. He had to get out of here before he broke down, too. "Hey, buddy, I'm going to get going. I'll call you and we'll have dinner another night."

He didn't wait for Sebastian's reply, just turned and hurried out. When he reached his truck, he sat for a long moment, his hands gripped on the wheel so hard that his fingers cramped. The ache filtered into his mind and into his heart, replacing the cloud of emotion.

"I'm not going to stop till I find you, Julie," he murmured.

JENNIFER STARED at her reflection in the tall three-way mirror, turning from side to side and smoothing her hands over her stomach. She sighed softly, then smiled. After trying on countless wedding dresses in every style imaginable, from ballgown to sheath, she'd finally found the one. It was perfect and the simple silhouette, an empire waist and a soft flowing skirt, hid the little bulge of her belly perfectly.

"This is it," she murmured. "This is the one."

Carmen circled her, perusing the style with a critical eye. "But, *hija,* it is so plain."

"I like plain," Jennifer answered, trying to keep the defensive edge from her voice. She'd assumed that choosing a dress would be simple. Just walk in the store, try a few on and buy one. But her mother had turned dress shopping into an exercise in frustration.

"I like the one with all the pearls on the front," Teresa chimed in.

"I like that ballgown with the big poofy skirt," Linda added.

"I'm not wearing pastels," Maria said with a pout. "Pastels are for babies. And I want black. Why can't I have black?"

Jennifer groaned. "Your dress is sapphire blue. Blue is a very grown-up color. And I think blue complements your beautiful skin and dark hair." Maria took some solace in the compliment, flopping down on a chair and continuing her pout.

Jennifer's family had gathered in Midland for the second Thursday in a row. Ryan had offered to buy another round of plane tickets, and Carmen had graciously accepted, anxious to be in on the selection of Jennifer's dress. The girls had come along to find their own outfits, as well.

"We should have gone to Dallas or Houston," Carmen murmured, plucking at the duchess satin skirt. "They have all the designer dresses there. Or at least San Antonio. Gina's Bridal has a much larger selection than this store. Even El Paso has more to choose from."

"Midland is fine, *Mamá*. There's plenty to choose from right here in this shop."

"But this is your wedding, Jennifer. The dress must be special. Perfect. After all, you will only be getting married once."

Jennifer turned around and pasted a smile on her face. If only that were true. But Jennifer wasn't sure what the future would hold for her, whether this sham of a marriage would end in a few months or a few years. Or whether, after it ended, she'd be brave enough to try again. "This dress *is* perfect," she said, determined to put her doubts aside.

Carmen shook her head. "I think you should try some others before you settle."

"No," Jennifer insisted. "This is the one I want. It's simple and comfortable and it hides my...condition. And it makes me feel pretty."

"*Hija,* please." She pulled another more elaborate gown from the rack and held it out. "Try this one—"

"*Mamá,* no! I don't want to argue about this any—"

"Hello, ladies!"

Jennifer, Carmen and the girls all turned to find Ryan standing just outside the dressing room door. He was wearing a suit and it looked as if he'd come directly from the office. Jennifer hadn't expected him to turn up and she winced, knowing there'd be one more voice to side with her mother.

"Hi, Ryan!" Teresa cried, running up and hugging him.

Ryan playfully tugged at her hair, but his gaze was fixed firmly on Jennifer. "Hello, beautiful. You look incredible."

Jennifer wasn't sure who he was talking to, but Teresa assumed it was her, and she twirled in front of him. "I'm going to be a flower girl. And we got a dress for that Lucy girl, too. It's blue just like mine. They're going to send it to the store in San Antonio." She pointed to her head, to the garland of silk flowers and ribbon that she wore. "We even get a hat to wear."

He dragged his eyes from Jennifer and turned to Carmen. "So has everything been settled?" Ryan asked. "The limo is parked outside and you'll have to leave within the next fifteen minutes if you're going to catch your plane back home."

"Nothing is settled," Carmen said, tossing up her hands. "You must talk to her, Ryan. She can be so stubborn."

"What's the problem?" he asked.

Carmen clucked her tongue. "That dress. It is too plain."

Ryan turned back to Jennifer, his gaze lazily drifting down the length of her body and back. A warm flush rose in Jennifer's cheeks and she crossed her arms beneath her breasts and rubbed the goose bumps that rose on her bare arms.

"I think it's perfect," Ryan murmured. "And if it's what Jennifer wants, then that makes it even more perfect."

Jennifer stared at him, unable to believe he was siding with her. "See, *Mamá.* I told you this was the dress."

Carmen sighed dramatically. "It is bad luck for the groom to see the bride in her dress before the wedding. You will have to choose another."

"This is the one, *Mamá,*" Jennifer repeated.

"All right, all right," Carmen said, shaking her head. "It is settled then. Come on, girls, get changed. We have a plane to catch." Carmen herded Jennifer's sisters out of the dressing room and back to their own, leaving Ryan and Jennifer alone.

Jennifer turned to the mirror and fiddled with the square neckline of the dress, adjusting the straps until they lay perfectly on her shoulders. "Thank you," she said, watching his reflection in the mirror.

"For what?"

"For backing me up. I'm glad to see that you're taking the rules seriously."

He slipped his hands around her waist and stood behind her. "I wasn't following the rules," he said. "I really think you look beautiful in that dress. Like a princess."

Jennifer slowly turned in his arms, her gaze nervously flitting over his features. She should have made a rule about saying nice things. Whenever Ryan did, it caught her off guard and she wasn't sure how to reply. "It is bad luck to see the bride in her dress before the wedding."

He rested his hands on her hips and stepped back. "How can looking at a vision in white ever be considered bad luck?"

"It's ivory," Jennifer murmured. "And I wish you wouldn't say things like that."

Ryan reached down and tipped her chin up until she was forced to look at him again. "If you make a rule against speaking the truth, you and I are not going to get along very well."

He bent closer and Jennifer was sure he was about to kiss her. And after their encounter in her car, it was all she could do to stop thinking about kissing him. She knew it was against the rules, but after arguing with her mother all afternoon, she need Ryan's strength, needed his affection. Just one little kiss wouldn't really be a serious infraction, would it? And if the kiss was too much she could—

"You two look lovely together!"

Jennifer jerked back, the warm blush flooding her cheeks with heat again. Carmen stood in the doorway, watching them both.

"Go ahead," she teased. "I did not mean to interrupt."

Her mother didn't move and Jennifer realized that she expected them to kiss! She sent Ryan a frantic glance and a satisfied smile twitched at the corners of his mouth. Now was no time to stick to the rules. If he refused to kiss her, Carmen would suspect they were angry with each other. And then, there'd be all sorts of questions to answer, questions she just didn't have the energy for right now.

"Kiss me," she whispered, soft enough so that her mother couldn't hear.

"Are you sure?" he replied beneath his breath.

"Just do it!" she said through a clenched smile.

Slowly, as if to taunt her, he leaned forward. And then his lips touched hers, and Jennifer's knees instantly went soft. It had been so long, days since they'd shared a kiss, and she'd forgotten how warm and delicious his mouth could be, how the simple touch of his tongue could bring desire rushing through her bloodstream. She clutched at the lapels of his suit as he pulled her body against his, deepening the kiss. And then, as suddenly as it started, he drew away.

"How was that?" he murmured, his breath soft in her ear.

"F-fine."

"Well," Carmen said, drawing Jennifer back to reality. "The girls and I are going to leave. Come here, *hija,* and give your *mamá* a kiss."

Numbly, Jennifer pulled herself from Ryan's arms and walked over to the door. She pressed a quick kiss on Carmen's cheek, then did the same for all three of her sisters. They hurried to the front of the store, and a moment later, they were gone.

Jennifer leaned back against the doorjamb and sighed. "I never thought planning a wedding could be so... stressful. The simplest decision turns into a major battle. What kind of cake to have, what style of dress, how big a bouquet to carry. We should have just eloped."

"We still can," Ryan said.

She shook her head. "No. As long as we're pretending, then we should do it up right."

His smile faded slightly. "Right. As long as we're pretending." He glanced around the dressing room. "So, are you almost done here? If you are, why don't we go out and get some dinner?"

Jennifer hesitated. She really should go back to the office and work. She was expecting a call from one of Wade Randall's ex-girlfriends and her contact at motor vehicles was tracing down the partial plate she'd got that night on her stakeout. She was so close and she was determined to solve the case before her wedding. "I really should go back to the—"

"You have to eat, Jen. Besides, it's nearly five. The workday is over."

"All right," she said, the rumble in her tummy changing her mind. She'd call the office for her messages, and if there were any, she'd go in after dinner. "I am a little hungry."

"I'll just wait outside," Ryan said, "while you change." He grabbed the door and began to pull it closed behind him, then stuck his head back inside. "You do look beautiful," he said with a wink.

Jennifer giggled as the door closed. She walked back to the mirror and stared at her reflection. She did look pretty. And the fact that Ryan thought she did pleased her. "I'll make him a good wife," she murmured, smoothing her hands over her skirt. "Whether we're married for months or years, I'll try to make him happy."

It was the only promise she could really make, for it was the only promise she could keep. And when she walked down the aisle and repeated vows that might be broken, she would keep that promise in her heart.

CHAPTER EIGHT

RYAN PULLED HIS CAR into the driveway of his condo. He smiled, noticing that Jennifer's convertible was parked out front. He turned off the ignition only to hear the sound of *tejano* music drifting on the evening air. He stepped out of the car, looking for the source of the sound. His attention fell on a black pickup truck parked thirty feet behind Jennifer's car. The driver was hidden by the tinted windshield, but Ryan watched as a cigarette butt dropped out the window.

He'd seen that truck before, in front of Jennifer's apartment. The guy with the tattoo. Ryan took a few steps toward the truck, intending to question the driver. But the driver apparently didn't want to talk to Ryan. An instant later, the engine roared to life and the driver threw the truck into Reverse. He backed into a nearby driveway, then roared off down the street.

Ryan stood in the street for a long moment. Was it just a coincidence that he'd seen the same black pickup truck twice? And what was the guy waiting for? Who was he watching? Realization pricked at his mind. "Kestwick," Ryan murmured. Could the man in the pickup be the father of Jennifer's baby? If it was Kestwick, why was he skulking around? Why not just get out and talk to Jennifer?

"Or maybe he has, and she hasn't told me," Ryan muttered. He stalked back to his front door, determined to question Jennifer. But as he inserted his key into the front door of his condo, the sound of music drifted through the thick wood.... *tejano*...very loud *tejano,* coming from inside his apartment. He slowly turned the knob and pushed the door open.

Ryan set his briefcase on the floor and wandered into the kitchen. He was brought up short by the sight of Jennifer, standing barefoot in the middle of a colossal mess, the back of her dress spattered with something red. His questions were quickly forgotten. "Jen?"

She spun around, the tomato sauce in the bowl she was holding sloshing over the edge and falling to the floor with a splat. "You're home!" she cried. "What are you doing home so early?"

"It's half past five. I'm usually home at half past five."

She gasped. "What? It can't be. The clock on the stove says three—" She groaned. "It's said three-thirty ever since I took the bread out. Oh, God, that clock doesn't work! I'm never going to be ready. They'll be here in thirty minutes and I haven't even changed."

"Who'll be here?" Ryan asked, wandering over to the stove.

"You have to help me," she pleaded. "There, in the big pot. Take those noodles out of the water and—I don't know, dry them off."

"Who'll be here, Jen?"

"I should have never tried lasagna. It's just too complicated. Anything with more than three ingredients isn't within my capabilities. A jar of sauce, a pound of hamburger, a package of noodles and a package of cheese. I thought it would be easy. Just put it together and stick it in the oven, but then I burned the hamburger and had to go out and get—"

"Stop!" he said, grabbing her by the arms. "Take a deep breath."

She did as she was told. He pried her fingers off the bowl of sauce and the plastic spoon she held, then set them down on the counter. "I'll finish the lasagna. You go get ready."

"You know how to make lasagna?"

"I think I can muddle through," he said with a grin. "Go ahead."

She pushed up on her toes and gave him a grateful kiss on the cheek, then hurried to the living room and picked up a garment bag she'd tossed across the back of the sofa.

"So, who's coming to dinner?" he called right before he stepped on a half-cooked lasagna noodle that had somehow ended up on the kitchen floor. He picked his foot up and shook it, trying to dislodge the sticky noodle. He then noticed that she'd managed to dirty nearly every surface of his usually pristine kitchen. There was sauce on the walls, cheese in the sink and some unidentifiable brown substance on the ceiling.

"Your parents," she replied.

He set his foot back down. "Who?"

"I called them this morning. I thought it would be the perfect chance to talk to them about the wedding. And the baby."

Ryan stalked out of the kitchen, slipping slightly on the pasta before regaining his footing. When he reached the living room, Jennifer was smoothing the wrinkles out of a pretty flowered dress. "You had no right," he said, his voice quiet and deceptively even.

"Well, you wouldn't call them, so I had to. Someone had to make the first move."

"I don't want to see them," Ryan said. "I agreed you could invite them to the wedding, but that was all."

"You have to forgive them sometime," Jennifer said. "You can't be a complete idiot for the rest of your life."

"You don't know anything about my life," he snapped, anger surging inside him.

Jennifer took a deep breath and let it out slowly. "Yes,

I do. I know a lot about your life, Ryan. And I know all the details of your adoption. And I also know your parents aren't to blame. Dr. Douglas Benton is the one you should blame. He stole you from your mother and father and gave you to the Madisons. He stole at least twenty babies from their real parents and gave them to desperate couples. The only thing you can blame Rhonda and Jeffrey Madison for is wanting a child.''

''And paying for that child,'' he said, pacing the length of the room. ''Don't you think they knew that what they were doing was illegal? Hell, Jen, I was delivered to them in the parking lot of a grocery store in exchange for cash. They never even legally adopted me. They have no claim on my life.''

''And if they had questioned Benton, do you think the good doctor would have returned you to your real parents? He just would have sold you to the next highest bidder. And that couple may not have been as loving as Jeffrey and Rhonda Madison.''

Ryan hadn't thought of it that way. Damn it, why did a woman who didn't have the common sense to cook lasagna manage to make so much sense when it came to his life? He raked his hand through his hair. ''I'm just not ready yet,'' he said. ''I still have some things to sort out.''

''When are you going to be ready?'' she demanded.

''I don't know.''

Jennifer tucked the dress under her arm. ''Well, you better figure it out. Before our wedding. Because whether you like it or not, they have to be there. And if you refuse to speak to them, my mother will get suspicious.''

''That agreement I signed does not give you the license to run my life,'' he warned. ''This is a direct violation of rule number six and rule number eleven.''

''This has nothing to do with finances,'' Jennifer shot back.

"That's rule number nine," he reminded her. "Rule number six is all family obligations must be negotiated and rule number eleven is no arguments about money, the wedding, the baby or family."

"I'm not arguing, you are."

"Rule number twelve. I'm thinking of an appropriate punishment for breaking not one, but two rules."

She stared at him for a long minute. *"Tu eres un hombre cabezudo, malicioso, con corazón de piedra."* She spoke so fast that her words sounded like one long string of syllables, broken only by emphatic hand gestures. She finished with a stomp of her foot before she spun on her heel and headed toward his bedroom.

"And you can add another rule to your list," he shouted after her. "This will not be a bilingual marriage. Either you speak English to me or I refuse to listen."

"You refuse to listen?" She hurried back to him, then stood toe to toe. "Well, here's a translation," she said, punctuating each word with a sharp jab to his chest. "You're a spiteful, pigheaded, coldhearted man. And if your parents were smart, they'd take you to that grocery store parking lot and give you back—" Suddenly, Jennifer's face went pale and she took a step back. She brought her hand to her stomach and held it there, her wide eyes telegraphing trouble.

Concern sharpened Ryan's senses and he reached out to grab her arm. "Are you all right? Jen, is it the baby?" He gently led her to the sofa. "Here, sit. I'll call the doctor. Or should I call an ambulance?"

She shook her head, tears moistening the corners of her eyes. "No, no, wait just a second." She rubbed her hand over her belly and a slow smile broke over her face. "He moved. I mean, not just a little flutter. But I felt it. He kicked me. Right here." She grabbed Ryan's hand and put it on her stomach. "Do you feel that? That's my baby."

Ryan let out a sigh of relief. She was all right—and the
baby was all right. As he rested his hand on her belly and
watched the expression of amazement on her face, Ryan
didn't have the heart to tell her that he'd felt the same last
week when she was lying in his arms. The baby moved
again and Ryan chuckled as he gazed into Jennifer's eyes.
"A future soccer star." He watched a tear trickle down
her cheek and he caught it with his thumb. "Hey, what's
wrong?"

"It's nothing," she said, turning away.

"Tell me," he urged in a quiet voice.

"Every day he gets more and more real. He's got a foot
and he's kicking me. And I'm scared."

He drew her into his arms and gave her a warm hug.
"You don't have to be scared. I'm here." He pulled back
then kissed her forehead. But he couldn't stop there. He
moved to her cheek and kissed away another tear, the salt
taste lingering on his tongue. Ryan wanted to comfort, to
reassure her that there was nothing to worry about. That
he'd protect her and keep both her and the baby safe.

His lips drifted down to hers and he gave her a gentle
kiss, fully intending that that would be the end of it. He
expected admonishment, another reference to the rules. But
the moment their lips met, he felt surrender, instant and
complete.

Her arms snaked around his neck and her sweet body
molded to his. At first, he thought she was deliberately
provoking him, waiting for the perfect moment to dance
away and leave him wanting. He spanned her waist with
his hands, bunching the soft fabric of her dress in his fists.
Her fingers flexed on his chest and then wandered to the
buttons of his shirt.

Slowly, she undid them, one by one, each button raising
his desire another notch. And when she brushed his shirt
out of the way and smoothed her hands over his bare chest,

he lost all semblance of control. This wasn't a game anymore and any rules they had were forgotten. With a low growl, he pulled her beneath him and settled himself alongside her body, the soft cushions of the sofa enveloping them.

Jennifer reached for his tie, but when she couldn't unknot it, Ryan took over, yanking and tugging until he managed to get it over his head. He held it out to her like a prize, and with a smile, she took it and threw it over the back of the sofa. His suit jacket followed, and then his shirt. And when his chest was bare, she traced a line from his collarbone to his belly with her finger.

"We shouldn't be doing this," she murmured, her tone holding a trace of challenge.

"I know, I know," Ryan replied, her touch causing a shiver to prickle his skin. "We should stop right now."

"Yes," she replied, her hand drifting down to his belt. With nimble fingers, she unbuckled it, then pulled it slowly from his pants, another piece to this two-person striptease they were performing. He was sure she'd stop there, but she didn't. Her hands brushed along the front of his pants, the warmth from her fingers seeping through to his growing erection. He groaned, desire welling up inside him.

What had happened to the rules? he wondered. Why had she suddenly decided to toss them aside? He really didn't care to learn the answers to his questions. Instead, he wanted to make her feel the same raging desire that coursed through his body. He was beyond control and Ryan knew that if she didn't stop him, he'd make love to her, right here and now.

He reached out and slowly unbuttoned her dress. This was what it was supposed to be like between them, this sweet yet enticing intimacy, this need that couldn't be ignored. He leaned over her and placed a single kiss on the warm skin between her breasts, right above the clasp of her bra.

She sighed and he took the sound as encouragement, running his tongue along the lacy fabric and across the soft swell of flesh. And then, he fumbled with the clasp and it popped open. Ryan's breath caught in his throat as his gaze took in her breasts, full and ripe, the nipples peaked. "I want you," he murmured, dragging her dress down over her arms and twisting her bra off. When she was naked from the waist up, his lips closed over one pink tip.

"I want you," she said, her neck arched, her fingers furrowed through his hair, drawing him closer.

He rolled on top of her, pulling her legs up on either side of his hips. The hard ridge of his desire burned between them, ached for the release he'd find inside her. But just as he was about to take the next step, an ear-piercing buzz cut through the quickened breathing and soft moans.

They both stiffened and the buzzer sounded again. With a cry, Jennifer wriggled out from beneath him, then tumbled off the edge of the couch. She quickly stood, but as she moved away from the sofa, she stubbed her toe on the coffee table. Silently, she jumped up and down and mouthed a vivid oath.

"Get up!" she muttered through a clenched jaw. "Your parents are here!"

Ryan grinned and rolled to his back, throwing his arm over his eyes. "If we don't answer, they'll go away."

Jennifer grabbed his arm and tried to pull him up. "No, I invited them to dinner. I can't just leave them out there."

"Why are you so determined to impress them?"

"I'm not," she said, finally pulling him to his feet. "I'm doing this for you. Now get up!" She gathered his clothes then hastily tossed them through the kitchen door. "You can get dressed in there. And don't come out until you're decent.''

JENNIFER RAKED her hands through her hair and tried to scrape the smudge of tomato sauce from the front of her dress as she ran to the front door. How had she let herself get so carried away? She was the one who had put the rules on paper and she was the one who was always breaking them. Fumbling with the buttons of her dress, she tried to restore order to her clothes. When she had, she turned to make sure Ryan had escaped to the kitchen.

He was standing in the doorway, arms braced on either side of the door, his chest bare and his pants showing off a flat belly and narrow hips and evidence of his arousal. A tiny thrill coursed through her body and she shivered, her mind still clouded by the passion they'd shared.

"Just get rid of them, won't you?" he asked. He turned and disappeared into the kitchen, the door swinging shut behind him.

Jennifer shot him an irritated glare then pasted a smile on her face and pulled the door open. She wasn't sure what she expected of Ryan's parents or what they expected of her, but they stood in the doorway for a long moment, neither one of them able to come up with even a polite greeting. They were an attractive couple. Rhonda was cool and composed and Jeffrey quiet and distinguished. They stared at each other for a long moment.

"You must be Jennifer," Rhonda Madison finally said.

"Yes! Yes, I am." Jennifer reached out and shook her hand. "Mr. and Mrs. Madison, please come in." She stepped aside as Ryan's parents entered the condo. "Please, sit down. Ryan is just...finishing up a few things in the kitchen."

She hurried over to the sofa and frantically began to fluff the pillows, then noticed her bra draped over one of them. She snatched it up and stuffed it down the front of her dress, then turned and invited them to sit. When Rhonda and Jeffrey were settled on the sofa, she offered them something to drink, then raced back to the kitchen.

Jennifer found Ryan standing at the counter, still half-dressed, patiently assembling the lasagna. "They're out there. Why don't you get yourself dressed and join us for a glass of wine?"

"I'm cooking," he muttered.

"I can't believe how stubborn you are."

Ryan glanced over at her as she unbuttoned the front of her dress. "As much as I'd love to continue our little encounter, don't you think you should attend to your guests?"

Jennifer glared at him, then turned around and slipped back into the bra he'd so recently removed. "I'm not going to argue about this. They're here, they're staying, and sooner or later, you're going to have to speak to them, even if I have to drag them in here to eat." She sent him a withering glare, then hurried back through the door, the wine bottle and three glasses clutched in her arms.

"It's so nice to meet you," Jennifer said. "I've been trying to plan a get-together for a long time, but you know Ryan. He's always so busy. It was impossible to find a date."

"And how did you get him to agree to tonight?" Rhonda asked.

Jennifer handed Rhonda a glass of wine and smiled. "I didn't tell him you were coming."

Ryan's parents looked stunned at first, then grimaced in tandem. "How has he been?" Jeffrey asked. "It seems like ages since we've seen him. Ever since that awful detective came and gave him the news."

Jennifer's smile faded. "Actually, Mr. Madison, I was

that detective. I'm a private investigator. I worked for Ben
Mulholland, Ryan's brother.''

Rhonda gasped. ''And you would upset your fiancé's
life with such news?'' she asked.

''Actually, he wasn't my fiancé then. I didn't really
know him. Ben's daughter had leukemia and he was looking for relatives who might be bone marrow donors.''
Though she'd hoped the explanation would soothe their
shock, Jennifer saw by their expressions that they weren't
pleased with the admission.

''If you didn't know him then, just how long have you
two been engaged?'' Jeffrey asked.

''A couple of weeks,'' she admitted.

''Did you tell them about the baby?'' They all turned
to watch Ryan stroll into the room. He'd managed to put
on his shirt, but he hadn't bothered to button it up. He
grabbed the wine bottle and filled his glass to the rim. Then
he flopped down into an overstuffed chair and took a long
sip of wine.

''Baby?'' Rhonda and Jeffrey said the word at the same
time.

''Mmm-hmm,'' Ryan said, taking another swallow of
wine. ''Jennifer is going to have a baby.''

''But how—'' Rhonda frowned. ''You said you—''

Jennifer watched the wheels turn as Ryan's parents tried
to count the days and the months, wondering how a couple
who met such a short time ago could already be expecting
a baby. ''I know this is all a little much to take in, but
we'd be very pleased if you'd attend the wedding. You
should get an invitation any day now.''

''The wedding is two weeks from tomorrow in El
Paso,'' Ryan said.

Rhonda and Jeffrey's jaws dropped and they glanced at
each other. ''Well, that's nice, dear,'' his mother said. ''So
soon.''

"Isn't it?" Ryan replied with a dry laugh.

Jennifer stared at him for a long moment. "Ryan, darling, would you help me out in the kitchen for a moment? I need to check on dinner." She reached down and grabbed his arm, then yanked him to his feet. When they gained the privacy of the kitchen, Jennifer turned on him. "Are you trying to start an argument? Or are you acting like a jerk for some other reason?"

"Just because you invited them doesn't mean I have to entertain them with sparkling conversation."

"I've only asked you for two things since the moment we met. I asked you to come to San Antonio for Lucy's sake and I asked you to go to El Paso for my parents' sake. And now, I'm asking you for one more thing, but you're too stubborn and selfish to give it to me. While I finish dinner, I want you to go out there and make peace. I don't care how you do it, but I want you to do it."

Ryan drew a deep breath, then let it out slowly, a properly chastened expression replacing his sardonic grin. "I'm sorry. You're right. I've been acting like a jerk."

Jennifer turned him around and shoved him toward the door. "That's the first sensible thing you've said all night. Now, leave me alone in here so I can finish getting dinner ready. And pour them both another glass of wine. Maybe it will loosen them up."

Ryan chuckled. "You don't know Jeffrey and Rhonda. This is as loose as they get." He pushed the swinging door open and left Jennifer alone in the kitchen. In truth, she was glad to step out of the fray for a few minutes. The fact that Ryan's parents blamed her for all their troubles didn't make chipper conversation very easy. And then Ryan had to make his big announcement of her pregnancy. They probably thought she was some gold digger who had trapped their son into marriage.

"Heaven forbid they ever learn the truth," she muttered

as she peered into the oven at the lasagna. "That this marriage is all a sham, an award-winning performance for the benefit of my very conservative parents."

But even she was having trouble convincing herself that everything she felt for Ryan was a fraud. Over the past couple of weeks she'd come to need him, to count on him for his understanding and his strength of will. He'd agreed to marry her, to smooth away the wrinkles from this part of her life. And for that, she'd be forever grateful. But where did gratitude end and true love begin?

After so thoroughly tangling him in the threads of her life, would she ever know for sure? There was definitely passion between them, so strong and overwhelming that neither one of them could control it once it was unleashed. Another shiver skittered down her spine as she remembered the sweet sensation of his mouth on her breast, the feel of his hands on her naked skin.

She leaned back against the refrigerator, suddenly feeling a little warm. Maybe it was the close quarters of the kitchen or the heat from the oven. Or maybe it was just the traces of passion that they'd left unfulfilled. Suddenly, she wanted this awful and uncomfortable dinner to be over. She wanted Jeffrey and Rhonda Madison to go home and she wanted Ryan to pull her back to the sofa and continue where he'd left off earlier.

Jennifer started to work on the salad, tearing the lettuce up and tossing it in a bowl. A few minutes later, Ryan returned to the kitchen, his wineglass in his hand. She glanced over her shoulder. "Would you set the table for me? The lasagna will be ready in another twenty minutes and I'll just finish up the salad and come right out."

"We won't need to set the table."

"We're not going to eat off paper plates in front of the television," Jennifer said. "These are your parents."

"They may be my parents, but they're also gone," Ryan said.

She froze, a handful of lettuce clutched in her fingers. "What?"

"They left."

"What did you say to them?"

"Nothing. That was the problem, Jen. We don't have anything to say to each other. We sat there staring at each other for a few minutes and then my mother started crying, my father cursed and they both walked out. I didn't say a thing, I swear." He paused. "And I don't think they'll be coming to the wedding."

Jennifer stared at him long and hard. Then, very deliberately, she shoved oven mitts onto her hands, yanked the oven door open and reached inside. She pulled out the lasagna and held it in front of him. "What are we going to do with all this food?" she asked, her eyebrow arched.

"I suppose we could freeze it?"

"I have a better idea," Jennifer said. She tipped the pan forward until the lasagna slid out and landed on his shoes. Steam drifted up from the floor and the kitchen filled with the scent of garlic and tomatoes. "I'm going home."

She stepped around him, past the mess on the kitchen floor, past the sofa where they'd nearly made love. Grabbing her purse from the table near the door, she walked outside. Her mother had always said that marriage was hard work, filled with ups and downs. Well, Jennifer had never liked roller coasters and arguing with Ryan was more exhausting than an entire day at the office. And they weren't even married yet.

"If this is what marriage is supposed to be like," she murmured, "I'm not sure I can survive the engagement."

JENNIFER LAY on the exam table at her obstetrician's office, her hand resting on her stomach. She'd been walking around all morning, waiting for the baby to move and delighting in it each time it did. She tried to imagine the tiny little person growing inside her, with his little arms and legs, his perfectly formed fingers and toes. For the first time, she wondered whether the baby would be a boy or girl, whether she would have dark eyes or tiny feet or he would have a dimple in his cheek or expressive hands. The baby was no longer just "it."

But her thoughts weren't always so optimistic. She still fought the fears and insecurities that came with being a first-time mother. Even now, she wished that Ryan was here, holding her hand and making her smile. She really shouldn't have stormed out like that, but sometimes Ryan could be so stubborn.

She sighed. All last night, she'd examined her own motives in their little family drama. In all honesty, she felt responsible for the rift between Ryan and his parents. If she hadn't come to Ryan and told him who he really was, he'd be happy now. His life would have continued on the same course and he'd still love his parents, never knowing the truth. But she'd changed the course of his life—in more ways than one. And she just wanted to put a small portion of it back the way it was.

"So, how are we today?"

Jennifer glanced over her shoulder as Dr. Kinsey slipped through the door. "We're fine," she said, her hand still on her stomach. "Better than fine. I felt the baby move last night. Not just a little movement, but it felt like he kicked me and then he flipped over inside of me."

Dr. Kinsey smiled. "There'll be a lot more of that. And you'll notice your baby will be more active at certain times of the day. He's still got some room in there and he's having some fun before it gets a little cramped."

Another knock sounded on the door and the nurse peeked in. "Jennifer? Your husband is here."

She pushed up, bracing herself on her elbows. "My husband? I'm not married."

"Then the father?" the nurse asked, stepping aside.

Ryan appeared from behind the door and gave her a wave. "Hi," he murmured. "Is it all right if I come in?"

Jennifer didn't know what to say. He was the last person she expected to see today and the only one she wanted to see at this very moment. "How did you know I was here?"

"I saw it in your date book the other day. If you don't want me to be here, I can wait outside."

She shook her head, then motioned him inside. Dr. Kinsey grabbed a chair and pulled it toward the exam table. Ryan sat down, a gift box clutched in his hand. He reached out to take her fingers in his. "I'm sorry about last night," he murmured, drawing her hand up to his lips and pressing a kiss on her wrist.

"I am, too," Jennifer replied.

"So, would you like to do an ultrasound today?"

Jennifer shook her head. "Only if you think it's necessary. My insurance has a really high deductible and I can't afford to—"

"Do it," Ryan said. "That is, if Jennifer wants it. I'll pay for it. There's no need to worry about money. Whatever she needs, she should have."

Dr. Kinsey turned to Jennifer. "Would you like to get another look at your baby?"

Jennifer gave Ryan's hand a squeeze in silent gratitude. How had she found such a sweet and caring man? Why couldn't she have met Ryan at that concert last May instead of— She pushed every thought of the man from her mind. Ryan was more a father to this baby than he'd ever be. "Yes," she finally said. "Do the ultrasound."

Dr. Kinsey pulled up Jennifer's gown and squeezed the gel onto her belly. She pointed to the monitor and Jennifer watched as a fuzzy image appeared. At first, it didn't look like anything, but gradually the doctor pointed out the baby's features. "Your baby is at twenty-three weeks. He weighs about a pound and is about eight inches long."

"Is everything all right?" Ryan asked. "I mean, are all the parts there?"

Dr. Kinsey chuckled. "All the parts are there—or not."

"Not?" Ryan said.

"Would you like to know the sex of the baby? We can sometimes see on the ultrasound if the baby is in the right position."

Jennifer looked at Ryan. "Should we?" It really was her decision, but suddenly she felt as if Ryan were in this with her. If he wanted to know, then so did she.

"I'd like to be surprised," he said to Jennifer. "I—I mean, if I were you, I'd want to be surprised."

Jennifer turned to the doctor and shook her head. "No, I think we'll wait."

"There aren't two or three in there, are there?" Ryan asked.

Dr. Kinsey handed Jennifer a paper towel. "Nope. Just one very healthy baby." She grabbed a tape measure and measured Jennifer's stomach. "You're still small," she said. "But I have a feeling within the next few weeks that's going to change. Now, I think you should sign up for childbirth classes. The baby is due in mid-February, but after the first of the year, the classes are always full because they're not held during the holidays." She handed Ryan a brochure. "Jennifer will need a coach. You seem to have a calming effect on her."

She turned back to Jennifer and handed her the photo that had emerged from the ultrasound machine, then checked Jennifer's chart. "Everything looks fine. The nurse drew blood and I'll call you if we find anything out of the ordinary. You can get dressed now and I'll see you in four weeks. And don't be afraid to call if you've got questions, no matter how silly they seem.''

Jennifer nodded, then lay back on the table as the doctor left. She held up the ultrasound photo and looked at it. ''I think the baby looks like me,'' she said, showing the photo to Ryan.

''Then she'll be the most beautiful baby in the world,'' he said. He stood, then pressed a kiss on her forehead. ''So, do you want a girl?''

''I know it sounds cliché, but I don't care,'' Jennifer replied. ''Just as long as it's healthy.''

Ryan reached around his chair and picked up the present he'd set on the floor. ''I brought this for you. I guess you could say it's an apology gift.''

''You didn't need to do that. I was as much at fault as you were. I shouldn't have invited your parents without asking you.''

''And I called them today and apologized. They invited us to dinner sometime next week, although I'm not sure I'm really ready for that. I said I'd talk to you. Rule number six.''

''I'd love to go,'' she said. ''Whenever you're ready.''

''Open your gift.''

Jennifer sat up and laid the box on her lap. She tugged at the ribbon and Ryan impatiently helped her pull it off, then took the box and removed the lid. ''It's a baby book,'' he said. ''See, there's a place for ultrasound pictures. And pages for you to write down your feelings during the pregnancy. And here's a spot to list all the names you're considering.''

''This is wonderful,'' Jennifer said. ''We can work on it together.'' She paused and sent him a sideways glance. ''I—I mean, if you want to.''

''I do,'' Ryan said, covering her hand with his. ''Now, why don't you get dressed and we'll get out of here. I think it's about time we started looking for some things for the baby.''

"You don't think we'll be jinxing things, do you?" Jennifer asked.

He pointed to the picture. "That baby is getting bigger every day. I think he's going to want a bed to sleep in and some clothes to wear when he gets here. And if you're worried, we'll just go out and browse.''

"That sounds like fun.''

Ryan gave her another quick kiss on the forehead, then slipped out of the room, but Jennifer didn't get up to dress right away. Instead, she lay back down and placed her hands over her belly. She waited for the baby to move again and then she smiled. "We're going to be all right,'' she said. "Everything is going to be just fine.''

CHAPTER NINE

"WHERE ARE we going?" Jennifer shouted, the wind whipping at her hair and bringing high color to her cheeks.

Ryan glanced over at her from behind the wheel of his company pick-up truck, struck by how beautiful she looked today. His gaze dropped to the gentle swell of her belly. Her figure grew rounder and more lush every day, a process he loved to watch. "We're almost there," he said. "Be patient."

It was a beautiful fall day in West Texas, the sky a brilliant blue and filled with fluffy white clouds, the kind of day Ryan wanted to spend outdoors with Jennifer rather than caught up in geology surveys at the drilling site. The heat that usually hung around well past summer was starting to abate, and the early mornings and late evenings had a fresh crispness to them that hinted at the approaching winter.

He'd surprised Jennifer during her lunch hour, spiriting her away from her desk with promises of a tasty lunch in a special spot. Though she had eaten a huge breakfast that morning at his apartment, lately Ryan noticed she was ravenous twenty-four hours a day. But he wouldn't tell her where they'd be dining, only that she'd have to wait for that piece of the puzzle.

Over the past few days, their life had settled into a regular routine. They had dinner together every night, reviewing their wedding plans during the meal. On some nights, they went to classes with the priest, and on others, they simply sat on the sofa and studied their baby books. And afterward, she'd curl up on his bed or he'd stretch out on her sofa and spend the night. Jennifer seemed to need him there while she slept. His presence on the sofa was reassuring to her, and Ryan wasn't about to argue.

Since that day in the doctor's office, they'd pushed aside the conflicts between them and grown even closer. On his birthday, she'd cooked him *pozole,* then presented him with a pile of presents, turning a day he'd anticipated with dread into a real celebration. This time together had given Ryan a taste of what a real marriage to Jennifer might be like. He'd come home from a busy day at work and she'd be waiting, her smile chasing away all his stress, her voice like music after a day at a noisy drilling site.

There was no doubt in his mind that he was completely in love with Jennifer Rodriguez. He didn't even make an effort to hide it anymore. In just three short weeks, he'd been bewitched by her, convinced that this was the woman he was meant to love forever.

Unfortunately, he still wasn't sure how Jennifer felt. At times, he'd look into her dark eyes and he'd see genuine affection. Other times, he'd find smoldering desire. But there was always a tiny part of her that she held back, a part that he couldn't touch. Ryan suspected she still harbored some deep doubts about their marriage and their future together, and some fears about the upcoming birth. But he was determined to erase those doubts and fears, to break down the invisible wall she'd built between them, and introduce her to the possibilities of the life they might share.

That's what this lunch was all about—making Jennifer consider the possibilities. Ryan pulled off the highway and followed a winding road into a beautiful subdivision on the outskirts of Midland. The streets were lined with stately homes, most with brick or stone facades and wide front lawns. Exquisite landscaping made the new homes appear as if they'd been built years ago.

He'd found the house ten days ago, and the moment he'd walked in the front door, he knew it was perfect for the three of them. He hadn't thought twice about buying it, and since it was already empty, the real estate agent and his bankers did their best to accommodate an immediate closing.

"I didn't realize there was a restaurant in this neighborhood," Jennifer commented.

"We're not going to a restaurant," Ryan said. He made another turn, into a lovely cul-de-sac, then pulled in the driveway of a two-story brick colonial. He looked at her, hoping to gauge her reaction. "This is where we're having lunch."

"Who lives here?" she asked with mild curiosity.

"Some people I know very well." Ryan chuckled. "They're expecting us." He jumped out of the truck and circled around the front to get her door. He helped her out, his gaze dropping to her belly. He imagined the day he'd bring them both home from the hospital, a slender Jennifer and a new baby wrapped in a blanket. The real estate agent had left the house unlocked and he'd had the catered picnic lunch delivered earlier.

"This is a beautiful house," Jennifer said as she rang the doorbell. "Are these friends of yours or business associates? Did we invite them to the wedding?" Ryan started to push open the front door, but she reached out to stop him. "We can't just walk in."

"I'm sure the owners won't mind." He followed her as she wandered into the foyer. The empty living room was to her right and the barren dining room to her left. And in the center of the foyer, a beautiful staircase wound up to the second floor.

She frowned. "What is this? It looks like the owners have moved out."

"Or haven't moved in yet," Ryan said, standing behind her. He wrapped his arms around her waist and rested his chin on her shoulder. "This house is ours, Jennifer. I bought it."

Jennifer gasped and spun around. "Ours?"

Unable to contain his excitement any longer, Ryan grabbed her hand and pulled her through the dining room to the huge kitchen at the back of the house. "Isn't this great? It's twice the size of both our kitchens put together. And these French doors overlook the backyard. There's plenty of room for the baby to play. Hey, we could even get a dog."

"Ryan, I—"

"Don't say anything yet," Ryan replied, pressing his fingers to her lips. "Let me show you the second floor." He drew her along to the stairs. "There are four bedrooms and two baths up here, and there's a powder room on the first floor. And there's a laundry room on the second floor, too." He pulled her toward the bedroom at the end of the hall. "But this is what I want you to see." He pushed the door open, then stepped aside. "This is the nursery. I remembered what you said about Lily and Cole Bishop, about how they were decorating a nursery for their baby. I thought we should have a nursery, too."

He'd closed the deal on the house on Monday and the painter and paper hanger had arrived the next day. The baby store had delivered and set up everything else early that morning. The nursery was now completely furnished with the things that Jennifer had loved during their shopping trip last week—the white crib with the little animal sheets and the mobile with the circus theme. The huge stuffed bear and the music box that played a lullaby. He'd bought it all for her—and for the baby.

"What do you think?" he asked. "I know you probably wanted to take care of all of this yourself and you can change it if you want. I just needed you to see the possibilities." He strode over to the window. "This room gets plenty of sun and it overlooks the backyard." He pointed to a rocking chair. "And the lady at the store said this is the best way to get the baby to—"

"Stop," Jennifer said, holding up her hand. "You don't have to convince me. This is beautiful. It's exactly what I would have picked."

Ryan frowned. "Then why don't you look happy?" he asked, reaching out to touch her shoulder. "Was I too presumptuous? When I found this house, I thought it would be—"

"I know," she said, her voice wavering slightly. "Perfect. And it is." She pulled away and slowly wandered over to the window, then stood absolutely still for a long time.

"You don't like it."

"I said it was perfect," she replied, an impatient edge to her voice. "Or it would be if we were the perfect couple waiting for our perfect baby. But we're not." She paused, then turned to face him. "I—I think we should go."

"What about lunch?" he asked.

"I'm really not hungry," she murmured, taking a last look around the room.

Ryan cursed beneath his breath. "Damn it, Jen, I'm not going to let you do this again—retreat into your own little world where you can shut me out. Tell me what you're feeling. I can't make you feel better if you don't talk to me."

"Since when has it been your responsibility to make me feel better?" she asked, her posture stiffening as if she were readying herself for an argument.

"That's not an answer. And you know I care for you. It's only natural I'd want you to be happy."

She glanced around the room. "So that's why you bought the house? So I'd be happy?"

"Yes," Ryan said. "I wanted us to have a nice place to live. A place that wasn't just yours or mine. A place that was ours and the baby's."

"And what if it doesn't work out?" she demanded. "What if we get divorced in a few months?"

Her words tore at his heart but Ryan refused to believe that their marriage wouldn't work. It had to work. He loved her too much to let her go. "Jen, it's just a house. I can always sell it."

"No, it's an investment."

He sighed in exasperation. "Maybe it is. But what's wrong with that?"

"It's too much...pressure. Too many expectations."

Ryan shook his head. "Pressure," he repeated. "We're getting married next weekend. And this *house* is too much pressure?"

"The marriage is just for now. This house is for the future. That's very different."

"Why? Is it so bad for me to think about a future with you? Hell, Jen, what if it *does* work out? Why always focus on the negative? Why not believe that we might make a go of this, that we might just get lucky and live happily ever after?"

"Because the chances of us having a future together are slim to none. There are couples who go into marriage madly in love and committed to a life together and they end up divorced. Ryan, we have an arrangement between us, a list of rules, not love. You've been searching for some kind of family since you learned the truth about your parents. And I'm pregnant with another man's child and afraid to face that alone. That's three strikes against us."

"That doesn't mean the game is over," he countered. "Can you open your mind to the possibilities?"

"Right now, all I can think about is getting through this wedding and then getting through this pregnancy. After the baby is born, my entire life will change. I can't make any promises. Not right now."

He crossed the room in three short strides, then grabbed her hands. "Just think about the house. You and the baby could be happy here. We all could."

Jennifer closed her eyes and sighed, then nodded. "All right. I'll think about it. Now can we go?"

"I think we should have lunch," he said. "Knowing how your appetite has been lately, I'd be willing to bet you're starving."

She shook her head. "No. I just really need to get back to the office. I've got a lot of work to do."

Ryan placed his hands on her shoulders and stared down into her eyes. "I'm glad that we talked," he said. "No matter how long we live together, we have to be honest with each other."

"I know," Jennifer murmured. She walked out of the nursery, then hurried down the stairs and out the front door. Ryan stopped in the foyer and looked around the empty rooms, wondering how all his good intentions had turned out so bad, wondering if they'd ever live in this house or if it would become a monument to his dashed hopes.

Maybe he'd misjudged the depth of her feelings for him. Maybe he'd misread the emotion he'd seen in her eyes. And maybe, to Jennifer, this was just all a convenient arrangement. Ryan shook his head. He couldn't allow himself to believe that.

If he did, he'd have lost before he really even started.

JENNIFER SAT at her desk at work, staring silently across the room, her thoughts occupied not with the Randall file spread in front of her, but with the events of her lunch hour. She'd been prepared for a surprise but not a surprise as big as a four-bedroom, three-bath house on one point five acres! How was she supposed to respond?

This had all gotten completely out of control. The longer they continued on this path, the harder and harder it would be to extricate herself. What would come next? Would they start taking family vacations together? Would he begin putting money in a college fund for the baby?

It was supposed to be a simple arrangement with an easy out clause. That had been the plan. But things had changed. Over the past three weeks, she'd felt her relationship with Ryan evolving into something more than just a platonic understanding or a list of rules scribbled on a piece of paper. They'd shared wonderfully close moments, moments of passion and moments of joy and moments of absolute contentment.

But a relationship that was once so simple and uncomplicated was now nearly impossible to define. She cared about Ryan more than she'd ever cared about any other man in her life. In truth, she'd fallen in love with Ryan Madison.

Jennifer groaned softly, then buried her face in her hands. How could she have let this happen? She knew from the start that Ryan had agreed to their arrangement for his own reasons. His family had suddenly been taken from him, the parents he'd loved his whole life exposed as strangers. He was so obviously searching for something, anything to give his personal life meaning. And she just happened to come along at the right time—or maybe, more accurately, the wrong time.

Playing the white knight to her damsel in distress gave him a purpose, a noble cause that could balance out the anger he felt for his parents. She should have known this would happen. What single man in his right mind would have so quickly agreed to pose as her fiancé? Or offer a marriage proposal after just a few days together?

If only they'd had an ordinary relationship, then maybe she might be able to gauge his true feelings for her. But their first meeting wasn't exactly storybook and their second meeting was even more unconventional. They'd had a nonexistent courtship and had gotten to know each other under very unusual circumstances. Nothing about their time together was ordinary.

She laid her head down on her desk and closed her eyes, trying to put order to the chaos she'd created. When she'd come to him with her plan to take a fake fiancé home, she'd had it all mapped out. But then Teresa had dropped the bomb about her pregnancy...and Ryan had sided with her parents about the wedding...and everything started snowballing until she couldn't stop it. And to make matters worse, he'd turned out to be a man she could truly love, a sweet and honorable and passionate man, the kind of man she'd only dreamed about.

She sat up, brushing the hair out of her eyes and turning her attention back to the Randall folder. She'd talked to co-workers, bartenders, ex-girlfriends, but Wade Randall always seemed to be one step ahead of her. Her one and only chance to find out where he lived had been lost that night in front of the Lucky Eight. The DMV check had yielded nothing and the ex-girlfriend she'd found hadn't had much to say. If only her car hadn't stalled or Ryan hadn't appeared—

The door of the agency opened and Jennifer quickly composed herself, pasting a friendly smile on her face. But when she looked up, her breath froze in her chest. The visitor slowly sauntered across the small reception area and placed his hands on her desk. He was huge, well over six feet, with bulging biceps and a neck that disappeared into massive shoulders. Her gaze fell on the macabre spiderweb on his left arm.

"I hear you're looking for me," Randall murmured, his voice low and menacing.

Jennifer stared up into eyes hard as ice and an expression that couldn't hide a vicious demeanor. Her heart slammed in her chest and her brain spun with fear. "Can—can I help you?"

He laughed. "Don't play dumb, lady. One of my buddies at the Lucky Eight told me you were looking for me. I wanna know why."

"I—our agency—was hired by—by an attorney." She swallowed, schooling her voice to hide her fear. She had to come up with a cover story—and quick. If Wade Randall knew what she was really after, she'd have every reason to fear for her life. "From what I understand," she began, "and—and I'm not actually the primary detective on this case...." She cleared her throat. "From what I understand, a distant relative of yours has died and left you a substantial sum in his will." Roy and Ralph had used the ploy hundreds of times before. People who took great pains to hide themselves could be incredibly stupid—and greedy—when it came to the possibility of a huge windfall.

"What relative?" he demanded. "None of my relatives has any money."

"I'm not sure who it is," Jennifer said. "You see, it—it's not my case. But Roy Morales will be back later this afternoon. If you'd like to leave your phone number, I could have him call you."

Wade Randall slowly shook his head as he straightened. His arm flexed and the spiderweb undulated, bringing a sick feeling to Jennifer's stomach. "I think I'll just wait, if that's all right by you." He slowly sat down in one of the guest chairs then twisted to reach for something in his back pocket. Jennifer's eyes widened when she saw he had a knife. With a flick of his finger, a blade sprung from the end of the handle, the sound echoing in the silence of the office. Randall leaned back and began to clean his finger-nails, but the threat was unmistakable.

"I—I'm not sure exactly when he'll be back. Per-haps—"

Randall stood up again and pointed the knife at her. "Why don't you tell me the truth," he said as he slowly stepped toward her. "Because I don't really believe the story you're tryin' to sell me." He brought his fist down and the blade of the knife stuck in the laminated top of her desk. "Did my ex hire you? Are you lookin' for the kid?"

"Kid?" Through the pounding in her head, she heard the doorknob rattle. Jennifer said a silent prayer, hoping that Roy or Ralph had returned early. Perhaps they'd sub-due Wade Randall with a quick punch to the nose.

But Randall heard the door, too. He deftly pulled the knife from the desk and hid it against his forearm. "Watch what you say," he muttered. "We haven't finished here. Not yet."

He slowly turned as the door opened. But it wasn't Roy or Ralph who entered. Instead, Jennifer watched as Ryan walked in the door. A myriad of emotions tumbled through her mind. Relief washed over her, mixed with a fair amount of worry.

Ryan already fancied himself her white knight, but the last thing she wanted was for him to save her now. She needed to get him out of the office before Wade Randall decided to turn his anger in a different direction. Randall took his place in the guest chair, watching as Ryan entered, his gaze narrow, his beefy body coiled like a tightly wound spring.

"Ryan!" Jennifer cried with false enthusiasm. "What are you doing here?" Her words sounded forced and Ryan noticed right away. She jumped up from behind her desk and gave him a hug.

He glanced over at Randall, then turned back to Jennifer, frowning. "I probably should have called," he said. "Are you busy? I wanted to talk. I thought we could go out and get an early supper, then maybe discuss the house."

Randall gave Jennifer a warning look. "Actually, I am busy. I've got to meet with a client. We'll have to talk when I get home." She glanced around Ryan's shoulder. "I'll be right with you, sir."

Ryan glanced over his shoulder at Randall, then reached down and gave Jennifer's hands a squeeze. "All right," he said in an even tone. "We'll talk later." He pulled her toward the door, then stepped between her and Randall. Drawing her close, he kissed her, then pressed his lips to her ear. "Are you in trouble?" he murmured, so softly that only she could hear. "If you are, kiss me again."

Jennifer glanced up into his eyes, then brushed a quick kiss across his lips. Her answer was clear. "I'll see you at home, darling," she said.

"Wait," Ryan said. "Before I leave, I'd better call the drilling site. I've got to talk to the foreman about a new survey I picked up. Can I use a phone?"

Jennifer nodded. "You can use the phone in Ralph's office," she said. "Just press nine for an outside line."

Ryan nodded, then gave her elbow a squeeze. He turned and walked toward the office. "Sorry," he said to Randall. "I'll be out of here in a few minutes. Just have to make a quick call."

Jennifer watched him disappear behind the door, then sat back down at her desk. "He'll be gone in a few minutes," she said.

"He better be," Randall muttered. "Because you and me have a lot to talk about. Like how you're going to tell my ex that you never found me. I think that would be the healthy choice—'' his gaze dropped to her belly and the knife glinted in his hand ''—considering your delicate condition.''

The sound of Ryan's voice from inside Ralph's office echoed through the door. What started out as a soft murmur, slowly grew louder and louder. ''I told you to wait until those surveys came in,'' Ryan said. ''I specifically told Carlos to pick up the surveys this morning. Now who the hell dropped the ball? No, don't give me excuses. Get Carlos. I want him on the phone now!''

Jennifer held her breath. He knew she was in trouble! Why was he arguing with his drilling foreman? But as the argument went on and on, she realized that he was buying time. Randall squirmed impatiently, but he was loath to make a move as long as Ryan was in the other office. He tucked the knife beneath his arm.

And then, after what seemed like hours—but was actually only five minutes or so—the door of the main office burst open. Jennifer screamed as three policemen rushed inside, guns drawn. At the same moment, Ryan stepped out of the office and grabbed Jennifer, then pushed her behind his back. Jennifer peered over Ryan's shoulder and watched as the police quickly subdued Randall, cuffed him and bagged the knife as evidence.

When it was finally over, Ryan turned to her and pulled her into his arms, hugging her fiercely. Then he gazed down into her eyes, smoothing his hand over her cheek. ''Are you all right? God, Jen, when I saw that guy in your office, I wasn't sure what to do.''

Jennifer nodded. ''How did you know?''

''I've seen him twice. Once he was watching your apartment, and the other day, he was in front of mine. I figured he was trouble. Who is he?''

''That was Wade Randall, the guy I was looking for.

He kidnapped his son.'' Jennifer glanced around the office, then grabbed the file from her desk. "I have to talk to the police. I have to tell them what I know. They still have to find the boy."

"Jen, there'll be plenty of—"

"Miss Rodriguez?"

Jennifer turned to find two of the officers standing at the door. She pulled out of Ryan's grasp and hurried toward them. "His name is Wade Randall. He has outstanding arrest warrants for assault and battery in two states. And he kidnapped his son. He came here and threatened me with a knife."

"A knife?" Ryan asked with a gasp. "Damn it, Jen, why didn't you—"

"We'd like you to come down to the station," the officer interrupted.

"I'll drive her," Ryan offered, stepping to her side.

"Actually, Officer Lopez can interview you here," the policeman said to Ryan. "After you're finished, you can pick Miss Rodriguez up at the station. Our interview with her will take at least a couple of hours."

Jennifer sent Ryan a weak smile as she followed Officer Wilson out. She could see the anger in Ryan's eyes and she was almost grateful to be leaving. "Roy is supposed to be back any minute. Tell him what happened and tell him to call Lily at Finders Keepers. She'll call the mother." She drew a ragged breath. "I'll be fine."

When she reached the squad car on the street, she leaned back against the hood and sighed softly. The file folder slipped from her fingers and landed on the street, and she bent to pick it up. Suddenly, a sharp pain stabbed at her stomach. Jennifer moaned softly and pressed her hand to her belly. But the pain didn't pass. It was as though the baby were tugging at her from inside. She braced her hand against the car and tried to breathe deeply and evenly. It would pass. She'd just moved a little too quickly.

"Just a little twinge," she murmured, her words meant to reassure herself.

But overwhelming her own words were Dr. Kinsey's admonishment. *If you have any questions...* And then her mind reeled back to the baby book she'd been reading a few nights ago. *Any unusual cramping or pain... Avoid stress...* Suddenly, all the warning bells sounded and a flood of information came rushing into her brain, all the awful possibilities that the baby books warned against but claimed were rare.

"Miss Rodriguez?"

"I—I think we better go to the hospital," she said, her hands pressed to her abdomen. "Something's wrong."

The officer quickly snatched up the file folder, then grabbed her arm and helped her into the back seat of the patrol car. "The hospital is only a few minutes away," he reassured her. "Don't worry, miss. I'll get you there safe and sound."

Jennifer forced a smile then closed her eyes. When she opened them, they were at the entrance to the emergency room of Odessa General. Officer Wilson raced around to her side of the car and helped her out, all the while shouting for a wheelchair. When she got inside, a nurse came to her aid, settling her in a wheelchair and quickly getting her doctor's name.

Officer Wilson insisted on staying with her, but Jennifer reached out and patted his hand. "I'm fine," she said, her fear causing tears to swim in her eyes.

"Is there anyone I can call? Where can I find your husband? I'll go pick him up. With lights and siren, I could have him here right away."

"No," Jennifer murmured, fighting the impulse to call

Ryan. "There's no one to call. It's not serious. I'll be fine."

Officer Wilson nodded and the nurse wheeled her into an exam room, helped her into a gown and got her up on the table. So much for her determination to regain her independence, Jennifer mused. The last person she wanted here was Ryan. First, he'd scold her, and then he'd make her feel guilty, and after that, he'd remind her that she had a baby to think about. She didn't want to hear it from him for she was already angry at herself. How could she have put herself—and her baby—at such risk? She knew Randall was dangerous and yet she continued to pursue the case on her own.

Jennifer covered her eyes with her hand, the warm tears spilling over and trickling down her cheeks. Though she didn't want to see Ryan now, she couldn't help but want him near. She wanted him holding her hand and smoothing her hair and murmuring calm and reassuring words in her ear. If he was here, he'd know what to do. He'd know if the baby was going to be all right.

Jennifer watched as the nurse hurried back into the room, pushing some kind of machine. She strapped a monitor on her belly, and a few moments later, the machine began to beep. The nurse smiled. "That's your baby's heartbeat," she said.

"It sounds so fast," Jennifer said.

"It's perfect. Now, I want you to relax. Your blood pressure is a little high. I've called Dr. Kinsey and she's on her way. Are you having any more pain?"

Jennifer shook her head. "Not since I left the office. I—there was a lot of—excitement. And I moved too quickly."

The nurse nodded. "Sometimes you'll just get muscle spasms. The baby is stretching out your abdominal muscles and they react. But Dr. Kinsey will examine you when she gets here." The nurse handed her a call button. "I'm

going to go get your paperwork started. I'll be right outside
the door. If you need anything or have any more pain, just
buzz.''

Jennifer nodded. When she was alone again, she stared
up at the ceiling, her mind racing and her hands still trembling. She tried to focus on the nurse's words. "Maybe it
is just a muscle spasm," she murmured, forcing her
breathing to slow.

She said a little prayer, then made a silent promise to
God. If the baby was all right, she'd put an end to all this
craziness—all the lies and all the pretending. She'd tell her
parents the truth. She'd put her life back in order and regain her independence. And she'd tell Ryan she had no
intention of entering into a sham of a marriage.

And then, only then, would she ever know if she and
Ryan were meant to spend the rest of their lives together.

RYAN RACED through the front doors of Odessa General
Hospital and skidded to a stop at the information desk.
He'd finished his interview with the police at Jennifer's
office and had arrived at the police station to pick her up,
when he ran into the officer who'd left with Jennifer. He'd
asked a simple question, wondering when Jennifer would
be done with her interview, only to learn that she wasn't
at the station at all but at the hospital.

"Obstetrics?" he asked, trying to catch his breath. "Or
maybe she's in the emergency room."

"Name?" the nurse asked.

"Jennifer Rodriguez."

The nurse pointed him down the hallway. "Emergency
room. Follow the blue arrows."

Ryan ran down the hall, taking several turns before
bursting through wide double doors. He reached the
nurse's station in less than thirty seconds. "I'm looking
for Jennifer Rodriguez."

"Are you her husband?"

"No," Ryan said impatiently.

"A relative?"

He cursed softly. "No."

"Her boyfriend?"

"No," Ryan repeated, then paused. Hell, if he didn't answer affirmatively pretty soon, they wouldn't let him in to see her. "Well, yeah, I guess I am. I'm her fiancé. Is that good enough for you?"

The nurse gave him a sour expression. "She's in Exam Room 3. Right down there."

He hurried toward the room, raking his fingers through his hair and praying that Jennifer was all right. All the way to the hospital, speeding down city streets and running stop signs, he'd been assailed by terrible visions. Jennifer in pain, the baby in trouble. If anything happened to the baby, Ryan wasn't sure what he'd do, besides make sure Wade Randall paid. He'd come to love Jennifer so much, counted on both her and the baby to be in his future. But without the baby, Jennifer would have no reason to need him. And he'd have no chance to make her fall in love with him.

As he approached her room, he made a promise to himself. If everything was all right, then he wasn't going to scold her over the whole Randall mess. Instead, he was going to tell her exactly how he felt. And if everything wasn't right, then he was going to do his best to convince her that they still belonged together.

When he knocked on the door, there was no answer. Then a few moments later, Dr. Kinsey pulled it open. She smiled warmly and he felt a small measure of relief. If the news was bad, she wouldn't be smiling, would she? He walked past her and saw Jennifer on the bed, a nurse standing beside her. "Sweetheart. I came as soon as I found out you were—"

"Ryan," she murmured, her eyes wide with surprise, "how did you know I was here?"

He took her hand and gave it a squeeze. "I ran into Officer Wilson at the station. What happened? What does Dr. Kinsey say? Is the baby all right?"

"I was standing next to the squad car," she explained, her voice trembling slightly, "and I dropped my file folder. When I bent to pick it up, I got this pain."

"What did the doctor say?"

"She took some tests and did an exam," Jennifer said.

"And the doctor says she's fine," Dr. Kinsey added.

Ryan distractedly glanced over his shoulder. "Fine? And the baby?"

"We have all the tests back and there's nothing to worry about. It looks like it was just growing pains." At his frown, the doctor continued her explanation. "There are two ligaments that attach to the uterus," she said, pointing to her lower abdomen, "and they can cramp and contract as the baby gets larger. The cramping often frightens expectant mothers, but after a time Jennifer will learn to recognize these pains from other pains. She was right to come in. It's always best to check these things out."

"Then the baby is all right, too?" Ryan asked.

"The baby is just fine," Dr. Kinsey said. She walked over to the bed, glanced at the monitor and scribbled something on the chart. "As soon as you're ready, you can go home, Jennifer." She removed the monitor. "Just take it easy for the rest of the day. And no heavy lifting for the rest of this pregnancy."

The doctor left and Ryan waited as the nurse finished all the paperwork with Jennifer, then walked with her to the door. "I'll be taking care of all the bills," he said.

"No," Jennifer called from the bed.

Ryan turned back to her. "Jen, I thought we—"

"No," she repeated to the nurse. "You can submit the bills to my insurance company."

With a nod, the nurse headed out the door.

Ryan slowly walked back toward the bed. Jennifer swung her legs over the side and sat on the edge, nervously avoiding his gaze. He caught her chin with his fingers and tipped her face up, forcing her to look at him. "I don't mind taking care of the bills. It's the least I can do."

Jennifer swallowed hard, then opened her mouth as if to explain. Instead, she shook her head and a long silence grew between them. She finally sighed softly and spoke. "Go ahead," she murmured. "Say it. I know you want to."

"Say what?"

"What you're thinking. How I put myself in danger with Randall. How this is all my fault. How I could have been hurt, even killed, if you hadn't shown up when you did."

"Jen, I'm just glad you're—"

"No," Jennifer interrupted, placing her fingers over his lips. "I can't. I can't do this anymore."

Ryan smiled and took her fingers in his. "You're doing fine. The baby is all right and you're safe now. And Wade Randall is in jail."

"I'm not talking about the baby. Or me. I'm talking about this. Us. The wedding, the house, the happily-ever-after. This is not what I wanted. I wanted you to pose as my fiancé for one day and suddenly we're getting married and moving to the suburbs and buying a dog. This is not what I wanted."

"I thought we agreed that—"

"No!" she cried. "I didn't agree. I got swept away. You made me feel safe and I thank you for that, Ryan. Because I really needed someone to lean on. And maybe you did save my life back at the office. But I can't go through with this. I can't marry you.''

Frustration surged up inside him. Lately, she'd become so emotional, her moods rising and crashing at the slightest provocation. He'd read in the baby book that it was best to be patient and to offer as much support as he could. ''Jen, think about it. You've had a terrible scare—first with Randall and then with the baby. Now is no time to make a decision like this. Not when you're so emotional.''

''This is the perfect time. Everything is very clear. I've come to depend on you and that's not right. This baby is my responsibility, not yours. And this life we've constructed isn't real. It's based on a lie. A lie we told my parents.'' She turned away from him and slipped the dress over her head. The hospital gown dropped to the floor at her feet.

When she turned back to him, her dress was buttoned and her expression was unyielding. ''I need you to take me back to the office.''

''The doctor said you need to rest. I'll take you back to my place where I can keep an eye on you.''

''No, I need to get my car. I'm going home to El Paso tonight. I'm going to tell my parents that the wedding is off.''

Frustration gave way to disbelief. She couldn't be serious! They'd come this far. Why would she back out now? Ryan stepped toward her. ''Jen, don't do this.''

''All this tension is bad for me and the baby. I need to stop this before we make a big mistake.''

He reached out and took her hand. ''This isn't a mistake.''

She tipped her chin up defiantly. ''I want you to answer one question. Do you love me?''

Ryan's mind raced, wondering which answer she wanted this time. Did she want the truth, that yes, he did love her? Or did she want a lie, that he was still marrying her as a favor, as part of some silly scheme? He opened his mouth, fully intending to tell her truth, then snapped it shut.

"Answer my question," she said.

"No, answer mine," Ryan demanded. "Do you love me?"

"No."

Her answer was like a punch to the stomach. But after the initial pain, Ryan realized that it had come a little too easily, a little too quickly. "Good," he murmured. "Because that would only get in the way, don't you think?"

"Then you don't love me?" she asked.

He shrugged, not bothering to answer one way or the other. If he was lucky, she'd take his reply for what she wanted. Or maybe he was just a coward, afraid to admit the truth—afraid that Jennifer didn't care for him the way he cared for her. He'd learned to harden his heart when it came to his parents. Maybe it was time he did the same with Jennifer, before he got hurt. "I guess it would be a real disaster if we actually developed feelings for each other," he said.

"How would we know if those feelings were real? You want a family, something to take the place of the family you lost. And I'm grateful to you and I've come to depend on you. But that's not love, Ryan." She grabbed her purse.

"I guess not," he said.

She nodded slowly, then drew in a sharp breath and forced a smile. "I have to go. I've got a long drive ahead of me and a lot to think about."

Ryan reached in his pocket and pulled out his wallet. He grabbed all the cash he had inside and held it out to her. "Don't drive. Buy a plane ticket."

"I don't want your money," she said.

"Take it. It's my fault everything went this far. If it

wasn't for me, there wouldn't be any wedding plans.'' He grabbed her hand and pressed the bills into it. ''And tell your parents that whatever the wedding costs to cancel, I'll pay for that, too.''

She nodded, then backed toward the door. ''I— I'll just call a cab,'' she said. ''I'm sorry. I'm so sorry.''

''I am, too,'' Ryan replied.

Jennifer blinked back the tears, then turned and ran out of the hospital room. He heard her footsteps echoing on the cool tile floors, then gradually fading. Ryan stepped back and sat on the edge of the bed, too numb to feel anger or regret. Hell, he'd known all along that this could happen. He should never have asked her to marry him so quickly. He should have bided his time, waited for her feelings to become clearer. Instead, he'd tried to force the issue, to make her love him. And in the process, he'd managed to make her mistrust his motives.

''I'm sorry, too, Jen,'' he murmured. ''I don't think you'll ever know just how sorry I am.''

CHAPTER TEN

THE TAXI pulled up outside her parents' house shortly after eight. Jennifer wearily paid the driver with part of the cash Ryan had given her, then trudged up to the front door. She'd stopped at her apartment in Odessa to pick up fresh clothes, stuffing as much as she could into an overnight bag, not really sure how long she'd be away.

Undoing a wedding that was scheduled to take place in a week would be a lot of work. There were the caterers and the musicians, the priest and the florists. And the guests, all those guests, left to wonder what had happened to her happily-ever-after. If only they knew the truth, that her dream wedding was just a mirage, meant to fool the people who loved her the most.

Jennifer stopped, her hand on the front door. She glanced over her shoulder, wondering whether it might be best to take the cab back to the airport and go home. "They're going to kill me," she murmured. "Or worse, they'll disown me."

Suddenly, she needed more time to decide what to say. Explanations wouldn't be easy, but they'd be impossible if she stumbled over her words or started crying hysterically. Jennifer peered through the narrow window in the front door. If she was lucky, her parents would be dining at the club and she'd have a few more hours to herself.

Or maybe she *should* just run away. She could disappear for a few weeks, slip into Mexico and hide out in some cheap hotel. Then when everything had cooled down, she could come back and make her explanations. It was the coward's way out, but right now, that option looked awfully tempting.

In the end, Jennifer gathered her courage and pushed the front door open. "Hello? Anybody home?" She heard footsteps running through the kitchen and across the wood floors of the hallway.

Teresa appeared from around a corner and stopped short. "Jenny! You're home. *Mamá*, it's Jenny. Jenny's home." She raced over to her and threw her arms around Jennifer's legs, giving her a bone-crushing hug. "My dress is all ready," she said, gazing up at her with excited eyes. "And I went with *Mamá* to look at pictures of the flowers and the cake this afternoon. And *Mamá* says we can skip school on the Friday before the wedding so that we can help her get ready. Maria still hates her dress and Linda got a bra."

Jennifer reached down and ruffled her little sister's hair. "It sounds like you've all been very busy."

"Where's Ryan?" Teresa asked, scampering to the open front door.

"Ryan is still in Midland. He had to work so I came by myself."

"Don't tell me you drove all this way alone! And at this time of night!"

Jennifer looked up and smiled at her mother, who stood at the end of the hallway. "No. Ryan gave me money for a plane ticket."

Her mother bustled up and took Jennifer's overnight bag from her hand. Then she reached up and touched Jennifer's cheek, a look of concern wrinkling her brow. "Are you all right? You look a little pale, *niña*."

Jennifer shook her head. "I'm just really tired. I had a long day at work and the flight was bumpy."

"What are you doing here?" Carmen asked. "You were

not due to come until next week. Are you worried about the wedding?"

Her shoulders lifted in an indifferent shrug. "I just needed to come home for a little while, *Mamá*. Is that all right?"

Her mother gathered her into her arms and gave her a hug. "Of course. I have been hoping to have some time with you before the wedding. I feel like I am making all your decisions for you." She drew back and smiled. "And we have not had that mother-daughter talk that we are supposed to have."

"What talk?"

Carmen patted Jennifer's stomach. "The one where I tell you all about sex."

Jennifer's breath caught in her throat and tears burned in the corners of her eyes. Up until now, her mother had been so disapproving of everything that had happened, about the mistakes she'd made and the shame she'd brought upon the family. But now, Carmen had made a little joke, and Jennifer realized that her mother wasn't speaking to her as she would a child. She was teasing her, woman to woman, equal to equal.

She drew a shaky breath and fought the lump of emotion clogging her throat. But it was no use. She couldn't stop the tears from coming. "Oh, *Mamá*. I'm sorry. I know I've disappointed you and *Papi*. But I'm going to make it right. I promise, I'll pay back every dime if it takes the rest of my life."

Carmen drew back. "What are you talking about, Jennifer?"

"The—the wedding," she said between soft sobs. "I—I want to call off the—the wedding."

"Call off the wedding?" Teresa cried. "She can't call off the wedding! I won't get to wear my new dress."

"Teresa, go to your room," Carmen ordered. "It is time to get ready for bed."

"But it's only eight o'clock," she whined. "My bedtime is at nine."

"Do as I say," Carmen insisted in an even voice.

When Teresa had stomped up the stairs and slammed her bedroom door shut, Carmen quietly led Jennifer to her old bedroom. She sat Jennifer down on the bed. "I am going to go make us some tea and then we are going to have a nice long talk." She opened Jennifer's bag and pulled out her nightgown. "And you get ready for bed before you fall asleep in your clothes."

Jennifer watched her mother leave the room, then flopped back on her pillows. She'd been holding back the tears for so long, the effort had exhausted her. Her head ached and her throat burned. She'd thought the stress of telling her parents she was engaged had been bad, but this was so much worse. She never should have let it get so far. But then, she'd always tried so hard to please Diego and Carmen, no matter what it cost her.

She closed her eyes. Images of Ryan flashed through her mind. He'd told her exactly what she wanted to hear. He didn't love her. She'd been so worried that he expected more than she could give. But now that she knew his true feelings, her heart felt as if it were breaking into a million pieces. She loved him and he couldn't return those feelings, or didn't want to.

Jennifer struggled up from the bed and grabbed her nightgown. The soft flannel felt good on her skin and she tossed her clothes over a chair and slid between the crisp, clean sheets. A soft knock sounded at the door and her mother slipped back inside, a tray in her hands.

Carmen sat down on the edge of the bed and handed Jennifer a cup of tea, then poured one for herself. After a quiet sip, she sent Jennifer a concerned frown. "You look exhausted. Did you have a fight with Ryan? Is that what caused this?''

Jennifer shook her head. ''Not really a fight. I just don't think we're ready to get married.''

''*Hija,* if this were just an ordinary wedding, then I would say, call it off. There is no good to come from a marriage that begins with doubts. But there is more to this wedding than a bride and a groom. There is a baby to think of. A baby who deserves a *mamá* and a *papi.*''

''I know,'' Jennifer said. ''*Mamá,* I—we aren't really—I have to tell you something and I don't want you to hate me.''

Carmen slipped her arm around Jennifer's shoulders. ''*Hija,* you are my daughter. I could never hate you.''

''I think you could,'' Jennifer murmured, resting her head on her mother's shoulder and twisting her fingers together until they were numb. ''Ryan and I—we aren't really—we just got swept up in this and the wedding seemed like the easiest solution. But the easiest solution might not be the best—for me or for the baby.''

She drew a ragged breath, prepared to tell her mother the whole truth—that she'd had an affair with a virtual stranger, that the baby wasn't Ryan's, and that the wedding was just a sham. Her mind whirled with disjointed words and phrases, but she couldn't find a way to put them together so they'd make sense. Even worse, she couldn't bear to see the disappointment in her mother's eyes.

''You are afraid,'' Carmen said in a matter-of-fact tone.

Jennifer nodded, frustrated by her inability to speak the truth. ''Marriage is such a big step. I think I'm just beginning to realize that now, the closer we get to the wedding.''

''You're afraid that you do not really love Ryan? And perhaps that he does not love you?''

She wasn't afraid since she knew precisely how she felt—and how he *didn't* feel. But wasn't this what she wanted? A marriage in name only, a relationship dictated by rules and restrictions? Her precious independence? "Everything is so mixed up, *Mamá.* I'm not sure how either one of us feels."

"*Niña,* I have seen the way he looks at you. He has deep feelings for you, feelings that will not fade over time."

"I know. But it's not love, Mama. I think he just wants to rescue me. It's like this misguided sense of chivalry. I want a man to marry me because he loves me, not because he wants to save me from a life as a single mother."

"And how do you feel about this man?"

Jennifer paused before she replied. Though she hadn't been completely honest with her mother so far, now was the time to tell the truth. Saying it out loud might help. "I'm in love with him," she murmured. "Hopelessly, completely in love with him. How can I not be? He's been so good to me and the baby. He bought us a house. Can you believe that, *Mamá?* A big expensive house with a beautiful nursery and huge backyard."

"I don't see the problem then."

"But what if I love him because I'm grateful to him? And he loves me because he wants to fill some void in his life? And we realize too late, after the wedding, that it's not enough. That it isn't true love and it won't last."

Carmen laughed. "Do you know why I fell in love with your *papi?* It was his clothes. He wore the nicest clothes. They were always clean and perfectly pressed, and his hair was tidy and his fingernails clean. I thought, any man who takes such good care of his appearance is a man who would make my girlfriends envious. That is how it started. I wanted to show off to my girlfriends. But then I got to know Diego, and soon, I did not care about the clothes. I loved the man. And you love Ryan."

"I'm not sure that's enough. I just wish we had more time. Then I would know for sure."

Her mother sighed softly. "Well, *niña,* you have all the time in the world. If you want to call off the wedding, then we will do that."

Jennifer gasped. "You will? You'd call off the wedding?"

Carmen nodded solemnly. "But there is one condition."

"What is that?"

"You have to go back to Ryan and you must talk to him—openly and honestly. You must tell him how you feel and you must see if you can get past this. And if you still want to call off the wedding, then that is what we will do. But not until you speak to him and you tell him how you feel."

"All right," Jennifer said. "I'll go. Tomorrow or the next day, I'll fly back to Midland and I'll talk to him."

Carmen smiled. "I think you and Ryan love each other very much. You are just too stubborn to admit it to yourselves. And to each other." She placed her hand on Jennifer's cheek. "Sleep on it, *niña.* Maybe things will be clearer in the morning."

Jennifer nodded and Carmen stood and carried the tray to the door. *"Hasta mañana, que sueñes con los angelitos,"* her mother whispered as she closed the door.

Jennifer sank back into her pillows. If she knew one thing, it was that she wouldn't be sleeping with the angels tonight. Now that she had permission to cancel the wedding, she was more confused than ever. This was what she wanted, wasn't it? A way out.

But what she really wanted was Ryan, his love and his passion, and a future together. And she wanted it without any risk to her own heart. Jennifer was coming to the realization that the only way to get her happily-ever-after might be to take the biggest risk of all—to marry Ryan now and hope that love would come later.

She rubbed her temples with her fingers and pinched her eyes shut. "I'll think about this tomorrow," she murmured. "*Mamá* is right. Everything will be clearer in the morning."

RYAN ROLLED OVER on the sofa, reaching out to balance himself as he opened his eyes. He raked his hands through his hair and groaned, exhaustion still muddling his brain. For the third night in a row, he'd fallen asleep in front of the television, fully dressed. It was the only way he could sleep at all, the idle drone from the cable shopping network replacing the noise that went on in his brain.

Since Jennifer had left, he hadn't been able to think about anything but her. When he wasn't wondering how he'd gone wrong, he was trying to figure out how he could make it all right again. And after an entire weekend spent mulling it over, he still hadn't come up with any good answers.

It all came down to that single question she'd asked— do you love me? Maybe there wasn't a right answer, at least not for Jennifer. Though she usually seemed so sure of what she wanted, as they got closer to the wedding, she had become increasingly indecisive. And since he couldn't read her mind, he was often left in the dark.

Ryan sat up and rubbed his eyes. It was time to stop feeling sorry for himself. He'd messed up another engagement, never mind that this was a woman he really wanted to marry—or that the engagement was a fraud. But he'd been relieved when he and Elise had broken up, he'd felt free and unencumbered. Unfortunately, he couldn't summon those feelings now. All he could manage was a keen sense of loss, as though something incredible had slipped through his fingers.

So how long would it take to forget her? Ryan wondered. To put aside all his regrets and get Jennifer Rodriguez out of his mind. Surely there would be some contact. After all, he'd offered to pay the costs for canceling the wedding. Given the choice, he'd rather not have to see her again and face the realization that she was walking out of his life forever. But he probably wouldn't have any choice in the matter.

Hell, maybe he should give up on relationships altogether. Two failed engagements were enough to make any man a confirmed bachelor. And there were certain benefits to a no-strings approach to the opposite sex. He'd never have to spend another sleepless night on the sofa, watching the cable shopping network and subsisting on pork rinds and warm beer.

A soft thud sounded on the front door and Ryan glanced at his watch. The paper boy was early this morning. He rubbed his bare chest, then fumbled with the buttons of his dress shirt as he stumbled to the door. Best to get back into his routine, he thought. The same routine he'd maintained before he'd met Jennifer. The paper, a few cups of coffee, a quick jog, then a hot shower before heading out to work.

He yanked open the front door, then froze as his sleepy gaze fell on Jennifer, standing on his front step with the newspaper in her hand. "You're here," he murmured, wondering if this was all just a dream and he was still asleep on the sofa.

Her eyes were ringed with red, her hair was tangled and she looked like she hadn't slept in days. She nodded, her gaze fixed on his. "I—I came back last night," she murmured.

"How long have you been out here?"

Jennifer shrugged and rubbed her arms through her thin

jacket, her teeth chattering. "Not long. Since just before dawn. I wanted to make sure I didn't miss you."

"Come in," he said, stepping aside. "It's chilly out there. I'll make us some coffee." He wanted to take her hand, to rub her fingers between his until they were warm, to fold her into his embrace and inhale the sweet scent of her hair. But Ryan knew better than to touch her. She looked like a tiny frightened animal, ready to scurry for cover at the slightest movement.

He hurried to the kitchen and flipped on the coffee-maker, then popped some bread in the toaster and poured two glasses of orange juice. Knowing Jennifer, she probably hadn't bothered with— Ryan cursed silently. He'd have to learn to stop worrying about her. She wasn't his responsibility anymore and he needn't be concerned about her diet.

He stuck a mug beneath the stream of coffee, then added the sugar and milk that Jennifer preferred. Then he took her mug, the toast and a glass of juice back into the living room. He found her perched on the edge of the sofa, her jacket folded in her lap, her hands clenched on top.

Ryan sat down beside her. "So I guess you told them," he said, handing her the coffee. "Were they angry?"

Her gaze dropped to the floor. "I told my mother I wanted to cancel the wedding," she began.

"And how did she react?"

"She surprised me," Jennifer said. "She told me if I wasn't certain I wanted to get married, then I should call the wedding off. But she also said I needed to come back here and make another attempt to work things out."

"And is that why you're here?" Ryan asked.

She shook her head, her hair tumbling around her face in soft waves. "I'm not sure why I'm here. It just felt like the right place to come."

He took the mug of coffee from her cold fingers, then

handed her the glass of orange juice. "Drink your juice," he said.

She did as she was told, guzzling the whole glass as if she hadn't had anything to eat or drink for days. Then she took a deep breath, burped softly, and set her glass down on the coffee table. "I don't want to cancel the wedding," she said in a quiet voice.

Ryan blinked, not sure that he'd heard her right. He bent forward, trying to read her expression. "I—I thought you went to El Paso to— I thought this was what you wanted."

"I don't want to cancel the wedding," she repeated. "I think, under the circumstances, it would be best if we went ahead with our plans."

He frowned. Her mother had given her the go-ahead to cancel. Why would Jennifer change her mind? "What do *you* really want?" Ryan asked.

"This is what I want," Jennifer replied, still keeping her gaze fixed straight ahead.

Ryan reached out and caught her chin with his finger, then turned her face to him. When she risked a look up, he could see the lies in her eyes and it made his stomach wrench. She didn't want to get married now any more than she did when she walked out on him Friday. But something had happened in El Paso: her parents had somehow convinced her that she had no other choice. And though they'd offered to cancel the wedding, she'd been pushed in exactly the opposite direction—into a marriage she didn't want.

Maybe *he* should just call it off, Ryan mused. Backing out would give her exactly what she wanted without forcing her to pay the price. Her parents and relatives could offer their sympathy and understanding while turning their anger on him.

His gaze wandered over her beautiful face, taking in the dark smudges beneath her eyes and the pale color of her cheeks. He'd grown to love her simple beauty, her infectious laugh and her passionate nature. And he didn't want to give her up, damn it. He loved Jennifer and he was willing to take her under any terms, even knowing that she didn't love him. "Then we'll get married," he said.

Relief washed over her features. "Really? You still want to go through with it?"

Ryan nodded.

Jennifer pulled in a ragged breath then smiled tremulously. But Ryan could see the tears glittering in her eyes. He reached out and cupped her cheek in his palm. "Don't cry," he said.

"I can't seem to help it," Jennifer replied, waving her hand in front of her face. "I've been crying all weekend and I can't stop." Laughter slipped from her lips. "I think the baby has his hand on the faucet."

Ryan pressed his forehead to hers and smiled. "I'm glad you came back," he murmured. Then, as if it were the most natural thing in the world, he came a bit closer and kissed her. The kiss was soft and fleeting, and so tantalizing. But Ryan knew when to stop. At least he thought he did. She stared up at him, her eyes wide, her lips damp. And she didn't breathe, as if she were waiting for him to kiss her again. He did, only this time Ryan lingered a bit longer, wondering how far she might let him go.

He didn't have to wait long for an answer. A tiny moan slipped from her lips and her hands fluttered from his chest to his shoulders to the nape of his neck. Desire washed over him like a wave, sharpening his senses, making him focus on the feel of her mouth, the heat of her tongue, the sweet taste of her. A floodgate had opened and all the emotion they'd kept so tightly controlled now swept them away from reality.

Ryan pulled her closer until her body pressed along the length of his. He knew this was wrong and that she'd probably regret it, but he vowed to deal with that problem later. He had Jennifer back, in his arms, and in six days, they'd be married. His hands smoothed over her, slowly and gently, memorizing every curve, reveling in the changes the baby had wrought on her body. And when she pulled back and looked into his eyes, he didn't see regret, but a need as piercing as his own. He reached out and drew a finger along her cheek to her jawline, unable to stop looking at her, needing to take in every detail of her features.

Jennifer's gaze dropped to his mouth and she moved to kiss him again, a kiss so exquisitely perfect that Ryan was content to leave it there. But then, she looked at him again and spoke. And he knew that they wouldn't end things with a simple kiss. This time they would share so much more.

"Make love to me," she murmured.

JENNIFER WATCHED his reaction as it reflected in his hazel eyes. She held her breath, praying that he wouldn't refuse, hoping against hope that his common sense had fled the moment their lips first touched. She'd lost herself in this perfect moment and she didn't want to be found. Not yet.

"Please," she murmured.

"Jen, are you sure?"

Jennifer nodded. With every ounce of her being, she knew this was what she wanted. There was no doubt, no hesitation. The rules didn't apply anymore for they'd all become pointless once she'd realized how much she loved Ryan Madison. And if this was all she'd ever have with him, then she'd be satisfied.

Ryan pulled her up from the sofa and took her hand, then led her to his bedroom. The growing light from the dawn filtered through the sheer curtains, illuminating the room in a warm glow. They sat down on the edge of the bed and Jennifer wasn't sure what to do first. She felt like an untried schoolgirl, full of desire but riddled with apprehension.

"Will this be all right?" he asked, holding on to her hand and studying her fingers.

Jennifer blinked. "It's not my first time, if that's what you mean."

Ryan chuckled and pointed to her tummy. "I kind of figured that. I meant is it all right with the baby and all?"

A smile curled the corners of her mouth and the tension seemed to dissolve between them. This was the Ryan she loved—the sweet concern mixed with a sexy confidence. "I think it would be all right," she murmured. With a hesitant hand, she reached out and pressed her palm to his chest. Beneath her fingers, his heart beat strong and true. Hers was hammering so hard she was certain he could hear it.

With a lazy ease, he reached out and touched her in the same spot, his fingertips skimming beneath the scooped neckline of her dress. Mimicking his caress, Jennifer slipped her hand beneath the open front of his shirt. For each action, there was another reaction. Before she knew it, his shirt fell off his shoulders and her dress was suddenly unbuttoned to the waist.

Ryan leaned over and kissed her bare shoulder, then traced a line along her collarbone. He stopped when he reached the soft cleft between her breasts. Every inch of her skin tingled from the warmth of his lips. She'd read in her books that pregnant women often felt unattractive, but the way Ryan looked at her, she felt beautiful and sexy and alive with desire. A sigh of contentment slipped from her lips as she furrowed her hands through his hair and tipped her head back.

They rolled onto the bed together, tangled in each other's arms, clothes half on and half off. Ryan's hands slid to the crease beneath each breast and he teased at her nipples with his thumbs until they reached a hard peak. Anxious for his exploration to continue, Jennifer reached down to unfasten her bra, allowing his mouth to find her flesh, craving the sweet sensations that would shoot through her body when he did.

But he brushed her hands away. "Let me," he murmured. When the silky fabric slid over her skin, he nuzzled her breast, then drew her into his mouth. Waves of aching sensation washed over her as he teased her nipple with his tongue. Suddenly, clothes became a barrier to more pleasure. Jennifer tugged at his shirt and he struggled out of it, then yanked her dress down around her hips. She didn't give a thought to modesty, so desperate was she to feel his naked body next to hers, to lose herself in his masculine beauty.

But Ryan was determined to take his time, exploring, learning every inch of her body with his fingers and his mouth. Jennifer couldn't be so patient. She ran her palm down his chest, then unbuttoned his trousers. The hard ridge of his desire pressed against the fine fabric and she allowed her fingers to brush him there.

With a low growl, Ryan sucked in a sharp breath. Taking his reaction as encouragement, Jennifer touched him again and then again, until she fell into a slow, enticing rhythm. He reached down and fumbled with his zipper, allowing her to touch him more intimately. And when she did, Jennifer felt powerful over his desire, yet powerless to control her own. She'd always blamed passion for the mistake she'd made five months ago. But compared with the way Ryan made her feel, that night hadn't been passion at all. Passion was wild and mind-shattering, it was a dance with fire, dangerous yet mesmerizing.

"You don't know what your touch does to me," he murmured, his voice ragged and deep. "What it's always done to me."

"Then let me touch you," she said, nuzzling his neck. "Everywhere."

He pushed off the bed, then stood beside it and stripped off the remainder of his clothes. Jennifer stared at him as he stood in the low light, her gaze flitting over the planes and angles of his body, his broad chest, his rippled belly, his narrow hips and his sex, hot and ripe.

Jennifer held out her hand and Ryan pulled her up to her feet. He slowly kissed his way down her torso, then grabbed the hem of her dress and drew it over her head. She slipped out of her bra as he skimmed her panties down her hips. And then there were no barriers between them, nothing left to stop them from the inevitable passion they would share.

She circled her arms around his neck and kissed him just once, short and sweet, teasing him to take more. The contact between their naked bodies was electric, and with a low groan, Ryan grabbed her waist and picked her up, settling her legs around his hips. Together, they fell back onto the bed, losing themselves in the feel of their bodies so close together.

Jennifer's senses spun out of control, taste and touch and sound swirling around her until she lost herself in a whirlpool of need. He touched her between her legs, finding the perfect spot, fingering her moist warmth. A cry of pleasure escaped her lips, delirious pleasure astonishing in its power over her.

He stroked her slowly at first, bringing her close to the edge, then drawing her back. Frustrated and eager for her release, Jennifer whispered his name over and over again, her breath teasing at his ear, an unspoken plea for him to end her sweet torment.

But instinct soon overwhelmed them both and they could no longer keep themselves from the ultimate intimacy. Ryan pulled her on top of him and brought her knees up alongside her hips. Jennifer knew she could have him then, quick and frantic, but she wanted to tease him as he had her. Slowly, she moved across the length of him, promising him entrance but then drawing away.

Ryan had no more patience than she did. He grabbed her hips and made her stay still. Their gazes locked, he slowly brought her down on top of him until she took him all in, exquisite heat searing to the core of her body. Jennifer held her breath. They hadn't bothered with a condom, there was no reason. This was the man she was about to marry, the man she loved.

As she moved above him, raw emotion suffused his expression. Jennifer watched him, his own desire reflected in her rhythm. At first her movements were slow and deliberate, but tension grew inside her with each thrust, and her control began to slip. She felt herself on the verge and watched as his need became fierce, wild, overpowering. Every nerve in her body crackled, every muscle ached, and when he touched her between their bodies, she had no choice but to let go.

Ryan arched beneath her, pulling her down against him as they reached their peak together, soft pleas mixing with harsh breathing. Again and again she came down on him until they were both completely spent. Time seemed to stop for them as they slowly drifted back to reality. Jennifer rolled into his embrace and he tucked her against him. She closed her eyes, absolute contentment draining the last bit of energy from her body.

There had been a time when she thought making love to Ryan would be a mistake. But now that it had happened, she couldn't believe it had been wrong. And no matter what the future held for them, memories of this time together would always remind her of the true power of passion and the depth of her love. And maybe, if she was lucky, this would be the start—of a love that would last a lifetime.

CHAPTER ELEVEN

RYAN PICKED HER UP for their flight to El Paso just after dawn on Friday morning. As they rode to the airport, Jennifer stared out the window, too nervous to make even a feeble attempt at conversation. In truth, since the morning they'd made love, neither one of them had brought up the subject of their little indiscretion. It had become their elephant in the living room, always there, impossible to forget and getting bigger and bigger every day.

In Jennifer's eyes, their morning together had been the most wonderful time of her life. Making love to Ryan had been everything she'd imagined it would be and so much more. They'd connected, both body and soul, and every touch, every sigh had been an expression of feelings too deep to fathom. For a few perfect hours, they'd existed in a dream world, where all troubles and worries had been pushed aside for sensual pleasures.

But with their morning of passion had come the realization that they'd broken the rules—*her* rules—once again. No kissing, separate beds, full dress around the house, those were the little rules and they'd broken them all in the first few minutes. But there was also the big, unwritten rule—no sex. She hadn't even bothered to write it down because it had been inconceivable that she'd allow herself to go so far. Now that she had—they had—Jennifer wasn't sure what to do about it.

Maybe if she didn't mention it, they'd enjoy the same pleasures again. After all, technically, there was no rule against wild, passionate sex. And as long as they did it fully dressed, on the dining room table, and without kissing, it wasn't against the rules.

She drew a deep breath and turned toward him, prepared to broach the subject for the first time. She wanted to do away with the damn rules, tear them up and never think about them again. But Ryan's attention was focused on the highway ahead and she wasn't really sure what to say. She couldn't admit she'd loved every minute of their time together, that it had been all she could think about for the past four days and nights. Or that she'd wondered what circumstances might cause another lapse like the one they'd enjoyed.

What she really wanted to ask was what had it meant to him. Though her own feelings were crystal clear, the only clue she had to Ryan's feelings came from his very own words—he wasn't in love with her. She had only imagined emotion in his eyes and in his touch that morning. "Wishful thinking," she murmured.

"What?" Ryan asked, glancing over at her.

"What? Oh, nothing," Jennifer replied with a shake of her head. "I was just—clearing my throat."

Silence descended on the car once again. Maybe she didn't want to know how he really felt. Maybe that's why she'd avoided him these past few days, claiming that she was too busy with plans for the wedding and cases at work. They'd spoken on the phone every night, but their usual routine of dinner and a chaste evening spent in the same apartment had been forgotten. Neither one of them wanted to tempt fate again.

"You're quiet this morning," Ryan commented. "Are you worried about the wedding?"

"No," Jennifer murmured.

"You seem a little tired."

"No," she repeated.

"Are you hungry?" Ryan asked. "We could stop to get something to eat."

"No."

He sent her a wry smile. "Do you think you could manage something more than a single-word answer? After all, you are speaking to your future husband here. If this is any indication of what life is going to be like, then I've got a problem."

"You've got a problem?" Jennifer asked, an edge in her voice. "What about me? What am I supposed to expect?"

"Expect?"

"The elephant in the living room?" Jennifer cried. "I laid out a perfectly good plan and you messed it all up." This was a good strategy, she mused. She'd just blame everything on Ryan. He'd get defensive, she'd egg him on and maybe he'd confess that he really loved her and he wanted to live happily ever after with her.

"I messed it up? Hey, there were two people in my bed. And I wasn't the only one breaking the rules."

"I just want to be sure that you never break the rules again," Jennifer said. "Do I have your word?"

Ryan laughed sharply. "Hell, no. I'm not going to promise anything. As far as I'm concerned, you can burn those rules."

Jennifer's heart leaped. "Are—are you saying you're going to deliberately break the rules again?"

Ryan glanced over at her, then shook his head. He jerked the steering wheel to the right and the car dropped off onto the shoulder of the road, gravel and dust blowing up behind it. "All right, you want to get this straight? Let's do it right here, right now. I happen to believe what happened between us was very nice. Better than nice. It was…extraordinary. And I'm damn well not going to feel sorry it happened. Nor am I going to do anything to prevent it from happening again. Now, if that's a problem with you, we can just turn around and drive back home. You can call your parents and tell them the wedding is off.''

She sat back in the seat and crossed her arms above her belly, trying not to smile. This was progress. He hated the rules as much as she did! ''I just think that things would run much more smoothly if we had—if we were—if there was—'' She cleared her throat. ''If we don't get going, we're going to be late for our plane.''

They drove in silence for a long time before Ryan spoke again. This time the anger and frustration were gone from his voice. ''I'm sorry,'' he murmured. ''I didn't mean to shout.''

''I am, too,'' Jennifer replied.

''Jen, I want you to know that you can get out of this at any time. I won't hold you to our agreement. In fact, maybe we should work out some kind of signal.''

''A signal? For what?''

''You can tug on your ear or touch your nose and I'll know that you want out.''

Get out? Jennifer's heart fell. This was not what she wanted. How could he be so glib, to talk about marrying her one moment and canceling the wedding the next? She bit her bottom lip and turned back to the window. ''I—I don't think that will be necessary,'' Jennifer replied, trying to keep her tone nonchalant.

''I just want you to be happy,'' he murmured. ''That's all I've ever wanted.''

She watched as the scenery sped by. Was it so easy for him to give her up? Just a tug of the ear or a touch of the nose and everything they'd shared would disappear in an instant? Maybe her suspicions about his feelings were right. He was just doing her a favor by marrying her, and she was showing him precious little gratitude for all his attention.

"Thank you," she said.

"For what?"

"For doing this for me. For putting up with my silly rules. I know I don't always seem very grateful, but I am."

He smiled at her. "Everything will be all right, Jennifer."

"How do you know?"

Ryan shrugged. "I just do. It doesn't seem like it now, but everything will work out the way it's supposed to."

If only she could be certain, Jennifer thought. There were times when she wanted to wipe out the past, everything that had happened between them, and start over again. She would have done so many things differently. She never would have asked him to pose as her fiancé, she would have told her parents about her pregnancy and faced the consequences on her own. Then, perhaps the attraction they'd felt at their first meeting might have grown in a different direction. Without all the confusion, they might have fallen in love for real.

But it was too late for regrets. She'd made this life for herself and she'd have to live with the doubts and the insecurities. Every day she'd be forced to look into her husband's eyes, hoping to find some trace of love there, and dying a little when she didn't. Maybe someday, things would change, but she would do her best not to hold her breath.

"Maybe someday," she murmured.

FROM THE MOMENT they'd arrived in El Paso, the day had been filled with nonstop action. Jennifer had pasted a smile on her face and tried to appear as if she were completely at ease with her role as the blushing bride. But Ryan could see the toll that her charade was taking and he couldn't help but worry that the facade would soon shatter.

After a quick lunch on the Rodriguez terrace, Jennifer had been whisked away by her mother and her sisters to complete last-minute plans for the wedding. He had wanted to go with her, to hold her hand and soothe her nerves. And he thought they'd have time together that afternoon until Tía Yolanda and a crowd of female relatives arrived for an impromptu wedding shower. There were games and gifts and fun, but Jennifer looked as if she were being hauled off to the dentist, sending Ryan a helpless glance as Diego and Joe dragged him away for a round of golf at their country club.

Ryan had no choice but to accept. And though he tried to act like the confident bridegroom, his thoughts had been completely occupied with Jennifer. It was clear that she was having some serious doubts about the wedding and he fully expected her to tug on her ear or touch her nose any second. He'd agonized through nine holes of mediocre golf, a few beers and a roundabout ride home, anxious to see her again.

By the time they got back to the Rodriguez house, she'd changed into a pretty ivory dress that she planned to wear to the rehearsal. He took a quick shower, dressed in a sport coat and slacks and met her out in front of the house. She stood next to the rental car and clutched a tangle of ribbons that had been strung through a paper plate. He was relieved to finally have her to himself, even if it was only for a short time.

"What is that?" Ryan asked.

"It's supposed to be a bouquet," she said with a rueful smile. "It's a tradition at wedding showers. It's made from all the ribbons from the shower gifts and I'm supposed to carry it down the aisle during the rehearsal."

Ryan pulled the car door open for her. "Did you have fun at the shower?"

She shrugged. "I got a lot of nice presents," she said.

Ryan closed the door, then jogged around and got in the car. "What kind of presents?"

"Nothing special," she murmured.

"No, I want to know," he said.

Jennifer groaned, a pretty blush coloring her cheeks. "It was a lingerie shower," she admitted. "Why they decided on that, I'm really not sure. I'm the size of a whale and they're giving me skimpy little things that wouldn't fit around my thigh. Tía Yolanda says I can wear them after the baby is born to rekindle the—" Jennifer stopped short. "Never mind."

"For what it's worth, I think you're beautiful just the way you are," Ryan said.

It was the perfect thing to say. He could see it in her face, in the tiny smile that twitched at the corners of her mouth. "Thanks," she said.

As they pulled out of the driveway, his mind wandered back to the morning they'd made love, replaying the memory again and again, going over every detail, and adding a few new details that involved Jennifer dressed in sexy lingerie…and Jennifer without sexy lingerie. In all his life, he'd never really made love to a woman. He'd had sex, but adding the emotional component changed everything. Jennifer had become part of him and he'd become part of her for one single, perfect moment. And he wanted to experience that again—and very soon.

But she was right, there was an elephant in the living room and they'd both been avoiding the subject. Talking about how great they were together wasn't going to help his cause. This decision to go through with the wedding was hers and hers alone. For the next twenty-four hours, until the moment they walked down the aisle, she held their future in her hands.

He peered out the window at a passing sign. "Can you tell me where we're going?"

Jennifer gave him directions through the downtown area, chatting aimlessly about passing sights as they drove. Though the marriage license was supposed to be purchased at least three days in advance, Diego had persuaded a judge who was a good friend to waive the rules since Ryan and Jennifer were from out of town. Jennifer's father had assured them that the process would take only a few minutes and they could meet everyone at the church afterward for the rehearsal.

Ryan pulled into a parking space near the county offices and turned off the car. Jennifer let out a deep sigh and tipped her head back on the headrest. "We should have eloped," she murmured. "We could have gone to Vegas and had a lovely little wedding in one of those twenty-four-hour chapels. Elvis could have married us. Our wedding dinner could have been an all-you-can-eat buffet, and for our honeymoon, we could have played the slots."

"We still could," Ryan said. "Las Vegas is...that way." He pointed to the north.

"Wouldn't that defeat the purpose of this whole charade?"

Ryan stared at his hands, gripped around the steering wheel. Why couldn't he seem to get a handle on her mood? She'd gone from indifference to gratitude to sarcasm all in the space of fifteen minutes. "Say the word, Jen, and I'll turn the car around and head for Vegas."

"Are you crazy? Have you seen all the plans that have been made? I walked out into that tent in the backyard. This is a major event. There's no way I could possibly call it off now. My parents have spent thousand and thousands of dollars. When my mother said this was going to be a small wedding, she was in serious denial.''

A long silence grew between them as they both sat, staring out the windshield. Add indignation to the list. Ryan turned to her, sliding his arm over the back of the seat. He wanted to touch her, but he was afraid of her reaction. ''Jen, I want to apologize,'' he said.

''You already did. And I don't mind if you shout.''

''I wanted to apologize for all of this,'' he said. ''I feel responsible, like I pushed you into this whole wedding thing.''

''You didn't,'' she said. ''I agreed to the wedding.''

He drew a deep breath and let it out slowly. ''I guess I didn't expect it to be so difficult. When it was just the two of us, back home, it was easier to pretend. But now, with everyone watching, I feel like I'm on a stage and I'm just some hack actor stumbling around and forgetting his lines.''

''You're doing fine,'' she murmured. ''Just keep reminding yourself this will all be over in twenty-four hours.''

''Over,'' Ryan repeated as he pushed the car door open. ''Right.'' It would be far from over. In truth, the wedding would just be the beginning of their problems. Even after the vows were spoken, he'd be living in constant doubt, wondering when Jennifer would decide she no longer wanted to be with him.

Someday, she'd feel courageous enough to live her life on her own. She'd take the baby and find a place of her own and he'd be forgotten, expected to go on with his life as if she'd never been in it. And that was the day that it would be over—for him.

As she stepped out of the car, Ryan was sorely tempted to gather her into his arms and kiss her. He could always tell precisely how she felt by the way she reacted to his

kisses. But kissing her—and breaking one of her rules—
might just push her past her limit. He dragged his gaze
away from her mouth, that sweet mouth, and glanced up
at the building that housed the county offices. "I guess
this is it," he said.

Jennifer gave him a curt nod, then started down the sidewalk. She was halfway up the steps before he caught up
with her. He pulled open the heavy door and let her pass,
her shoulder brushing his chest. It was the first time they'd
touched since they'd made love and it wasn't enough,
Ryan mused. A warm flood of desire raced through his
bloodstream, but he had no choice but to ignore it.

Though it was nearly 5:00 p.m. on a Friday evening,
the clerk had promised to wait until Ryan and Jennifer
arrived. He had all the paperwork ready, and once they
produced their identification, their social security numbers
and a small fee, they were ready to sign the license. The
clerk handed the pen to Jennifer first, pointing to the spot
where she was to sign.

Ryan saw her hand tremble slightly as she stared down
at the marriage license. Was this going to be it? Was this
the spot where she backed out? She hesitated, holding the
pen over the paper for a long while. Then with a sharp
intake of breath, she scribbled her name across the bottom
and pushed the pen at Ryan.

Suddenly, the impact of what they were about to do hit
him full force. He'd thought it would come when he saw
her walk down the aisle or when they said "I do." But it
came now, earlier than expected, and the realization took
his breath away. They were really going to get married!
They would sign legal documents, stand in front of a priest
and promise to love each other for the rest of their lives.
Though it had seemed like a good plan a few weeks ago,
Ryan's feelings had changed. Marrying Jennifer under
false pretenses felt wrong, deceitful and hypocritical.

"Aren't you going to sign it?"

Startled out of his thoughts, Ryan glanced over at Jennifer. "What?"

"You have to sign it," she said, "or it's not legal."

Ryan nodded, then scribbled his signature next to Jennifer's. The clerk stamped the documents, handed Ryan their share of the paperwork and wished them both luck. Then he walked away from the counter, leaving Ryan and Jennifer alone. Ryan held the papers out to her. "You can rip them up anytime," he said.

Jennifer frowned. "That's the second time today you've offered me a way out. Maybe it's you who would like to call this whole thing off?"

Ryan smiled and shook his head. "Like you said, it's a little too late for that." With every second that passed, the magnitude of what they were about to do increased. He was getting everything he ever wanted—the woman he loved, a family, a chance at a future—yet it was tainted with doubts and insecurities.

"Let's go," he said. "We're going to be late for the rehearsal."

BY THE TIME they reached St. Benedict's, everyone else had arrived—all the cousins and the aunts and uncles and Jennifer's parents and her siblings. They'd assembled in the vestibule and Jennifer's mother was going over the order of the processional with the wedding party and the organist. When she caught sight of Jennifer, she came scurrying over, her eyes alight with excitement.

"*Hija,* we were beginning to think you were not coming!"

The rest of the crowd laughed at the little joke, but only Jennifer knew how close her mother had come to the truth. If she'd had the courage, she would have turned and run at that very moment. Ryan's words kept tumbling around in her brain until she was so confused she wasn't sure what she was supposed to do. It had all been so much simpler when it was just a game with a set of rules she'd made up. But now, she wasn't sure she wanted to continue playing.

This was so real and so...final. It was easy to say they could end it with a quick divorce, but Jennifer knew that any divorce would be painful. She glanced over at Father Juan, who stood at the outer edge of the vestibule, and forced a smile. Ryan had found Ben and was talking to him just inside the doors, and Lucy was running around, laughing, with Teresa hard on her heels.

"You look tired."

Jennifer glanced over her shoulder and found Carolyn Mulholland standing behind her. Carolyn held out her arms and Jennifer gave her a hug. "Everyone keeps saying that, but I'm fine," Jennifer assured her. "Just a little nervous."

"Don't worry. I went through this last month, and even though Ben and I got married in Lucy's hospital room, I still had butterflies. Just remember to take some time and enjoy it all. It's a day you'll never forget."

Whether she ran out before the ceremony or went through with it and regretted it later, Jennifer couldn't see that she'd be looking back on her wedding with anything close to fondness. "Lucy looks wonderful," she said, anxious to change the subject.

Carolyn gazed across the vestibule and smiled warmly. "She does, doesn't she?" She turned back to Jennifer and pointed to her tummy. "And I'm so happy for you. Ryan told Ben about the baby when he visited us in San Antonio. I'm glad to know Lucy will have a little cousin to play with."

"Ryan visited you in San Antonio?" Jennifer asked, frowning. "When was that?"

"A few weeks ago. He was in on business and he

stopped at the house. We had a nice dinner. And then he and Ben got together another time, too, about a week later, and they had a few beers. Didn't he tell you?''

"No," Jennifer said, her tone flat. If he hadn't told her about something as important as seeing his brother, then what else was he keeping from her? Her confusion grew, and suddenly, she was beginning to feel like she didn't know the man she was marrying at all. "If he told you about the baby, then you probably know everything else."

Carolyn reached out and rubbed Jennifer's arm as she nodded. "You love him, don't you? I mean, you wouldn't go through with this if you didn't, right?"

Jennifer nodded. If there was one thing she was sure of, it was that she loved Ryan Madison. And though the rest of her life was a chaotic mess, she found herself clinging to that fact like a life preserver in a stormy sea. "I do. At first, I wasn't sure if I loved him for the right reasons, but now it doesn't make any difference why I love him. I just do. He's such a good man and he'll be a wonderful father for my baby."

"And he loves you," Carolyn said. "So what's the problem?"

Jennifer bit her bottom lip then shook her head. "But he doesn't. He doesn't love me."

"Of course he does," she said with a laugh. "He told Ben he loved you. Why would he say that if it wasn't true?"

Jennifer gasped. "Ryan told Ben that he loved me?" Her gaze jumped over to Ryan, then back to Carolyn. "Then why would he tell me—"

"All right, everyone!" Carmen called. "It is time to begin. Ryan, you and Ben should go with Father Juan. Yolanda, bring the twins to the door. The *pajines* need to get their little pillows. Girls, I want you to line up over here, and the rest of you, go find a place in the church."

She hurried over to Jennifer and took her arm before Jennifer had a chance to finish talking to Carolyn.

"We'll talk later," Jennifer called as her mother pulled her away.

Carolyn waved, then turned her attention to Lucy, who had managed to rumple her pretty dress and knock her little hat askew. There'd be plenty of time to talk at the rehearsal dinner, Jennifer thought. She'd find out exactly what Ryan had said, every word. And if Carolyn was sure of her story, then Jennifer would confront Ryan and get the truth straight from the source, before they walked down the aisle. A tiny shiver skittered through her. Could she hope that it was true, that Ryan really did love her?

"Stand up straight, *niña*," her mother whispered. "And walk slowly." Yanked from her thoughts, Jennifer did as she was told, then slipped her hand through her father's arm. With her mother on her other side, she began her walk up the aisle. Her knees wobbled and her palms began to sweat. She glanced down at the ribbon bouquet and noticed it trembling in her hand. If he loved her, then everything would change.

By the time she reached the front of the church, she was so caught up in thoughts of Ryan that she was only faintly aware of what was going on around her. She tried to remember everything she'd said and done before that moment when he admitted he didn't love her. What could possibly be his motive for lying to her?

She listened distractedly to the instructions from Father Juan as he ran through the order of the service. Diego would give the bride away and then Jennifer was to take Ryan's hand and come forward. The moment Ryan grabbed her fingers, she was jolted back to reality. Just the feel of his fingers clasping hers sent tingles up her arms.

As the priest reviewed the order of the vows and the exchange of rings, her attention settled on the way Ryan slowly stroked the back of her hand with his thumb. She wanted to believe that the simple caress was one of affection, that the man who held her hand also wanted her heart. If what Carolyn said was really true, then this wedding could have meaning. They'd have a future together and a chance for true happiness. Her heart skipped a beat and her breath caught in her throat. If only it was true. If only…

"Jennifer?"

She blinked, then dragged her gaze away from their hands and looked up at Ryan. "What?"

"The vows," he murmured. "You have to repeat what the priest says."

"I—I do," Jennifer stammered.

Father Juan gave her an odd look, then went on, reading through Ryan's half of the vows. She heard Ryan say "I do," and then Father Juan skipped through all the familiar words—*love, honor, cherish, sickness and health, till death do us part.* She repeated them all, not really hearing what she was saying, unable to make herself believe in the meaning. She could feel Ryan's gaze on her, but she kept her eyes cast downward. They knelt and the *padrinos* practiced stringing the *lazo* around their necks.

And then it was over. The *lazo* was gone and they stood. Father Juan gave her a few more instructions about lighting the candle for Mary before he stepped back. "And then, I will say 'I now present Mr. and Mrs. Ryan Madison.' And then you kiss your bride."

Jennifer froze, her eyes wide. They'd managed to skip over everything else. Why did they have to practice the kissing part? The church was silent as everyone waited. Jennifer glanced up at the organist, who watched them all from the organ loft. Even he was waiting for the kiss before he started the recessional.

"Usually, this is the part that the bride and groom like

the best,'' said Father Juan. He glanced back and forth between them, then smiled. ''Go ahead. Whenever you are ready.''

Ryan glanced down into Jennifer's eyes. ''I'm ready,'' he murmured. ''Are you?''

Jennifer nodded, and a moment later, his lips were on hers. This was all part of the charade, she told herself. This wonderful kiss and all the sensations that came with it. Still, Jennifer lost herself for a long moment in the feel of his lips on hers. For a moment, she believed he really loved her, that what Carolyn had told her was true.

She drew back. The lie had become so convincing, she couldn't tell where playacting left off and true feelings began. The organist launched into the recessional and Ryan took her hand and tucked it into the crook of his arm. Jennifer had no choice but to paste a smile on her face and walk down the aisle. But with every step, she vowed that tomorrow would not be like tonight. There would be no more playacting. Tomorrow would be real, and if she couldn't make it so, then she'd refuse to walk down the aisle at all.

CHAPTER TWELVE

RYAN PACED the length of the anteroom, his footsteps echoing off the rich wood paneling to the high gothic ceiling. He'd arrived at St. Benedict's nearly a half hour before with Ben, determined to talk to Jennifer before the ceremony. But he'd been shuffled off to talk with Father Juan. And when he'd finally broken away, he'd been kept from Jennifer by her very determined maid of honor, Maria, who insisted that it was bad luck to see the bride before the wedding.

Since the rehearsal last night, they hadn't found a single opportunity to be alone. They'd been whisked from the church to the restaurant, Joe driving their rental car and Maria keeping up a constant stream of chatter from the front seat. And once they had sat down at the long table, there had been numerous toasts and requests for kisses, and relatives stopping by the table with wishes for a long and happy life together. Jennifer had maintained an indifferent attitude toward him throughout it all, her plastic smile never fading for the audience.

Later, they'd returned to the Rodriguez house and she'd been taken away again, Carmen insisting she get to bed early. So Ryan had waited until she arrived at the church on the morning of the wedding, then appealed to Carmen. Jennifer's mother had assured him that he could speak to Jennifer through the door, just as soon as she was dressed and ready. Diego and Joe hadn't been much help. They just chuckled and shrugged, unwilling to go up against the Rodriguez women.

He'd been so thoroughly thwarted that the only option left to him was writing her a note, but he wasn't sure what he'd say. "Dear Jennifer," he murmured. "I love you, but if you want to back out of the wedding I'll still love you." He'd thought about this all last night while he lay awake in a bedroom down the hall from her. And his sleepless night had made him even more determined to set their relationship straight before they walked down the aisle.

A soft knock sounded at the door. "Jennifer?" Ryan quickly crossed the room, then yanked the door open, fully expecting to see his bride. Instead, he found his parents standing nervously on the other side. His father was dressed in a dark suit and tie and Rhonda wore a pretty mauve dress with a beaded jacket. He waited for the customary surge of anger, the wave of resentment that always accompanied seeing them. But it didn't come.

"Hi," he murmured.

"Hello, Ryan," his mother said, her nervousness making her voice tremble.

They stood in the doorway for a long time before Ryan spoke again. "Come on in," he said. "I—I wasn't sure you were coming."

"We wouldn't miss this for the world," Rhonda said. Her eyes glittered with unshed tears. "You look very handsome." She reached up and straightened her son's bow tie, smoothed her hands over his lapels, then realized what she was doing and drew away. The act was so instinctively maternal, so full of love and affection that Ryan couldn't fault her for it.

He touched his tie. "Thanks."

A faint blush colored Rhonda's cheeks. "I didn't think you'd ever let me do that again."

"Do what?" Ryan asked.

"Touch you. I thought everything had been ruined between us."

"Not ruined," Ryan said. "Just a little...tarnished." He smiled at his mother, then looked over at his father, who stood nearby. "To be honest, I'm glad you came. I've been doing some thinking lately. Reevaluating my reaction to this whole thing. And I've come to a few conclusions."

"And what are those, son?" Jeffrey asked.

"I can't blame you for this mess. It's not fair. I blame Douglas Benton."

"Who is Douglas Benton?" Rhonda asked, the name causing a curious lift of her eyebrows.

Ryan realized that he'd never bothered to tell his parents the story of how he came to be in the grocery store parking lot, the story that Ben and Carolyn and Jennifer had pieced together. "He was the doctor who took me from my mother, forged a birth certificate, and sold me to you for ten thousand dollars. He was probably the man you met in that parking lot."

"The man in the parking lot told us he was a lawyer," Jeffrey said. "He said that he'd taken care of all the adoption papers. He gave us a birth certificate with our names on it and he explained that it was customary to change the birth certificate to protect the identity of the mother. We thought your mother was a teenage runaway. If we knew the truth, we never would have—"

"Don't," Ryan said. "I know." He glanced between his mother and his father. "Jennifer helped me see that you're not to blame in this. Hell, Jen's baby isn't even born yet and I want so much to be a good father. I don't even know whether it's a boy or a girl, but I already know I love that baby. I can understand how you could love me and want me so much that nothing else matters."

A tear slipped from the corner of Rhonda's eye as Ryan embraced Jeffrey, then his mother. "I'm so sorry, sweetheart,'' she said. ''I know we can't bring your real parents back, but Jeffrey and I want you to know that we'll be there for you, for whatever you need.''

Ryan nodded. ''I know. I think I knew that all along. It just took a while for it to sink in.''

Rhonda rose up on her toes and gave Ryan a kiss on the cheek. Then, with a pretty blush, she sniffled and wiped her tears away with her fingers. ''Now, we better go find our places. We stopped in and introduced ourselves to Jennifer's family. She looks radiant, sweetheart. You're a very lucky man.''

Ryan's hopes rose. ''You saw Jennifer? I really need to talk to her. Do you think you could go back to the bride's room and tell her that I want to see her before the ceremony?''

Rhonda laughed and patted him on the cheek. ''Don't be silly. You can't see the bride before the ceremony. It's bad luck.''

Ryan sighed. Since when had everyone turned so superstitious? ''There's a reserved pew in the front,'' he said as his parents walked to the door. ''It's for family. I want you to sit there. Just tell the ushers that you're my mom and dad, all right?''

When he was left alone, he searched for a piece of paper. Maybe he could get a note to Jennifer. His mother would do him the favor and she'd already gotten past the guards once. He found a pad and pen and began to scribble a letter, but five minutes later, he'd left five different drafts crumpled on the floor.

The door creaked again and Ryan turned to see Ben slip through, a wide smile on his face. Like Ryan, he was dressed in a simple but elegant tuxedo. ''Hey, brother. Glad to see you haven't run off,'' he joked.

''Very funny,'' Ryan muttered. ''Are Lucy and Carolyn here yet?''

Ben nodded. "They went right to the bride's room. Carolyn said Lucy was so excited that she could barely sit still on the ride from the hotel. And now that she's made friends with Teresa, she had all sorts of things she wanted to tell her. They share a fondness for ponies. And I just met your folks. Nice people. Your mother was already sniffling. So, how are you doing?"

"Not good," Ryan said. "I'm not sure this wedding is going to happen. I know Jen is still wavering and I'm fully expecting to stand up in front of all these people and be stood up! If I could just talk to her, I'd be able to look into her eyes and see how she feels. And I want to tell her how I feel."

"Then go find her," Ben said.

"She might as well have a pack of pit bulls surrounding her." He paused. "But I could get a message to her through Carolyn. Maybe they'd let you talk to Carolyn and you could tell Carolyn to tell Jennifer that I—"

"Stop," Ben said, laughing. "This sounds like high school. What the hell is so important that you can't wait until after the wedding to tell her?"

Ryan thrust his fingers through his hair. "I have to tell her that I love her."

"I'm sure she knows that."

"I don't think she does. Probably because I haven't really said it. I mean, not in so many words. Not in any words."

"Geez, Ryan," Ben said with a gasp. "No wonder you're worried she'll run off. What the hell were you thinking? I'll go find Carolyn and see what I can do."

Ryan clapped Ben on the shoulder, relieved that someone was taking his request seriously. "Thanks. I knew there was a reason I asked you to be my best man."

Ben stopped and turned back to Ryan before he reached the door. "Hey, I saw Dylan on my way in. He and Lily and Cole flew in this morning and came right from the airport. He said he had something to tell you. Said it was really important. Could be news on your case.''

Ryan slowly straightened, his troubles with Jennifer instantly pushed aside. "Where is he?"

"Last time I saw him, he was standing out in front of the church."

Ryan hurried out of the anteroom through an outside door and strode down the sidewalk alongside the church, his heart racing in anticipation. He was almost afraid to hear what Dylan had to say, knowing what he'd learned could be bad news as easily as it could be good. He found Garrett leaning up against a fancy rental car, talking to a tall, broad-shouldered man dressed in a suit. Ryan assumed the man was Lily's husband, Cole Bishop. "Dylan," Ryan called as he crossed the street.

"Hi, Ryan. How ya doing?"

"Pretty good, considering I'm getting married in less than a half hour. I'm not sure I'm supposed to be this nervous."

"Ryan Madison, this is my brother-in-law, Cole Bishop, Lily's husband. If you've got any questions about wedding stuff, Cole's the one to ask. He and Lily just tied the knot in September and he hasn't stopped smiling since."

Cole reached out and shook Ryan's hand. "I'm not an expert on the subject," he said. "But I can tell you that marriage is the best thing that ever happened to me."

"Cole, can you excuse us for a few minutes?" Dylan asked. "Ryan and I have some business to discuss."

Cole nodded. "I'm going to track down Lily. Good luck today, Ryan. And don't forget to take a little time during the day to enjoy yourself. A guy only gets married once— if he's marrying the right woman."

Ryan smiled. Cole's words echoed in his mind. Hell, he was sure as he could be that he was marrying the right woman. He had no doubts in his mind. It was Jennifer he was worried about. Did she truly believe she was marrying the right man? Or was he simply the only man who had offered?

"I've got some good news for you," Dylan said, drawing Ryan around to the other side of the car. He reached inside his suit jacket and pulled out an envelope, then handed it to Ryan.

"What's this?"

"It's what you've been waiting for. All signed, sealed and delivered."

Ryan gasped. "You found him?"

"I'm a good P.I.," Dylan teased, as if Ryan had insulted his professional competency.

"What did you find out?" Ryan asked.

"Captain James Kestwick. He lives in Virginia and serves on a carrier out of Norfolk. I tracked him down, told him what I wanted, and he was quite happy to agree. He's got a fiancée from a very wealthy Virginia family and he doesn't want to screw that up. I think he might also have political aspirations. An affair and an illegitimate child might not sit too well with the voters."

"So, what's the procedure here?"

"You'll have to talk to a lawyer once the baby is born. That letter states that Kestwick is willing to give up all parental rights to the child. It's been notarized, but he may still have to show up in court. Although, if he's out to sea, that might not be necessary."

"That would be nice," Ryan said. "I'm not sure I want Jennifer facing him in a courtroom. I'm not sure *I'd* want to face him. I wouldn't know whether to punch him for all the pain he caused her or thank him for deserting her."

Dylan glanced at his watch. "Well, I better get inside. Lily promised to save me a spot." He held out his hand to Ryan and Ryan shook it. "Good luck."

Ryan watched him cross the street to the church. He didn't know Dylan well. Hell, he barely knew him at all. But both times he'd spoken to him, he'd gotten the impression that the guy was hiding some deep pain from the world. Today, it had been even more evident. When he'd wished Ryan luck, Ryan had almost sensed envy in his words.

"Hey, brother!" Ben stood at the front door of the church. "Come on, they're ready for us."

Ryan glanced down at his watch. He'd completely lost track of time. He had only five minutes left before the start of the ceremony and he still hadn't talked to Jennifer! He ran across the street, and when he got inside the church, he headed off toward the bride's room. But Ben grabbed him and pulled him in the opposite direction. "Come on, we have to get up front. Father Juan is waiting."

"But I have to talk to—"

"You can't talk to Jennifer now," Ben said. "Besides, it's bad luck to see the bride before she walks down the aisle."

JENNIFER HURRIED down the hallway, the skirt of her gown clutched in her hand. She'd lost track of time! One minute, she'd been looking for her shoes and zipping up her dress and adjusting her veil, and the next minute Carmen was pointing to her watch and ordering the girls to the church vestibule for the processional.

"I have to talk to Ryan," Jennifer insisted when she reached the vestibule. The florist handed her a bouquet then scurried off to distribute the rest of the flowers. Jennifer glanced at Maria and then Carmen and then her father, but no one was paying attention to her. Linda was fluffing Teresa's hair and Carolyn was helping Lucy with her basket of rose petals. And Tía Yolanda was there, too, clucking over her twin six-year-old grandsons, Raul and Rico, who would serve as the *pajines*.

"I have to talk to Ryan, now!" Jennifer shouted, stomping her foot.

Everyone stopped chattering then turned to look at her. "*Hija*, he's waiting at the front of the church," Carmen said. "The organist is about to start the processional. You have your whole life to talk to him."

"But this is important. I have to tell him something. And it can't wait."

"What could be so important?" Carmen asked in a placating tone.

"I have to tell him that I love him," Jennifer said.

Carmen patted Jennifer's hand patiently. "I am sure he knows."

"But he doesn't," Jennifer cried. "I've never told him before."

"You never told Ryan you loved him?" Maria asked.

"Are you calling the wedding off?" Teresa inquired, her eyes wide and ready to fill with tears. Lucy hurried over to Teresa's side and stared up at Jennifer with another pair of pleading eyes.

The doors to the church swung open and Jennifer heard the first strains of the processional. This was all happening too fast. She had so much to tell Ryan, so much to get straight before they repeated marriage vows. And now it was too late. The twins started down the aisle, followed by Teresa and Lucy. Jennifer felt a knot of tension growing in her stomach. Linda, then Maria stepped into the church and began their walk down the aisle, and Jennifer felt as if she were going to throw up.

"Are you ready?" Carmen asked, taking Jennifer's arm and leading her toward the door.

Diego took her other arm. "You're a good girl, Jennifer.

And you've found yourself a good man. He will make a fine *esposo*.''

Unable to stop what was happening, Jennifer numbly started down the aisle, walking through the rose petals that Lucy and Teresa had sprinkled on the white carpet. Step by step, she walked, her eyes firmly fixed ahead. And then, before she knew it, she was at the front of the church. Diego lifted her veil and kissed her cheek, then Carmen did the same. Jennifer turned to Ryan, nerves fluttering inside her stomach. Slowly, as she looked into his eyes, the rest of the world faded into the background.

"I need to talk to you," she whispered. "Now. Before we do this."

Ryan frowned. "I need to talk to you, too."

Jennifer's heart stopped at the serious expression on his face. Oh, God, he didn't want to go through with it. She'd finally realized how much she loved him, how much she wanted to marry him and build a life with him, and now he was going to dump her at the altar—or in some room close to the altar.

Jennifer slowly turned and faced the congregation as the last notes of the processional reverberated through the church. "I'm sorry," she called. "If you can just wait for a bit, Ryan and I need to talk." She grabbed Ryan's arm and dragged him to a small room to the right of the altar.

When they were safely inside, she closed the door behind her and leaned back against it, afraid her mother or father might come bursting in to demand an explanation. She lifted her veil and brushed it back over her head, then met his gaze squarely. It took all the courage she had to speak. "All right," she said, her voice trembling. "You can say it."

"Say what?" Ryan asked. "You're the one who wanted to tell me something."

"You can tell me you don't want to go through with

the ceremony, that you don't want to marry me. I'll understand if you want to just leave right now."

Ryan laughed. "I thought that's what *you* wanted to tell *me*. That you've had second thoughts or cold feet or a change of heart."

"*I* don't have cold feet," Jennifer said, astonished. "I just don't want to get married. Not like this."

Ryan's amusement faded and he shook his head and cursed beneath his breath. "I should have known," he murmured, shadows of regret etched across his handsome features. Jennifer reached out to touch his cheek, but he evaded her fingers. "I figured something like this would happen. That when it came right down to it, you wouldn't be able to say the vows."

"I *do* want to say the vows," she insisted. "But if we say them today, in front of all these people, I want them to mean something." She placed her hand over his heart. "I—I love you, Ryan. I didn't want to love you, but I couldn't help myself. And I don't love you because I'm thankful to you or because you can offer me a nice house and paid health care. I love you because you make my heart beat faster and my head spin. I love you because you're the first person I want to go to whether I'm feeling sad or happy."

A slow smile curved Ryan's lips and he let out a soft sigh. He grabbed her hands and slowly bent to one knee. Then he gently slipped off the engagement ring he'd given her that day outside her parents' house. "Let's do this right," he said, holding up the ring. "Jennifer Rodriguez, I love you. I've wanted to tell you that for such a long time. And I love you not because I'm looking to fill a hole in my life, but because you've become my life. Jen, I want you to marry me. For real. Forever." Ryan paused. "Please, say yes. You'll make me the happiest man on the face of the earth."

Jennifer felt the breath leave her body, and for a moment, she couldn't speak. "You—you love me?"

Ryan nodded. "Yes, I love you."

"And I love you," she cried. "And yes, Ryan Madison, I will marry you. Right here and right now. For real and forever."

He slowly slipped the ring back on her finger, then stood. With a soft cry of excitement, Jennifer threw herself into his arms. He picked her up and twirled her around, laughing as he nuzzled his face into the curve of her neck. Then he set her back on her feet and captured her face between his hands. His mouth came down on hers in a kiss so tender it nearly brought tears to Jennifer's eyes.

It was as if they were kissing for the very first time, for she was kissing him with the knowledge that their feelings were deep and abiding and meant to last a lifetime. Overwhelmed with emotion, she began to laugh, joy bubbling up from inside her, her lips still pressed to his. Ryan loved her and she loved him! And somehow, in the midst of all their silly agreements and rules, they'd managed to find each other. Now that she'd found him, she never wanted to let him go.

"Have I told you how beautiful you look today?" he murmured. "When I saw you coming down the aisle, you took my breath away."

Jennifer's eyes went wide. "Oh, no! You're not supposed to see the bride before the ceremony. This is bad luck."

"Technically, the ceremony has already started." Ryan kissed her again, then growled playfully. "Besides, this can't possibly be bad luck. In fact, I think this is just about the best luck I've had in my entire life. I found the woman I want to spend my life with, she's dressed in a beautiful white wedding gown, and there's a church full of people waiting outside the door. I'd say it's pretty lucky that you and I want to get married today.''

His mouth came down on hers, only this time the kiss wasn't sweet and gentle. It was filled with a hunger Jennifer knew would be sated later that night, when they were alone together. It was a desire she couldn't imagine ever fading between them, even when they were old and gray and sitting on a porch watching their great-grandchildren play at their feet.

"Ryan!"

They slowly drew out of their kiss and turned to see Ben standing in the doorway. Jennifer giggled, a blush warming her cheeks, and Ryan glared at his brother. ''This better be important,'' he said.

''You've got a couple hundred people waiting for you two to make this official. Do you plan to come out anytime soon? Because if you don't, Jennifer's mother is going to need a tranquilizer and I'm going to have to stop Diego from running home and fetching his shotgun.''

"Tell them we'll be out in a few minutes," Ryan said. Ben nodded, then closed the door behind him, and Ryan looked down into Jennifer's eyes. ''Are you ready to marry me?''

Jennifer nodded. ''I'm ready.''

Ryan reached behind her, carefully took hold of her veil and lowered it over her face. Then he smiled at her and took her hand. ''Then let's get on with the rest of our lives.''

With that, they stepped through the door and out into the church. As Jennifer walked back toward the altar, she felt the power of their love surround them. She murmured a silent prayer of thanks for the good fortune that had brought her into Ryan Madison's life and for the love that had grown between them.

And when her *padrinos* draped the *lazo* around her and

Ryan's shoulders and they said their vows before the
priest, every word came straight from her heart. She promised to love and honor and cherish Ryan for the rest of her
life—and she hoped that her life would be very, very long.

THE RECEPTION was in full swing beneath a huge tent in
the backyard of the Rodriguezes' home. Colorful *faroles,*
strung from the ceiling of the tent, illuminated the dance
floor, which until just an hour before had been filled with
candlelit dinner tables, set with silver and china and sparkling crystal.

The guests had dined on a mix of traditional Mexican
wedding dishes and elegant American fare. Jennifer and
Ryan had been seated at the head table and, throughout
their meal of *mole de gallina* and *frijoles borrachos,* had
been subjected to numerous toasts and requests for impromptu kisses. Jennifer had enjoyed every single kiss, but
it only made her long for the moment when she and Ryan
would be alone.

After dinner, Jennifer had danced with nearly every
male member of her immediate family and Ryan's—Diego, Joe, Ben, and Ryan's father, Jeffrey. The band had
played *boleros,* slow romantic ballads, and *rancheras,*
lively polkas. She'd even made it through a *huapango,* a
fast two-step, with Dylan Garrett, who had been a dancer
of formidable skill. Ryan had made his turns around the
floor with Carmen, Rhonda and all of Jennifer's sisters,
then found Carolyn and Lily. Now he was sweeping Lucy
around the floor in his arms, her legs dangling and her
laughter mixing with the music.

Jennifer was struck by the picture they made. She could
almost see Ryan with a little girl of his own. He would be
a wonderful father, attentive, generous, and totally besot-
ted. He'd spoil his daughter terribly. Jennifer wasn't worried about having a boy first. Ryan would make a won-

derful father either way. Besides, she intended to have more than one child. Four or five would be nice.

After the *huapango,* the band settled into a gentle country ballad called a *corrido,* and Jennifer found herself in the arms of her husband again. "Hello, *mía esposa,*" he murmured, his breath tickling at her ear.

"Hello, *mío esposo,*" she replied. "You know, I've decided that I really like this married life. But I don't like being away from you for so long."

Ryan nibbled at her earlobe as he swung her around the dance floor. "Well, I don't have any intention of letting go of you for the rest of my life. Now, do we have any other official duties to complete? Or can we get on with the honeymoon?"

"We took care of the grand march, and the garter and the bouquet," she said. "I've danced with everyone I needed to dance with. We just have to cut the cake."

"That can wait," Ryan said, taking her hand and leading her off the dance floor. "Come with me. I have a special wedding gift I want to give you." He grabbed two glasses of champagne from a table as they passed and handed her one.

"A wedding gift?" Jennifer moaned. "But I didn't get you anything."

"Well, actually you have. You could say it's on order."

"But I didn't—"

"Come on," Ryan insisted as they slipped off into the shadows surrounding the tent. "Before anyone notices we're gone."

When they'd found a quiet spot near the pool, they sat down on a chaise. Jennifer glanced around. "This is the same spot we sat that night before Maria's *quinceañera.*" She peered up into the trees. "Teresa?" she called. There was no answer. "I think we're alone."

Ryan leaned forward and pressed a kiss to her lips, his

tongue teasing at hers before he drew back. "I've wanted to do that all night long."

Jennifer giggled. "That's all we did during dinner. I barely got anything to eat."

"That was different," he teased. "Kissing for demanding friends and relatives isn't nearly as exciting as kissing for fun."

"Then kiss me again, husband. And this time, make it a good one."

Ryan more than made up for the chaste pecks he'd given her during dinner. His kiss set her pulse racing and her head spinning and she wondered if she'd always react with such passion to the taste of him. She was willing to wager he'd still have the knack for piquing her desire, even after thousands of kisses.

"So, where's my gift?" she said, when he finally gave her a chance to take a breath.

"You're not satisfied with my kisses?" he asked.

"I'm just curious," she said. "I'm also curious as to how *I* got *you* a gift and I don't remember shopping."

Ryan reached inside his tuxedo jacket and withdrew an envelope, then handed it to her. Jennifer hesitantly took it, then opened the flap and removed a single piece of paper. She unfolded it and squinted as she tried to read the tiny print by the blue glow of the swimming pool lights. "What is this?"

"It's an affidavit," Ryan said. "A notarized document that says that Captain James Kestwick officially gives up his parental rights to Baby Girl or Baby Boy Rodriguez."

"My baby? Our baby? What does this mean? How did you get this?"

"Dylan found the guy and he was quite happy to sign. And this means that the day our baby is born, we can start legal proceedings for me to adopt him—or her." He reached out and took her fingers in his hand. "We'll be a real family. If that's what you want."

Tears clouded Jennifer's vision, and she could barely find the words. "A—a family? All three of us?" She wrapped her arms around his neck. "I want that. I want that very much."

As he held her in his embrace, a wave of memories flooded Jennifer's mind. She remembered the moment she walked into his office at the dusty drilling site. She'd never dreamed she'd find a husband and a father for her child that day. But she had. And as his strength enveloped her and his warmth seeped into her skin, Jennifer wondered what she'd ever done to deserve such happiness.

Just a month ago, her life had seemed like such a mess. She'd been confused and frightened and so lonely she could barely face the day. But suddenly, she was here, newly wed and hugging her husband, embarking on the happiest time of her life. "This is the most wonderful gift," she said, pressing the paper to her heart. "I couldn't have asked for anything more." She sighed. "I only wish I had something as wonderful to give you."

Ryan drew back and dropped a kiss on her lips. "But you do. You have a present that I never imagined I might have." He reached down and placed his hand on the swell of her belly. "We're going to have a baby, Jen. And we're going to make a family. And that's the only gift I want."

"Well," Jennifer said. "Just as long as I don't have to limit myself to one gift. I think we should plan on at least two or three more gifts, to be delivered every few years."

Ryan tipped his head back and laughed. "Why don't we wait until this little package is unwrapped. Then you can talk to me about more."

Jennifer smiled, then shrugged. "I guess we do have time to discuss this."

"Sweetheart, we have the rest of our lives."

TRUEBLOOD, TEXAS *continues*
next month with
THE COWBOY'S SECRET SON
by Gayle Wilson

Mark Peterson had never gotten over Jillian
Salvini's desertion ten years ago. She and her
family had left in the middle of the night. Mark's
heart hadn't recovered. Now she is back. Is a
second chance possible?

Here's a preview!

CHAPTER ONE

"Come on, Mom," Drew encouraged. "You can do it."

And the faster she did it, the faster she would reach him, she told herself, and the safety of the ground. And the less cowardly she would seem to the two of them.

She lowered herself again, and then again, knowing that each step brought her closer to the ground. Closer to safety. Closer to Drew and to Mark. And with each step the subtle sway of the ladder lessened. Felt steadier. Nearer to the precious, solid earth. And although she was still careful, she began to move faster as her confidence increased.

His hands fastened around the outside of her thighs, offering support. As she lowered her body, they moved upward—to her hips and then her waist. And finally, the toe of her boot made contact with the ground.

She turned into Mark's arms without hesitation, and they fastened around her, holding her tightly against his chest. Despite how calm he'd sounded, she could feel the pounding of his heart under her breasts, and the tears she had denied at the top of the ladder welled upward again, in gratitude this time.

She rubbed her face against the smooth cotton of his shirt. The feel and the smell of him was like a long-forgotten dream, so sharp and so clear she wondered how she could ever have forgotten it.

Laundry soap. A brand she knew, but couldn't have named right now to save her life. Underlying that was the fragrance of his body. She would have been able to recognize him in a crowd of a thousand men. There was a hint of the soap he'd used this morning. The pleasantly clean, slightly salt-tanged aroma of a working man's perspiration. Subtle horse smell. Oiled leather.

She closed her eyes, letting the pleasure she felt wash over her in a wave of security. She was safe. Just as she had known her whole life long, in Mark's arms she was safe.

After a moment, he put his hands on her shoulders, pushing her away. And then the import of his hands' urging registered. In obedience she took a step back, looking up to meet his eyes, which were suspiciously bright.

"You okay?" he asked, his voice very gentle.

She nodded, not trusting her own. Drew laid his head against her side. She reached out to pull him close.

"What the hell happened up there?" Mark asked.

"I forgot to turn on the pump before the horses arrived."

"I mean with the ladder."

So much for her confession, which he obviously didn't need or want to hear.

"The bolts must be rusted," she said. "One of them broke or pulled away."

Mark looked up, his eyes tracing up the length of the ladder. She had no inclination to let hers follow. She didn't need to know exactly how high up that missing rung was.

"I'll take care of the horses," he said after a few seconds, finally lowering his gaze to her face. "Why don't you take Drew inside? Make us some coffee."

Inventing something for her to do to get her out of the yard? Even if he was, it didn't seem like a bad idea. Drew needed reassurance that everything was all right. And the way her knees had begun to tremble again, she could use a chair.

So she nodded. She began to move toward the house, talking quietly to Drew the whole way, her arm around his shoulders. Her legs were still shaking when they reached the back door.

She opened it, directing the boy inside with her hand on his back, before she turned to look at Mark. He was standing beside the ladder, his fingers busy with one of the bolts on the eye-level rung, working it out of the hole.

"Mom?" Drew said.

She turned to smile at him, and then she, too, entered the house, closing the back door behind her.

Mark had said he'd take care of the horses, Jillian had absolutely no doubt he would. The horses and anything else that needed taking care of. Judging by his ongoing examination of that ladder, right now, "anything else" apparently included her.